I0450859

Two Timing

Audra North

For A.B.

Chapter One

"What do you mean, you don't know where Melanie is?"

Derek Brewer glared at his brother, but Alden was looking down at the table, his gaze focused on the sugar packet he was playing with, rolling it back and forth between his fingers.

Derek huffed impatiently.

Alden shrugged and dropped the packet, then laid both of his hands flat on the table. Big hands that *should* have looked exactly like Derek's.

But there was that crooked pinky finger on Alden's right hand…the veins on the back that stood out in vivid blue over too-pale skin…the slight shaking whenever he didn't have them pressed flat on a surface, like they were now—these signs of hard living might not be noticeable to most people, but it made Derek feel like it didn't matter that they had the same hair, same eyes, same big nose, same lopsided smile. He and his twin may as well be strangers.

After eleven years of drug addiction, Alden had gone clean over a year ago, but Derek still felt like he'd lost his brother.

Alden sighed. "I've looked everywhere."

For a moment, Derek wondered whether Alden had read his mind and was confessing some deep, soulful feeling—that he felt like he had lost himself, too, and had looked everywhere to no avail. But then Derek remembered, *No, we were talking about Melanie.* Alden's ex-girlfriend and mother of Emma, their three-year-old daughter. Those two had broken up shortly after Emma was born, and Melanie had fallen off the wagon a few months before Alden had struggled onto it.

While Alden had improved every day, Melanie had been sucked deeper into her addiction.

Derek immediately suppressed the familiar surge of irritation at Alden in response to that thought. It wasn't his brother's fault that Melanie had taken the opposite path.

"Are you sure she didn't pick up a shift at one of the clubs and end up going home with a jo—uh, patron?"

It wasn't like she hadn't done it before.

When she was sober enough, Melanie worked as a stripper. But when the addiction got to be too much, she'd disappear— sometimes for days. Derek himself had even picked her a couple of times along the Strip, a section of Main Street on the south side of town that was known for its sex traffic. Back when she and Alden were still together, it was bad enough that the two considered getting high to be their favorite couples' activity. Having to book his brother's girlfriend for prostitution added a whole extra layer of shit to the situation.

Alden shook his head. If it bothered him to hear that Melanie was known for certain types of behavior, he didn't show it. "She worked the night before last and was scheduled again last night at Jerry's, but she didn't show up." He frowned. "I combed the Strip and all the clubs along Airport Boulevard. She hasn't been around any of those places in weeks. Nino told me that if she didn't get her ass into Jerry's soon, he'd actually fire her this time."

Derek snorted. *Yeah, right.* Nino, the manager at the joint where Melanie usually worked, was notoriously lax when it came to the strippers who did him sexual favors.

He switched into cop mode. "What about Melanie's mom? Did you call her? She might know whether Melanie has been seeing anyone new. Barring that, has anyone actually called the station to report her missing? I didn't see anything come in, and you know that the guys would have told me, even though it's my day off."

Alden shook his head. "June is the one who called me, in fact. Phoned me up this morning to say that Melanie had left Emma over there last night, but she told June she'd gotten a private gig she couldn't pass up so she was gonna blow off

Jerry's. But then she never came back."

Fuck. This whole thing was getting more tangled by the second. At least Emma had been left in reasonably responsible hands.

Then again, June Dickinson was either a saint…or an idiot. Or both. Derek respected Melanie's mother for putting up with her daughter's problems, but the woman was getting on in years and there was too much going on in her own life to manage her junkie daughter's and her toddler granddaughter's, too.

"She could have been telling the truth, or she could have been lying so June wouldn't think she was going to go out and get high." Derek sighed and shrugged. "Look, I'm sorry, but I can't put any energy on this until we have an official missing person's report. You know that. If you're so worried, quit dicking around and get down to the station and put it in right away. Don't believe any of that 'you have to wait twenty-four hours' bullshit you hear on TV."

Being a SWAT officer and a detective in the street crimes unit of the Greenbriar Police Department sometimes felt like being a doctor in a family full of diabetics—he was the one everyone came to when they needed free advice.

Alden nodded. "I know, I know. But I hadn't wanted to worry anyone before now. I'm still not sure I want to file it, since you know how she is. This isn't the first time she's gone on a bender. It could be days before she stumbles back home totally safe after a few days of tripping, and then your guys will have wasted their time on it for nothing."

Derek didn't bother to protest. If it became an official case, the other officers would give it their attention out of respect for him but, like Alden had said, this wasn't the first time something like this had happened.

On the other hand, it *was* the first time it had happened since Emma was in the picture. If Melanie was so far gone that she forgot she had a daughter who needed her, who knows what other terrible things could have happened to her?

He'd seen plenty in his career. He didn't even have to strain his imagination to know.

"File the report," he told his brother.

Alden shrugged. "If you say so. But that's not what I really need help with. I've got that contract starting tonight—"

Oh, right. Alden was supposed to start nightly cleaning services for an insurance company downtown. He'd started his own janitorial service company after no one would hire him because of his prison record. He'd been in and out of minimum security on drug raps, but that was enough to deter most employers.

Derek had helped him set up the company—helped his older brother by seven minutes get his first contract.

Sometimes he hated having to always be the good goddamned twin.

"I can't. Emma freaks out every time I so much as walk away to go into the other room. I think this shit with Melanie is really affecting her."

So *that's* why Alden had brought Emma along this morning. She was sitting at the table next to them, coloring the child's menu with a pack of crayons Alden had pulled from his jacket pocket when they'd arrived, after being told to "be a good girl and let Daddy talk to Uncle Derek about grown-up stuff."

"Besides, June is working a bunch of back-to-back night shifts at the gas station now, so she can't keep Emma anymore this week, anyway, or she'll be out of a job, too. The contract starts tonight and I can't bring Emma to the job site."

Ah. Fuck. Suddenly, Derek knew where this was leading. Something like dread settled deep in his stomach. He'd go to great lengths to make up for what he'd done to his twin, but this would be pushing even those limits.

Don't ask me. Don't ask—

"Can you cover for me?"

Fuck.

Derek huffed. "I'm not going to pretend to be you. We haven't done that since we were fifteen."

Since the year you got involved with drugs and I stopped knowing who you were.

"Only because I was so wasted that we looked too different," Alden protested.

It was weird to hear him speak that way. Now that he was clean, he was brutally honest when it came to his past. But when he had been in the grips of it, he'd denied his problem at every turn.

The truth momentarily stunned Derek into silence.

Alden flashed him a grin. "I've been working out again, though. I'm almost as cut as you are now. We could pass for each other, especially for this gig. I've only met the guy over at Sentinel once, and he said almost no one works late. Plus, it's not like any employees who might be there after hours actually care what the custodian looks like."

Derek meant to shake his head, to shut it down right away, but instead he found himself offering an alternative. "Why don't I watch Emma and you go do the job?"

"Because I'm telling you, she can't deal with me leaving her."

"But we look exactly alike." Derek shook his head. "It's not like—"

"You're trying to tell me you won't try to pass yourself off as me on a cleaning job, but you'll do it to your own niece?"

The look Alden was giving him…it made Derek uncomfortable and pissed him off at the same time. How many times had Derek saved his brother's ass in the past? He was the responsible one. The one who didn't throw away his life one hit at a time. How *dare* Alden?

But he kept his anger in check. Good twins didn't get angry over shit like that. They didn't lose their temper. They didn't cause harm. They controlled themselves.

He gave a little shrug. "I'd rather deal with a crying kid

than get written up by Chief Travers for moonlighting."

Alden frowned. "Look. I know it's a lot. But I'm trying to do right by Emma. By everyone, including myself. It's not like she's only a *little* upset when I leave. It's really affecting her and I can't do that to her. She knows the difference between us. You would upset her more than you think."

Damn it all. Alden was right. About one thing, at least. Derek would probably upset Emma. She'd never quite taken to her uncle, even though he tried hard to always smile and speak gently around her. But apparently, kids weren't fools. Emma probably could sense the horrible mess he carried around inside of him. The gnawing, heavy guilt over how much he hated his brother for being so irresponsible and foolish that Derek had to be that much more *good* to prove to others he wasn't a loser. The rage he felt whenever he thought about how his best friend and twin hadn't been strong enough for so long to *just stop*. The need to hunt down and destroy every dealer he could find in the desperate quest to bring Alden back from that shadowy place that Derek could never—*would* never—understand.

No matter how closely he resembled her Daddy, Emma was one of the few people who seemed to understand the truth. And she was a vulnerable little child.

No, he wouldn't subject his niece to his madness.

Alden sat quietly, watching his younger brother with a look that said, *Exactly.*

"Fuck you." Derek ran his hand over his face.

Alden paled. "I can't lose this job, Derek. I can't. Melanie hasn't been sober in months and now she's missing. I've gotta to take care of Emma. *Please.*"

"Oh, man. Alden—"

"*Please.*" Alden's voice strained. "I'm not even asking you. I'm *begging* you. Mom and Dad won't give me the time of day. Dad's never even met Emma. I have nothing else left except for her and I can't be there for her *and* keep this contract. I haven't even started it, for chrissakes."

Derek blew out a ragged breath and shook his head. "I don't know, man. This is really shady. Even if I weren't a cop, this would be shady. If this affects my work as an officer—"

"It's nothing illegal. I promise. It's my company, after all, even if it's only a one-man show. The property management company is paying Brewer Cleaning, not me directly. I'm trying to make a go of it. I'm trying to do the right thing. *Please*."

He couldn't take those *please*s anymore, coming in uncomfortable regularity out of his brother's mouth. Derek rubbed his neck, feeling his muscles tensing all over.

"All right. All right, I'll do it."

"God. Thank you, Derek. Thank—"

"But you figure this out as soon as possible, do you understand? I've got your back on anything that has to do with Emma. But I don't like this switching places thing. It's wrong. Deceptive and sneaky and…Jesus fucking Christ, we're *not* fifteen anymore."

Bright blue eyes exactly like his got watery and Derek had to look away. He'd seen his brother cry before. When they were little, of course. But also back when he was high on whatever the latest pills were that were going around, he used to cry, and Derek would set his face in stone and turn away. He couldn't bear to see that kind of whining, mewling dependence smacking him in the face.

But this was different. Now he couldn't bear to look at it because it meant Alden was human again. And then Derek would have to apologize for all those wasted years he'd resented Alden for not having the courtesy to disappear completely, and Alden would hate him.

And then he'd lose his brother all over again.

Toni pushed back from her desk and rubbed her forehead, trying to ease the headache she'd been fighting for the past few hours to no avail.

Faintly, she registered the sound of someone vacuuming on the other side of the floor. She checked her computer's clock. Quarter to seven already? At this rate, the cleaning crew would finish their work and shut off the lights before she made enough progress to go home for the day.

All the other cubicles were empty, the last stragglers having left nearly half an hour ago. She desperately wished she could leave, too—to go home and fall into bed until tomorrow morning, but she needed every hour at work that she could manage to squeeze out if she wanted to have this project proposal ready by next week. If it was accepted by the main office, the project would be hers—not to mention the promotion and a pay raise that came along with it.

Yeah, yeah. More stuff that bores you to death. What does a better title matter when you don't like your job, anyway?

Her head throbbed. She brought her fingers to the bridge of her nose and pinched hard, trying to concentrate.

Sal. You're doing this for Sal.

A promotion would mean being able to pay for the rehab program she'd heard about a few months before. The one that had a seventy percent success rate.

The one she hoped would free her older brother from his addiction.

Taking a deep breath, she slid her chair closer to her desk once more and lifted her hands to the keyboard, steeling herself to continue working on the proposal until she'd reached her goal for the night, no matter how long it took.

But just as she opened up a spreadsheet and began reviewing the numbers in it, the whirring of the vacuum she'd heard earlier suddenly filled the row of cubicles where she sat, startling her and making her head react with a sharp burn of pain.

Maybe the rest of the night was a wash, after all.

Sighing, she shut her laptop and stood up to see a

custodian a few feet away, his back to her, headphones in his ears, vacuuming the floor of her coworker's cubicle.

A custodian with a *really* nice back.

Wow.

It had been such a long time since Toni had been attracted to anyone—she was simply too tired and stressed about Sal's worsening addiction—that the jolt of lust that hit her felt like a shock to her entire system. She stood rooted to the spot, all thoughts of work, exhaustion, and her pounding head fleeing from her mind as she stared at the stranger.

He had brown hair cut military short and was wearing a dark green T-shirt that stretched tight over a broad back, framing muscles that flexed and bunched in the most alluring ways as he moved the vacuum back and forth over the industrial carpeting. Was that how he'd gotten in such good shape? From vacuuming? She'd never been so fascinated by anyone's rear view before, and even then, with the height of the cubicles, she could only see him from the waist up.

But he was beautiful.

His head bobbed slightly as he listened to the music coming from his headphones. She let out a little soft sigh of appreciation, so small a sound even she barely heard it—and he couldn't have, either—but he must have *felt* something because all of a sudden he froze, jerking the headphones from his ears even as he whirled around to face her.

Wide cheekbones, square jaw, a slightly overlarge nose...ocean blue eyes so sharply focused and intense she nearly had to cover her face against the sheer intimidation he managed to project in that single look. But she didn't shield her eyes, because some bright flash of recognition had materialized in her brain when she saw his face, and instead she yelped in surprise.

"Oh, my gosh! *Alden?*"

It was. It *must* be. Alden Brewer, her brother's fellow junkie friend. She hadn't seen him in years, but even when he and Sal used to hang around their house, stoned and a little goofy, Alden had been gorgeous enough to retain a permanent spot in her memory.

That had been right after her brother had dropped out of college.

Now…it had to have been nearly a decade since they'd last crossed paths, but Alden *appeared* to have gone clean in the best possible way.

His intense look faded, replaced with a blinking confusion.

He doesn't recognize me.

It shouldn't have been surprising, given the state he was in every time he hung around with her shiftless brother. Still, it was embarrassing to have been so easily forgotten by a boy on whom she'd once had such an intense crush.

He was definitely not a boy any longer, though. He was an alluring, sexy man. Who didn't remember her.

Are you really surprised? He barely even noticed you back then.

Well, that wasn't completely true. Once, when he'd first started coming around their house, Sal had made some offhand remark about how annoying she was and how much he hated having a little sister, and Alden had taken him to task for it.

Don't talk that way about her, man. Sisters, brothers—you gotta have each other's back.

She'd been embarrassed by his kind words and after that, every time he'd been over, she'd been too intimidated to spend much time with him and Sal. Even so, given how intensely she'd lusted after him back then, she was momentarily thrown by the realization that he didn't seem to know she even existed.

She gave a little wave. "I'm, uh, Toni Park." When he still didn't nod in recognition, she added. "Sal Park's little sister?"

Sal.

Saying his name out loud had called her back to herself enough to grow afraid, the sudden fear making her duck her head and pull her gaze from Alden's. He might *look* clean now, but given how violent Sal had become—raging at the slightest, most unexpected provocation—it was better to become as invisible as possible and then get the hell out of there.

The proposal would have to wait until tomorrow. She'd as much as decided already, anyway, what with her shut laptop and all.

Now she only had to get past Alden and make her escape. It was for the best that he didn't remember her.

That was what she told herself, anyway.

A tense, awkward moment passed during which she held her breath while he regarded her.

Thankfully, he didn't seem to be high. At least, he didn't shout and throw something at her head. In fact, he seemed to sense her trepidation, because he stayed where he was, two cubicles away, and after a few seconds he cleared his throat, and said softly, "I'm sorry, um, Toni. I had a few rough years and don't remember as many things as I should."

The way he said it—as though he was reluctantly choking out the words—made her feel sorry for him. It must not be easy to have to say such a thing to people who had known you, once upon a time. Especially if you couldn't remember even knowing *them*. It made her heart constrict in sympathy, relieving much of the tension that had gathered in her muscles.

"You look familiar, though," he added, as though trying to make *her* feel better.

He seemed to be carrying on a reasonable conversation. His eyes were alert, too. Not glassy or wild. Which meant he probably was *not* a meth head now, like Sal had become. Sal's drug use had evolved over time, and he'd started using meth a couple of years ago. Was that why he and Alden had stopped hanging out together? It was difficult, if not nearly impossible, to break out of that drug's hold. Maybe Alden had gotten away before he'd gone down the path of using meth.

She gave him a small smile. "I get that a lot."

Even Sal had said it to her once.

You look familiar. Do I know you?

He'd been high. Of course he had. He hadn't meant

anything by it, but his question had broken her heart.

Sal had been lost to her for so long she couldn't keep from asking Alden, "I know it's been a few years, but do you still, um—do you remember my brother?"

Will you share some stories about what a good guy he used to be?

She wished she could turn back time.

"Who's your brother, again?" Alden stepped out from the cubicle he was in and started walking toward her. For a moment, she was mesmerized by the slow, stealthy way he moved—surprisingly graceful for such a big man.

Of course, given his past habits, he probably had a lot of practice sneaking around. Goodness knows he and Sal had done more than their fair share of it at her parents' house. Once, she'd even caught them trying to steal money out of her piggy bank, and at sixteen years old she had been so infatuated with Alden she'd simply let them take it.

They'd probably used the money to buy more drugs.

Toni frowned. She didn't like remembering *that*. It was hard not to feel guilty, as though she had traded her brother's sobriety for a stupid crush on a wholly unsuitable man.

"Sal Park," she replied, saying his name softly, almost as though she were speaking of someone who had died long ago.

In a way, he had. And if something drastic didn't happen soon to get him off this terrible path, he'd be gone, anyway. That's why she was here tonight, after all. That was why she'd moved back home in the first place.

To save her brother's life.

Alden blinked at her, then frowned. "Sal Park is a known methamphetamine addict."

It didn't answer her question, exactly, and the way he said it was weird—so clinical and official-sounding. She wasn't sure when he'd developed that manner of speaking, but seeing his face as he'd said it—those full lips and sharp brows drawing his face into a look of clear disapproval—was enough for her to assume he hadn't associated with Sal in a while.

She nodded. "Yeah. Since two years ago or so. I guess it happened after you guys stopped, um"—she wiggled her fingers toward him, as though trying to find the word to describe getting stoned on Vicodin—"hanging out."

He gave a tight nod. Not approving. More like...sympathetic. "A couple years, huh? Which means he's probably in pretty deep by now."

Oh, God. She and her parents had borne the weight of it between the three of them for so long now that hearing another person—someone outside their tiny circle—simply speak the words was enough to make her heart clench and her breath catch. She had to shut her eyes for a moment against the sudden surge of pain, biting back the desire to sob out the words *And he's dragging us under along with him.*

"You okay?" He pitched his voice low, the understanding in it making her soften and lean toward him. It had been so long since anyone even *tried* to comprehend the nightmare she and her parents were going through. Her friends had slowly fallen by the wayside as Sal had spiraled further into the grip of his addiction.

Not that she blamed them.

But, God, she was starved for a little compassion. She wished, for once, someone would think she was worth the troubles that came along with her brother. All she wanted was for someone to think knowing her was enough of a reason to stick by her.

Of course she didn't confess that, though. Instead, she simply nodded and, desperate for some way to occupy her mouth that wouldn't result in her saying more than she should, slowly licked her lips.

Well. That was a mistake.

Because Alden's eyes immediately went to her mouth, tracking the movements of her tongue, his face firing with so much hot intention she had to fight the urge to fan herself with her hands.

He made a sound, low in his throat, that jumpstarted a

pulse point between her thighs.

"Sure you're okay?" The gentleness was gone now, replaced with a rough growl that scraped over her skin, leaving goose bumps in its wake.

She squeezed her legs together to try to ease the increasingly throbbing ache. "Y-yes. I'm fine. Why?"

She didn't mean for her voice to get all squeaky at the end, but he chose that moment to step even closer, moving to stand on the other side of the low cubicle, and a prickle of awareness raced up her arms, her head snapping back on a sharp inhale.

This close, he seemed much bigger than he'd looked when he was standing at the other desk. The man was seriously *built*. Much more than she would have expected from a guy like Alden, who had been pretty lean back when she'd known him. Maybe it really was from vacuuming. Or maybe he went to the gym a lot. He had to, given how big and hard and strong—

"You're sweating a little." He was leaning toward her, an odd look on his face.

She shook off her lust daze, blushing. The expression on his face was nothing like the one he'd worn a moment ago, when he'd been watching her mouth. *Oh, no*. Had she completely misread that situation? How embarrassing.

She really needed to go home and forget this day ever happened. She'd make up the time tomorrow.

She must have taken too long to respond, because he suddenly pulled back and blew out a breath. "Hey. Sorry. That was rude of me. I'm used to hanging with the guys from the sta— I mean, I forgot I'm not supposed to comment on a woman sweating."

Oh. He thought he'd offended her.

She wished he'd kissed her.

But that would have been crazy, and she didn't need to add any crazy to her life right now. So she pushed away the attraction that was making her a fool and forced a laugh. "Uh, thanks. I think."

He chuckled in reply, but shook his head. "Don't mention it. I better get back to work before I end up putting my foot in it again. I'm trying to clean this place, not muck it all up."

She grinned at him. "Well, make sure you clean really well on the desktops. You can't see it, but the cleaning product commercials have taught us that seemingly spotless surfaces are where all the germs are. You know, bad guys lurking in plain s-sight and all, uh…all that."

She stumbled over the last couple of words, realizing too late that he might think she was talking about *him* and his checkered past. She didn't want to offend him.

God, this was awkward.

But he just gave her a small smile. "No worries. I'm a very thorough kind of guy."

Oh, holy Christ. The way he said that was making her shake with barely suppressed *want*. She wanted him to be thorough with her.

"Don't stay too late or I'll have to clean your desk with you still in it," he added.

She tried to laugh at the supposed absurdity, but all she could think of was the sheer muscled bulk of him dominating her space…his big, masculine hands rubbing over the surface of her desk…that strong, broad back flexing as he stroked…surfaces…

A strange choking feeling rose in her throat and she had to strain to keep it from gurgling out of her. Her senses were utterly overloaded and he was standing there patiently, waiting for her to clear out.

Great.

Humiliated, all she could do was shake her head and fumble around for her bag, sliding her laptop into it with shaking fingers. "No, no, I had a few things to catch up on and… Well, I was about to leave, actually. It was—it was nice to see you again, Alden. Take care."

"I will. You watch out for yourself, too, okay?" He turned

away and moved to put his earbuds back in, but she paused for a second.

Well, that sounded rather ominous.

But he'd said it so innocuously, so casually, that she must be imagining there was some kind of message behind it. So she simply nodded and slung her bag over her shoulder, grabbed her jacket, and fled.

Chapter Two

It was taking Derek way too long to stop thinking about her.

Toni Park. The incredibly gorgeous-bodied, pouty-lipped, God-help-him-he-wanted-her-so-much woman who had fired something in him that he'd never known existed.

The need to take. Possess. Without thought and without consequences.

The intensity of the foreign feeling she'd inspired in him threw him off, starting with the surprising haze of lust that had fogged his vision as soon as he'd turned around and caught her staring at him over the cubicles. Light beads of sweat atop full red lips. A slight flush in her porcelain-skinned cheeks. Dark brown eyes that had gone wide and black. She'd looked like Snow White, up to no good, and his body had taken over his mind for a long moment before he'd been able to fight off the urge to do something *bad*.

Fucking. Alden.

Thankfully, Derek had managed to remind himself that he was here to do a job, not pick up a woman, and certainly not a woman who thought he was Alden. He wasn't the kind of guy who had sex with strangers under false pretenses. He was the good twin, damn it, and he always would be.

This Toni person had caught him off guard, that was all. She'd left and he'd…

Well, he'd managed to get back on track.

Derek hurled the last bag of trash into the dumpster and wiped his hands on the pair of old black jeans he'd dug out of his closet for this job. Thankfully, the shift schedule had him working most days and only one night. It hadn't been too hard to convince Captain Travers to let him switch out Friday's second shift for the morning; Derek was senior enough he usually got his preferred shifts, anyway, unless he was investigating a case. His reputation as a skilled detective had been built with a combination of hard work, a killer instinct, and his insistence on always behaving above reproach. Despite his momentary lapse in judgment with this whole Alden charade, he would not allow this moral gray ground to bleed into the rest of his life.

You're allowed to be attracted to her, asshole.

The voice in his head sounded remarkably like that of Warren Davis, another SWAT officer and a surly son of a bitch. Of course, ever since Davis had started dating Beatrice Lawrence, a photojournalist with the city paper, he'd mellowed quite a bit. The thought of someone like Davis, who'd spent years being all-around angry and tense, finding *joie de vivre* in a relationship with such a shy, quiet thing like Beatrice made Derek grin as he walked toward his truck.

Davis would probably approve of Derek having a girlfriend. But he probably wouldn't approve of the fantasies that had shot through Derek's mind upon meeting Toni tonight, despite the heated looks she'd been giving him, as though she wanted to put every part of him in her mouth. Not that he wouldn't thoroughly enjoy being eaten up by her, but getting involved in any way was a bad idea. He'd only been here tonight for one reason, and it didn't involve fast, rough sex with a stranger atop a flimsy cubicle desk.

Derek coughed and shifted his stride. It had become suddenly uncomfortable to walk normally, and this time she wasn't even around. If mere thoughts of her could do that to him, he really needed to stay away.

Well, maybe he wouldn't even need to come back here tomorrow. There was a chance Melanie might have come home. Or maybe Alden had managed to figure out a solution for what to do with Emma.

If you believe that, you should be stripped of your detective rank.

He climbed into his truck and dialed Alden's number,

putting the phone on speaker and setting it on the seat next to him as he started up the engine.

Alden answered after one ring. "Did it go okay?"

Well, damn. Alden was nervous. Hadn't been nervous about anything in a long time—hadn't *wanted* anything enough to get nervous about, except for drugs. Hearing that tension in his big brother's voice threw Derek back in time, and he had to grip the steering wheel hard to push the sudden shaking from his hands.

He took a deep breath before answering. "Yeah. It was fine."

Alden's heavy sigh of relief filled the cab of the truck. "Thanks, bro. I owe you. I owe—"

"You don't owe me anything." Derek's voice came out sharper than he'd intended, but he couldn't take hearing those words from Alden.

I forgive you because I am the good twin. You're not.

He took out his frustration on the shift lever, throwing the truck into drive and heading for the parking lot exit. His next words came out more gently. "Any contact from Melanie?"

There was a brief pause, but then Alden said, "Nothing. June called me this afternoon on her way into work and told me she'd filed the missing person report, though. I couldn't do a whole lot today because Emma was acting up so much. I think she senses that something's wrong."

Derek nodded, even though he knew Alden couldn't see. At least it was a step forward, even if it didn't necessarily solve the problem of swapping identities. "I'll probably be assigned to the case. It's either gonna be me or Davis, anyway. I'll talk to him about it. Meanwhile, how's Emma?"

"Sleeping. Finally. She—" Alden stopped and drew a ragged breath, and Derek could practically see Alden running his hand through his hair, leaving the short strands spiked up and sticking out every which way. It was a gesture they both did frequently, in exactly the same way. "We both had a rough day.

And then tonight as we were getting her ready for bed, she cried for a long time because she thought I was going to bring her back to Melanie's place while she was sleeping, and she doesn't want to go back there. I mean, I know she's only three, but she told me she's scared of Melanie's friends enough she doesn't want to ever go home again, and I believe her. I think that's part of why she's afraid I might leave even for a second."

Derek's hand tightened on the steering wheel. He knew where this was leading. "So I take it this means you won't be taking over the cleaning job tomorrow night. How much longer am I going to have to play the part of Alden Brewer?"

There was a long pause, and Derek bit back a curse. He knew it was probably too much to ask for that Alden would have solved everything in one day, but it still fucking sucked.

"A couple more nights," Alden insisted. "Three, four at the most, since that's when June is off work again. Maybe Melanie will come back before then. But even if she does, I don't think I can let Emma go back to her, so I've got to find another solution. There's gotta be *someone* out there I can find to watch over her without leaving her scared."

Poor Emma. Derek's frustration ebbed at the reminder this was all for the sake of his niece, who deserved to feel safe. He blew out a breath. "But if Melanie comes back, she has custody…" he trailed off, not wanting to say the words that had to be really upsetting for Alden.

"Yeah. But I'm sober now. She can't use those old arguments against me. And this time, *she's* the one who's missing on some bender."

Derek gave a dark laugh. "You never disappeared like this, at least." Melanie had pushed the courts for full custody when Emma was a few weeks old, since Alden had been too drug-addled to do anything except complain every time his daughter cried. They'd broken up, she'd kicked him out, and the request had been filed all within six hours.

At the time, Alden hadn't even seemed to register what was happening.

What a difference between then and now.

Alden was quiet for a moment before he said, "I feel as if I disappeared like she's doing now, though. And sometimes I think I still haven't fully come back." The words were so faint, nearly a whisper, that the sound from the road as Derek drove almost covered it over.

Fuck. There was no way Derek could respond to that without getting into a much longer conversation than he had energy for tonight. After a full shift at work and three hours of cleaning an office on top of that, he was finally feeling the exhaustion creeping in.

He swallowed against the tightness in his throat. "I think you need to get a lawyer."

A heavy sigh came through the speaker. "I know. I've got an appointment with one tomorrow. I'm taking in a copy of the missing person report and June will back me up. Against her own daughter. God, this is a mess."

"Yeah." Derek was glad Alden wasn't the cause of the mess this time around. It was easier to clean up when there was enough distance between you and the shit that you could see all of it. Leave no stone unturned.

Bad guys lurking in plain sight.

Toni's words skittered through his mind. "Hey, do you remember a kid named Sal Park?"

And his hot little sister?

He had to stop thinking about her that way. Maybe when he got home, he should call up that woman he'd been casually dating—which pretty much amounted to meeting up at her place, having a glass of wine before fucking, then leaving.

But…no.

No, he couldn't see her tonight. It was one thing to hook up when he was feeling generally horny. But it wasn't right to use one woman as a stand-in for another, especially when he hadn't seen her in weeks.

He wondered if Toni had a boyfriend or even a fuck

buddy. He'd seen the way she'd looked at him earlier. Would she think about Derek—*hell*, she thought he was actually Alden—tonight while some other guy thrust into her body? Would she think about him as she slid a finger over her—

"I know Sal." Alden's voice interrupted Derek's imaginings, and Derek blinked at the realization he'd lost track of both the conversation and his driving route. He'd missed the exit to his house. He should take it as a sign that sleep was more important than sex at the moment.

"I used to, anyway," Alden added. "But it's been years. He's real fucked up now. Meth head."

Derek took the next exit and looped around. "Yeah, I know. I've booked him a couple of times on minor shit, and he always walked free. But the guy is as good as gone." He'd dealt with too many meth addicts to believe Sal would manage to escape its hold, especially if he'd already been using for a couple of years. Meth heads were dangerous and scary and their addiction was so intense it was nearly impossible to break until they were wearing a tag on their toe. "Anyway, I thought about him because his sister works at Sentinel. I ran into her tonight."

"Toni?" Alden gave a lot whistle. "Toni is hot. Sweet, too. She used to have a crush on me. Sal told me."

For some reason, that made Derek feel strange and prickly, but he kept his voice calm. "Well, she didn't seem to realize I wasn't you. She recognized me. I mean, you. But of course I didn't recognize her. Told her I was too fucked up for so long."

"Dick." Alden threw the word through the speaker, but there was no heat behind it, and Derek laughed. "Why are you asking, anyway? Want to ask her out? She's a goody-goody from what I remember. Straight As and barely associated with her brother's druggie friends. Definitely your type."

"No, it's nothing like that," Derek lied. "But I wonder if Sal might know where Melanie is. He's pretty heavy into the scene. If you guys all knew each other way back when, she might have contacted him. Might even have gotten into that shit, too. It would certainly explain why she can't control herself even for Emma's sake."

He could hear the heavy breath Alden pushed out, coming like wind through the receiver. "You might actually be on to something. But I don't know. Even when I was so far gone I barely knew my own name, I knew not to touch meth. Melanie and I talked about it. She knew, too. That junk will kill you fast."

"Well, since I'll be heading back to Sentinel tomorrow, if Toni is there again, you want me to ask her? See if she knows anything?"

Alden hummed in thought. "I don't know. I don't really want to get her involved. Even if she was a good girl, she was always really cute, and her parents are great. Nice people. A lot older. I don't know what's going on with Sal, but I can't imagine their family is actually managing to cope with all of this."

Is this really Alden I'm talking to? Derek realized there were changes in Alden, but it was still hard to get used to his brother having compassion and empathy again. Those functions had been all but eliminated these past years, with the vike taking over everything that had once made Alden a real person.

Derek rolled into his driveway and turned off his truck. Ran his hand through his hair, like he'd imagined Alden doing earlier. "All right, I won't say anything to her. She was the only one there tonight, but even then she was about to leave when I ran across her. So she probably won't even be there tomorrow night, anyway." He ignored the weird pang of disappointment those words brought him. "And tomorrow I'll figure out what's going on with the case. If Davis is on it, I'll talk to him about the missing person report, fill in anything June might have left out."

"Thanks, Derek."

"And give Emma a hug from her favorite uncle."

Alden snorted. "Whatever, man. G'night."

The line disconnected and Derek grabbed his stuff out of the cab, then headed inside, ready to collapse.

Toni shut the door softly behind her and threw the deadbolt, pausing for a moment in the front hall to let her eyes adjust to the darkness. Not surprisingly, Mom and Dad were already in bed. She'd called them when she left the office, to tell them she wouldn't be home until much later, even though living at home and having to check in with her parents made her feel like she was sixteen instead of twenty-six.

Except it wasn't quite the same, really. This was a choice she'd made. A small way of reassuring them they still had one child with both feet planted fully in the land of the living. By the time she'd graduated from college and come back to Greenbriar, Sal had been arrested three times, been through a few rehab stints, and managed to alienate one of the best psychologists in the state.

And those were only the attempts at getting him help that she knew about. When she'd been away at school, her parents had kept it from her as best they could. But she'd seen the toll it had taken on them, dealing with everything alone. They had enough to worry about without her going AWOL on them, too.

She'd come back to save them all.

The situation made it difficult, though, to do anything like date or even go out with friends. Most guys who were interested in her even after they found out she still lived at home with her parents weren't the guys she was interested in.

No, you want men like Alden.

God, she was messed up. Alden might be the kind of guy who was willing to fool around with her a couple of times, but he probably already had enough baggage of his own to be taking on hers, too.

Of course, maybe that meant he might be more understanding than others had been…

Stop thinking about him!

Tonight she hadn't been able to come back home immediately after she'd finally left Sentinel. It had seemed too oppressive all of a sudden as she'd walked out of the office with thoughts of Alden crowding her mind, jostling up against the excitement that she would finally be able to get Sal into a reputable rehab program and dread of having to wrestle him into it.

If she could even find Sal first.

Unable to deal with the warring lust, fear, and frustration, she'd called home, told her parents she'd be late, then driven around the city just thinking. She'd thought about Alden and how *sexy* he'd turned out. She vaguely remembered a couple of years ago, before things had gone from bad to worse, Sal had mentioned Alden in passing because he'd had a daughter. With someone else who had run with their group for a while.

But Alden hadn't been wearing a ring tonight. Was he still with the mother of his child? Was he single?

Toni sighed. *Honestly*. She shouldn't be thinking about him that way. Not seriously. Not even as a passing infatuation. Not only because of his rough past, but because in some ways, his intense stares and chiseled, hulking body scared her even more than Sal did. And she found herself enjoying it.

You're sick.

She shook her head. No, it wasn't like that. He wasn't scary. He was intimidating, but not threatening. At least, not toward her. He was strong and hard and he could protect her—

No. No. *Stop trying to find a savior to sweep in and rescue you.*

She was on her own on this one. God help them all.

After a moment, she was able to make out the shapes of furniture in the living room to the left, and she could see the stairs at the end of the front hall, leading up to her bedroom. Slowly, she walked forward, trying not to make a sound that might wake her parents. Her laptop bag swung gently against her hip, the rasp of nylon against her corduroy pants sounding deafeningly loud in the tight silence. She grabbed the bag, holding it tightly in place before tiptoeing—

Bang!

A noise sounded in the kitchen, startling her so badly she wasn't able to stifle a sharp scream. It came out like the noise of a screeching cat, but at least she cut it off quickly, then covered her mouth with a hand, her breath coming fast and loud through her nose as she stared, wide-eyed, at the doorway to the kitchen.

Oh God oh God.

Had Sal gotten into the house somehow? They'd changed all the locks and put bars on the lower windows but that didn't mean anything if he was getting as desperate as he'd seemed lately.

Someone flipped on the hall light and Toni practically dove backward, plastering herself against the wall in a futile attempt to blend in with the floral paper.

And then... "Toni?"

The soft voice floated over to her, breaking her fear apart, and the breath whooshed out of Toni in such a rush she nearly fainted. Thank God she had the wall to hold her up.

"*Mom.* God. I-I thought you were Sal."

The shadowy figure of Isabella Park appeared in the doorway to the kitchen, behind the stairs. A second later, Toni's mother stepped into the hallway. Mom was wearing her faded flannel pajamas and holding a mug of something steaming in one hand.

"I'm sorry, sweetie. I didn't mean to scare you. I didn't even hear you come in." Her mother's face was drawn, revealing the abundance of worry lines around her mouth and on her forehead. Not for the first time, it struck Toni how *old* her parents had gotten in the past two years. Her mother's long, dark hair was streaked with gray, and deep wrinkles had marred the glowing olive skin that was a source of pride for the women in her Italian family.

A surge of helpless anger rose, making Toni push away from the wall and clear the horrified expression she could still feel on her face. No use in adding to her mother's agony.

"It's okay. It was my fault. I thought you would be sleeping, so I was trying extra hard not to make any noise. I didn't mean to scare you, either." She managed a small smile for her mom's benefit and gestured to the mug. "Hot milk?"

Mom nodded, and then her face broke out in a smile, bigger and brighter than Toni's. It was so good to see her mother smile she almost didn't hear the soft addition of "With a generous splash of rum."

Surprise had Toni laughing in response. "Mom! Seriously? And here I thought you were turning into Nonna Maria with your cozy pajamas and steamed milk."

"Who do you think I learned this from? My grandmother might have seemed like an innocent little old lady, but she was a firecracker until the end." Mom shrugged, her voice going reflective. "Just goes to show you things aren't what they seem on the surface, I guess."

Toni felt a weird sense of déjà vu creep down her spine at those words. Hadn't she said something like that to Alden tonight, when she'd warned him about all those invisible germs on the desks?

Speaking of…"Mom, do you remember a guy who used to hang around with Sal? Alden?"

To her surprise, Mom smiled. "Oh, of course I remember him. Alden Brewer, right? He was a sweet boy." But then her expression suddenly turned to alarm. "Oh, no. Is he mixed up with meth, too?"

"No." Toni shook her head. "He went clean. I ran into him tonight at work. I mean, he's a custodian, and since I was working late—"

"Alden went *clean*?"

The look on Mom's face said it all. Wistful longing, hope, and even what looked a bit like jealousy had settled into the lines around her eyes.

"Yeah," Toni said softly. There was no use asking anything

more about Alden. It would only hurt to have to talk about who he was now and give Mom a glimpse of how much better things could have turned out for Sal.

But at the same time, maybe he could help, somehow. Maybe Alden had a cure for this horrible life Sal was living. If he could help find Sal and convince him to go to rehab, maybe guide him when he got out…if they could get her brother the help he was demanding without having to involve the police or a horrible, state-sponsored lockdown rehab clinic…then maybe she could give her parents back their pride. Maybe she could return the kind of peace to this house that didn't make people age beyond their years or scream at every little bump and movement. A little salvation after years of suffering.

"Anyway, I'm really tired," Toni lied. She wasn't. Her headache had disappeared when she'd been talking to Alden in the office and she was still so keyed up, even after driving around town for so long, but she needed to be alone for a while. "I'd better get to bed."

Her mother nodded. "Of course. Good night. Sleep well, dear."

"Good night, Mom. I love you."

"I love you, too."

Toni practically ran toward the stairs, not bothering to look back as she disappeared into the darkness upstairs.

Chapter Three

Big brown eyes looked up from where she knelt on the floor in front of him. Those beautiful lips puckered, and Toni leaned forward to place a soft kiss on the fabric of his sweatpants, against the jutting head of his hard cock.

Derek groaned.

Take it out. Please, God, take it out and touch me, he silently begged. *Lick me*.

It was as though she could read his thoughts, because one slender hand reached up and tugged at the waistband, making the soft weave of his sweats rub over the sensitive head of his dick, creating both too much feeling and yet not enough. He gasped for breath, reaching down to help her push the pants off, sighing in relief when his erection sprang free, bobbing right above her lips. Tempting, straining—

Riiing!

Toni disappeared into vapor, and only then did Derek realize he was surrounded by some kind of strange, hazy fog. *What. The. Fuck.* He struggled for a moment, flailing his arms, trying to figure out where he was and where she'd gone.

Riiing!

Derek opened his eyes, breathing hard. *Shit. Shit shit shit.* Of course it had been a dream. It had been too good to be true.

Riiing!

"Aw, shut the fuck *up.*" He rolled over to grab the phone next to his bed, realizing belatedly the sweats he usually slept in were pushed down around his thighs, gently trapping his legs together, and his cock was still half-hard. *God, what a dream.*

He hit the talk button and put the phone to his ear,

grabbing at his pants with his free hand and yanking them up as he stood. "Hello?"

"Brewer, what the fuck is going on with your brother's baby mama?"

He was going to *kill* Donahue for interrupting that dream.

Derek scowled. "What the hell are you talking about? And why are you calling me this early?"

"I'm talking about Melanie. She's the reason why I'm calling you. One of the hookers who works down on the Strip got picked up early this morning. When Crewes put her in a holding cell, she said she was surprised Melanie wasn't already in there."

Wait. What?

"Did Melanie get picked up and no one told me?"

"No. Bit slow on the uptake this morning, huh? The other night, this hooker saw Melanie get into a car with a john but never come back. She figured Melanie had gotten herself arrested. That was the night she was supposed to be working a private gig, right?"

"I don't know. Damn it, I—hold on and let me think."

Donahue made an impatient sound on the other end. "Well, wake the fuck up, get your ass down to the station, and we'll interview the girl about it. It's nearly seven o'clock, anyway."

Goddamn. Derek usually rolled in around eight but always woke up well before then. The cleaning gig must have taken more of a toll than he'd realized. And he hadn't *wanted* to wake up…

His cock hardened again, starting to push up against his sweats in a torturous repeat of that glorious dream.

"Hey. You still there?" Donahue sounded a little worried now.

Derek bit back a groan. He didn't want the guys to start fussing over him like little old ladies. They'd be all up in his business in no time, and given they were some of the best cops on the force, it wouldn't be too difficult to take it from there and find out about his moonlighting.

Derek shook himself. "Yeah, I'm here. I didn't sleep well, is all. But I'll be at the station in half an hour."

He clicked out of the call and threw the phone down on the mattress. How was he going to survive this two-timing gig? He was tired, he was worried about his brother and his niece, and he'd gotten a hard-on from merely *thinking* about Toni Park. While on the phone with Donahue, for fuck's sake.

Enough complaining. You don't go back on your word. You're the good brother.

That's what he'd been telling himself for fifteen years, anyway. Maybe it was the exhaustion, or maybe it was latent rebellion he needed to quash right away, but Derek was having a hard time *feeling* it right now.

Then again, if Alden hadn't done the wrong thing all those years ago, he might never have lost half a lifetime to drugs. He'd had a chance back then to do the right thing and hadn't. And that had changed everything.

Derek couldn't afford to make the same mistake. He blew out a breath, then stretched and yawned. *Better get moving.* He had a long day ahead of him, and even though he had no business thinking about her, he found himself hoping he'd see Toni again at the end of it.

"How's the proposal coming, Toni?"

Toni turned to see her boss, Doug, standing in front of her cubicle. She tamped down the frustration she was feeling with work and gave him a small smile.

She hadn't slept well last night, alternately plagued by soul-freezing nightmares about Sal and body-burning dreams featuring Alden. She'd woken up late and had to rush to work, arriving to a mountain of emails and regular work that had to be taken care of before she could get back to developing the proposal.

She'd be staying late again tonight. And this time she couldn't afford to leave because of little things like a headache or a raging attraction to the janitor.

"It's going well, Doug." She nodded as though it might help add sincerity to her words. The presentation *was* going well, after all. It just required a lot of hard work to make sure things stayed that way. "And I want to thank you again for this opportunity. I really—"

He held up a hand and let out a soft chuckle, stepping into her cubicle and bending to her ear, pitching his voice low. "I know you don't really love this career. We've talked about this, remember? But you're still the smartest, hardest-working team member I've got. You're the right person for the job and you're doing me as much a favor as I'm doing you. We both know it, so save it."

He immediately backed off when he was done, but it hadn't been menacing, anyway. He'd probably not wanted all the other operations team members to hear, even though Doug was a good guy who usually preferred honesty and the straight-shooter approach to smarmy sucking up. If the others knew what he thought of her, she'd probably suffer even more barbed looks and behind-the-hand gossip than she did already. She tried to ignore it and was always friendly and polite to her coworkers, but she noticed that they'd cooled off in their treatment of her ever since Doug had started to take an interest in her professional development.

That had been a surprise for her, too, though. Doug had been a good mentor when she'd confessed during one of their review meetings that she'd taken the job only because it would mean being able to be near enough to her family, and that it wasn't her choice of profession. He hadn't held that against her. If anything, he'd given her something to take away the sting of putting aside her dreams to help her brother and parents.

She took a deep breath and nodded. "Either way, I'll be ready for next week."

Doug gave her thumbs up, then patted her on the shoulder and left.

Regardless of what he said, she really did owe him. Another reason why she'd need to work late again tonight. This proposal couldn't be merely good. It had to be exemplary, to show the higher-ups that Doug had made the right choice and that they could have as much faith in him as he'd shown to her.

That's not the only reason you want to be in the office after hours...

Her cheeks heated at the memory of some of the dreams she'd had of Alden last night. There was no use denying she was attracted to him—not like she wanted to pretend otherwise to herself, anyway. But if she did see him again, what did it matter? Alden Brewer had gone *clean*. She couldn't imagine he'd want her in his life, with the errant baggage of Sal and his addiction that Alden had somehow managed to kick off and emerge so much the better for it.

She turned back to her desk and ignored the stirrings of what felt like another epic headache coming on.

Chapter Four

Derek set down the vacuum in the short corridor that connected two sides of the building floor and rolled his shoulders, trying to work out the kinks that seemed to have settled down there overnight.

When he'd gotten to the station this morning and interviewed that hooker, she hadn't been able to tell them much more than what Donahue had shared over the phone. But given that Melanie had gotten into a car with someone and had never come back, it was starting to look more like foul play than a case of a junkie on a bender.

He didn't want to be the one to tell Alden, but he wasn't going to shy away from his responsibilities, either. He'd call Alden tonight after he finished the cleaning gig and talk to him about Melanie. Hopefully his brother would be ready to pick up this contract as soon as June had her nights off.

Derek had finished most of the floor already but hadn't been able to find Toni. He had gone by her cubicle and seen her purse and a pair of high heels there—the heels had made his blood race a bit faster as he'd pictured her slipping them off—but her laptop wasn't on the desk and he hadn't seen her anywhere.

Disappointment had slowed him down, but now he had only a couple more offices and a conference room to clean and he was done. He headed down one row of cubicles to a nook set back from the rest of the floor where the remaining three rooms were, but to his surprise the door to the conference room was shut and there was a light on inside, shining through the narrow window next to the door.

Toni.

He couldn't see into the room from where he stood, but he knew it was her.

The image of her from his dream this morning slammed into his mind's eye with all the finesse of a baseball bat to the face. Desire flooded through his body, making everything strain with the need to *take*.

He immediately fought the feeling, though. It wasn't right. This wasn't him. He wasn't impulsive or selfish like Alden was, and even if he was attracted to her, he shouldn't be lingering outside the door, thinking about chatting her up before taking her home to relieve some of this impossible ache.

She was too sexy for his own good.

But—no, *that* wasn't right, either. He couldn't blame it on her. The reaction had to be part of this horrible slippery slope he'd agreed to traverse when he'd temporarily taken on Alden's custodial services contract. The very idea of posing as the bad twin must be tampering with his mind.

Yeah. That was probably it. As long as he fought these urges for the next few days, everything would be fine.

Disappointment shifted into discomfort, and he bypassed the conference room in favor of cleaning the offices first. She was in there, anyway, and he didn't want to disturb her.

Yes, you do. You want to disturb her until she's begging you not to stop, never to stop, to disturb her morning, noon, and night, in your bed, on the floor, bent over the—

"Alden?"

Hearing Alden's name from her lips was like being soaked through with freezing cold water, but it was a good reminder not to let his lust run away with him. He could hardly give his brother's secret away, but he couldn't allow himself to get involved with Toni while he was lying about his own name, for fuck's sake.

He straightened up from where he'd been setting the small office trash can back in its place and turned to face her.

Aw, damn, she was beautiful. He'd already forgotten how

gorgeous she was, even though in his imagination she was already the hottest thing he'd ever seen.

"Toni. Hey." He made his face relax into a smile. "Another late night, huh?"

She lifted one shoulder in a semi-shrug. "I had a call with our West Coast office about some of their processes for…"

She trailed off and seemed to give herself a mental shake, because in the next second she gave that little half-shrug again and waved her hand in the air. "I'm sure you don't want the details."

"I'm interested in hearing about it, actually." He was studiously casual with the remark, knowing he was a fool for wanting to keep her around for a while longer.

She hesitated, though, and he made a show of gathering up his cleaning supplies from where he'd set them on a chair, placing them back into his bin. Did she think he wasn't intelligent enough to be able to understand? Was she trying not to spend any more time with him than what bare minimum politeness required?

Right before he was about to tell her to forget it and get out of his way, she spoke, surprising him.

"I'm working on a proposal for a new process rollout that would help new clients enroll in our medical insurance program. It would be company-wide, so all the office locations would use it. But it has to be cost-effective as well as easy to integrate with our existing staff and systems, so I've been number-crunching, talking to managers in all the other offices, and getting information that I'll hopefully be able to put together in some semi-coherent way in order to wow the executives, not embarrass my boss, and earn a promotion."

She threw it all out at once as though she'd been bottling it and he'd released some kind of fizzy thought substance into the room simply by showing a little interest…

He paused for a second, studying her. It was almost as if she'd been *saving* that speech for someone who showed interest.

Had no one else asked her about it? Her family? Her friends?

It struck him that it didn't *seem* like they had, anyway.

And she was biting her lower lip in a way that made her seem nervous.

Nervous and really sexy. He was having a hard time not getting hypnotized by the soft pink fullness of that poor, teeth-abused lip. He wanted to reach out and soothe it with his finger, and then with his lips, and then with the head of his cock and his lips again and then his tongue and—

"Are you okay?"

Her question jarred him back to reality. Thank God he was standing behind the large trash bin on wheels or he'd probably have a lot more explaining to do.

He blinked at her, then smiled a little when he realized she'd asked him the same thing he'd asked her last night. *When she'd been sweating.* He nodded. "Yeah, uh, sorry. I was thinking about how much responsibility that must be. A project like that. Do you have much left to do on it? You must be exhausted, having to work late like this."

Her shoulders dropped a fraction as though some tension had escaped from her. So she *had* been nervous.

"I'm in a good place with it tonight. I'm presenting it next week—Tuesday—so I don't think I'll have many more late nights. At least not after the meeting." She gave him a shy smile. "I'm tired, yes, but these long hours seem to have yielded some definite benefits." The meaningful look she flashed him from under her lashes had him nearly lunging over the bin to grab her.

No. No, you're pretending to be someone else. No, she's overworked and tired and feeling vulnerable because of her brother. It would be wrong.

At least he was no longer questioning whether she was attracted to him, too.

Still, he swallowed hard before saying, "It sounds like you love your job."

There went her one shoulder lift again. He wanted to curve his hand over that shoulder, pull the collar of her shirt down, and sink his teeth into the soft skin at the curve of her neck.

Goddamn it.

He was fantasizing about sex with a practical stranger who thought he was someone else while they were alone in a room together and he was hiding his erection behind a trash can. This was not the code of conduct he had promised to adhere to barely ten minutes ago.

He was going to *kill* Alden for putting him in this position. His cock was so desperate for release it hurt. He was almost tempted to rub it against the hard, curved plastic of the bin simply to get some temporary, albeit rough, relief.

"Do you love yours?" Toni asked, and for a bare second he thought she was asking whether he loved his cock before he realized they'd been talking about her job.

"Yes," he told her immediately, and with conviction, because he did love his job. His real one, though. Being a SWAT officer had been his dream growing up—or at least since he was fifteen. He didn't consider his answer a lie, though neither did he clarify that being a janitor wasn't actually his job.

She raised an eyebrow at him—probably more at the vehemence of his response than that he, by all outward appearances, seemed to have told her that he loved cleaning up after supposedly professional people who behaved like pigs in their workspaces.

Thankfully, his erection had subsided, and he took the opportunity to gesture toward the door. It was getting late and he did need to finish cleaning. Working double shifts was exhausting enough without drawing out the time he spent on physical labor.

As he followed her out of the office, shutting off the light as they left, he happened to look down and notice that her feet were bare—of course, she'd left her shoes at her desk—and he barely suppressed a groan of arousal at the sight of those delicate, toes covered over with a layer of sheer nylon.

Pink painted toenails, too.

He moved to the next office, and she stood in the doorway for a moment. "Well, it was good to see you again, Alden."

He grit his teeth against the desire to tell her to call him Derek, because that was name he wanted her to scream out when she came all over his cock. Telling her such a thing probably wasn't right for more than one reason—instead he gave her a tight nod. "Goodnight, Toni," he managed to get out.

A look of confusion flitted across her face, but she gave him a small wave and turned away, heading off toward her cubicle. A minute later, he heard the back door open and shut, and then the office filled with the silence that comes only when a place is truly, completely devoid of any other life.

He realized only then that she hadn't responded to his statement, about how it sounded like she loved her job, and for the first time, it struck him that maybe she was trying to avoid lying, too.

When Toni got home, Mom and Dad were sitting in the living room, watching television, but her dad switched it off as soon as she stepped into view.

"Toni. We didn't hear you come home."

She fisted her hands at her sides, her nails biting into the soft flesh of her palms as she tried to control her emotions. That hadn't been pleasant surprise in Dad's voice.

It had been fear.

We didn't hear you... What if it had been Sal and we hadn't heard... We didn't realize we might have been in danger... We didn't hear you...

By some stroke of luck, she managed to keep her expression neutral. At least, it felt that way on her face. "I'm sorry, Dad. It's my fault. I've been working later than usual and it's throwing off the routine."

I'm usually here to act as another set of eyes and ears. I'm usually here to help watch over you. I wasn't here tonight. I—

Her feelings must have been easy to read, because Dad stood up and made his way over to her, pulling her into a gentle hug before letting her go and looking at her in concern.

"Hey. Toni. I'm sorry. It's not your fault." Her father's voice was gravely but firm. "I didn't mean to make you feel that way."

Mom stood up, too, and padded over to stand next to Dad, linking her arm through his. Oddly, though, it felt almost as though they were forming a wall *against* her.

She really needed to go to bed and forget this whole thing happened. Rest and hopefully regain control over her explosive feelings.

"Sweetie. Your dad is right. We've—well, we've come to depend on you too much, I think. It's not fair to you and I don't want you to think that it's your responsibility to look out for us. If anything, it should the other way around!"

Mom sounded frustrated at the end, and Toni knew it was because her mother was frustrated with herself. She knew both her parents were being rational and kind. It was what parents were supposed to do.

But she still couldn't erase the sense of panic that was pushing at the boundary of her skin.

If she wasn't responsible for them, why did she give up that amazing chance at the distribution startup back in San Francisco where she could have built a company from the ground up? If she didn't have to look out for them, why did she leave the friends who supported her, the professional contacts she'd made, to come back to Greenbriar? Why had she shut out all possibility of having someone else in her life by coming home every day at six o'clock to make sure her parents were safe?

And even while her thoughts were screaming at her to

walk away and get some sleep and forget it, some deeper, more primal part of her was reminding her that there was someone in the world who might be able to understand her particular situation in life. Someone who had walked this road before, even if it had been on the opposite side.

Alden Brewer.

The mere thought of him helped to calm her. She wasn't doing this for nothing. She was going to put a stop to Sal's addiction and end his terrorization of her family. If Alden could do it, there was hope for Sal through the help of rehab. Between her raise and what remained of her parents' savings after his other trips through different facilities, she was confident that this time, he would turn it around.

"Want to join us for a bit and watch this show? It's pretty good." Mom was doing a good job of keeping her tone light, but Toni could see the stress on both her parents' faces.

All she wanted to do was go upstairs, soak in the tub, and fall asleep. But seeing them there, so desperate for the comfort of normalcy, made her nod her head and say with a smile, "I'd love to."

She made her way over to the couch and snuggled between them, allowing herself to pretend for a short time that they were a happy, carefree family of only three, simply enjoying one another's company. She had a feeling that her nearness also allowed her parents the temporary escape that the pretense offered, and she settled herself more deeply into their sides, feeling Mom, then Dad, slowly relax against her.

Maybe she wasn't responsible for them, but they needed her.

And *that* was a responsibility she didn't take lightly.

Chapter Five

It had felt strange to wake up this morning as himself. Derek had rolled out of bed with the odd sensation of wearing an ill-fitting outfit that would never be comfortable no matter how hard he tried to break it in.

He'd never felt that way about himself before. Sure, he'd felt at times like maybe he was missing out on some of the things he wanted, because being different enough to go after those things would mean being too much like his twin. But he'd never felt like who he was might not be the *right* person to be.

Right and wrong. Good twin. Bad twin.

Speaking of bad twins…

He had to call Alden.

He was in his car on the way to work, fighting the heavy fatigue that he'd woken up with. Last night, he'd basically blacked out until his alarm went off shortly after six, then he'd dragged himself to the gym for half an hour before his shift started and now he regretted not sleeping in and skipping the workout. His exhaustion was intense.

Alden picked up right away. "Derek. Hey. Is there news?"

What was—oh. Of course. How could he have forgotten about Melanie? He was supposed to have called Alden about it last night but he'd forgotten.

It wasn't like him. Given the delay, he also should have called one of the guys before calling Alden this morning, in case there were any updates. *Shit.* He was losing track of his responsibilities on both ends. At least he only had a few more days of this before he could go back to normal.

He sighed. "Not yet. I'm sorry. I'm working on it, though.

The hooker I talked to yesterday couldn't give us any new information. We have the description of the car she was seen getting into and I'll be heading down to the Strip later today to interview more folks, to see if any of them recognized the driver of the car. They might, if he's a regular."

There was a long pause, and Derek was pretty sure he knew what his brother was thinking.

That Melanie might never be coming back.

Given the timeline and the circumstances, the chances were getting smaller that they'd find her alive. This didn't sound like a regular bender. But he wasn't willing to make that assessment yet.

"I understand," Alden finally said. "Speaking of Melanie, though, did you happen to see Toni again last night?"

Hell yes I did.

Aw, man. Derek had managed to not think about her for a solid five minutes and now she was back on his mind in full force.

But he knew that wasn't what Alden was talking about. Derek cleared his throat, trying to loosen up the tightness of lust. "I did see her, but there wasn't really a chance to ask her about Sal or Melanie."

I was too busy trying to hide my rampant erection.

He quickly changed the subject, not wanting to talk about Toni anymore lest he give too much away. "How was the meeting with the lawyer yesterday? It was yesterday, right?"

Luckily, Alden didn't seem to notice the abrupt switch. "It was good. Promising. He said he'd put in a motion right away for temporary custody. I'm supposed to hear from him this morning, confirming that he filed it yesterday. He said he'd get the ball rolling on the rest."

At least that part of Alden's life seemed like it was under control. "Cool. I hope you can get it done quickly. How's Emma?"

"She's okay, I guess. I mean, she's fine as long as I'm with her, but she still panics and cries if I leave. Not like before, because at least I can go to the bathroom and she doesn't worry now. But I still can't, like, go to the grocery store without her."

"That's shitty, man." Derek meant it. No matter how inconvenient this whole setup was for him, Emma was a sweet, innocent child who didn't deserve to suffer.

"Yeah. Listen, Derek. I owe you so big. I can't"—Alden let out a breath so strong it was audible through the phone—"I can't even begin to explain how much I appreciate this."

Derek cringed. *Here comes the abject thanks again.*

"I mean, I'm thankful not only for me but for Emma. She needed the time and you've been a lifesaver. I don't know how to—"

"It's okay," Derek interrupted. *Fuck.* Hadn't Alden realized yet that he didn't want to hear that kind of mewling gratitude? The implicit dependence of it?

"It's *okay*?" Alden echoed. "I—" He stopped for a second, and Derek could practically hear him trying to calm himself on the other end of the line. "Not that I'm...objecting." Alden's slow speech meant he was choosing his words carefully now. "I thought you were pissed off at me for putting you in this position and I didn't want it to come between us."

Derek grunted. Yes, he was annoyed, but holding a grudge over it and torturing Alden as part of some sick debt? For fuck's sake, he wasn't a jerk. He was the good guy, here.

Wasn't he?

He pulled his truck into the Greenbriar Police Station employee parking lot. "Yeah. It's okay," he repeated.

It sucked, but there really was no other way. He couldn't blame his brother for trying to do the right thing for Emma. *Okay* was the best it could be. He swallowed a yawn. After this was over, he was going to sleep for a week.

Maybe Toni would be there again tonight. That would definitely keep him awake.

Damn it, he was thinking of her again.

He'd hated having to lie to her last night. He'd tried not to. He'd tried to come up with as many creative ways as possible to answer her questions without actually lying, speaking as much in the abstract as possible and trying not to say "I" at all. But there were a few moments when he'd had no choice, and it made him feel like shit. He didn't *want* to be like Alden. It was why he'd wanted to avoid taking this job in the first place.

A few more nights and then it would be over. Alden would take over and Toni wouldn't work late again, at least for quite some time. She'd never know the truth and he could walk away with a clear conscience.

Keep your hands off her and everything will be fine.

It bothered him to even think of hurting her.

But it wouldn't be you who hurt her. It would be Alden...

He shook the shady thought out of his head and sighed. "Look, I have to go. I just got to work and I have a lot of shit to deal with today."

At least *that* was the truth.

"Toni. May I talk to you for a minute?" The hushed tones of Dad's voice were enough to indicate that this was a conversation he didn't want her mother to overhear.

Toni had just come downstairs to grab a bite to eat before leaving for work when her dad had stepped out of the kitchen to make his request.

"Sure," she murmured, grateful that her emotions were much less volatile this morning. A good night's sleep had cured most of her feelings of panic, but she hoped the sensation would stay at bay at least through this talk with Dad.

"What is it?" she asked as soon as he'd led her into the office and shut the door behind them. She noticed with a sad sense of inevitability that most of his hair was now white, making him look much older than his fifty-eight years.

"I wanted to tell you something. I thought about it last night after we talked. We really have put too much stress on you, Toni. I don't think it's fair and I'm ashamed of myself for allowing it to happen. I know you've been doing so much, working so hard, to help pay for this treatment, but I've come to a decision."

Uh-oh. This did not sound good. Especially when the decision was something Mom wasn't supposed to hear.

But he didn't seem to notice her tension, instead continuing in the same resolved manner, "We're going to sell this house. We can use the money we get from it to fund Sal's rehab."

Sell the house?

But it was all they had left! Their retirement savings had already gone toward helping Sal, and look where that had gotten them.

Toni shook her head. "Dad, I don't mind. Really. I want to help. I want Sal to get better and you guys have already spent so much on those other rehab programs. It isn't fair—"

"It isn't fair to *you*," her father interrupted. "This is not the kind of parent I want to be. That *we* want to be. Mom and I both agree that we have to be better than this. We—"

"How come she doesn't know what you're talking to me about, then?" Toni challenged.

For a moment, her father seemed stricken, and she cringed at her insensitivity.

"Dad. I'm sorry. I didn't mean to sound like I was accusing you or trying to make you feel bad. I'm *sorry*."

He sighed, his shoulders drooping wearily. "I didn't tell her my idea right away because I didn't want her to use up her energy trying to convince you that it's the right thing to do. You know she would agree and would spend so much focus and emotion on getting you to accept it. She's already so fragile. Adding this on top of everything else would only wear her out faster."

Toni nodded and swallowed the urge to apologize again, trying to move on. "If you sold the house, where would you go?"

"We could rent an apartment for a few months while we waited to see how the rehab goes for Sal. If it works, we could look into buying in a new area. If it doesn't, it might be better for us to start over somewhere else." Her dad shrugged as though he wasn't quite certain, but his answer seemed well thought out.

In fact, he presented it with enough practical detail that it took her a moment for the real meaning to sink in—if the rehab program worked for Sal, they'd stay, presumably for his sake. But if it didn't...

"You'd *give up* on him?"

Her dad turned to look out the window, out through the iron bars that kept Sal at bay, and Toni immediately wanted to take back the question. She already knew the answer, and there was no need to make her father say it out loud.

Of course they'd give up on him. Not because they didn't love him—she'd seen what they'd gone through for his sake. But because they would have tried everything at that point, and there would simply be no more hope for him if this last resort didn't work.

Dad inhaled a shuddering breath, his back to her, and she imagined that he was fighting back tears. He'd never cried in front of her and she didn't want him to start now. It would be too...well, too *real*, somehow.

"I know what you've sacrificed for us, Toni." His voice was soft, but it carried. "No matter what, you can go return to California and get back that life you never should have left behind. I wish I could give you more than my regrets and apologies, but it's time for us all to do what we need to do."

Go back to California?

Leave?

Abandon her parents and brother?

Maybe a month ago, Toni would have jumped at the chance to return to the very different life she'd left behind. But now, seeing what might be—with her so close to getting a promotion that might help Sal get the treatment he needed without having to bankrupt her parents in the process—only strengthened her conviction that this was the right thing to do. Sal might still come out of this okay, and if that happened, they'd all need to be strong for him.

When that happens. Not if. When. Don't give up on Sal.

Alden had succeeded in breaking free, after all, and he'd made a better life for himself. It was possible. There was still hope.

"I'm not going anywhere," she insisted.

Dad turned around and she caught the sheen of wetness in his eyes before he blinked it away. "Toni—"

She pressed forward. "Wait a little while, okay? Like you said, Mom is fragile. Why don't we agree that if I get this promotion, I'll pay for the rehab. If it works, you can pay me back. If it doesn't…well, we'll deal with that when we get there. Okay?"

He regarded her for a minute, but finally gave her a slow, reluctant nod. "Okay. But don't tell your mother about any of this. I don't want her to worry herself sick."

She gave him a small, sad smile. "I won't tell. Thank you for not giving up on him yet, Dad."

But her dad only turned toward the window again, and after a moment Toni murmured a goodbye and slipped out the door to go to work.

Chapter Six

"Brewer. Coffee."

Derek had been at the station for all of two minutes when Ben Crewes, his partner and fellow SWAT officer, walked in and set a lidded paper cup on the bench behind Derek's locker.

Sweet Jesus, he's a lifesaver.

Derek grabbed at the cup, saluting Crewes with it. "Thanks, man." He put his mouth to the hole in the lid and took a deep swig, uncaring of the burning heat of the liquid.

He was too fucking tired to waste time on letting it cool down. He needed the caffeine.

Crewes raised a brow at him, but didn't say anything, and Derek nodded another thanks. It was one of the many reasons that Crewes was a good friend in addition to a good partner at work. He understood when not to push.

Crewes leaned against one of the other lockers and gestured toward Derek. "Hurry up. We gotta be across town in twenty minutes."

Derek pulled his uniform shirt on over his white tank undershirt. He'd meant to be here earlier so he could be dressed already, but he didn't realize how much more slowly he was moving than usual. He'd lost track of time while he'd been on the phone with Alden.

"What have we got going today?" He buttoned up, grabbed his cap, then took another big gulp of coffee before slamming his locker shut.

"We got a domestic call about ten minutes ago. In Northside."

Derek let out a harsh breath. Man, he hated domestic

disturbance calls. Too often they ended in nothing but an abused woman's fearful silence. "All right," he growled, turning toward the exit. Crewes fell into step next to him and they headed to the cruiser in silence.

But at the car, Crewes slid into the driver's seat without warning, leaving Derek standing next to the door, trying to process what was happening. He always drove on Wednesdays. Not that he enjoyed it—they both hated having to be behind the wheel. But it was his turn and he wasn't going to shirk his responsibility.

"What are you doing? It's Wednesday." Maybe Ben had forgotten.

But his partner rolled his eyes and jerked his head toward the passenger's seat. "There's no way I'm letting you drive in the state you're in."

What the hell? That raised Derek's hackles. "What are you trying to say? Are you seriously accusing me of being intoxicated? Or *high?*" Ben had to know he'd never do such a thing. How could he—?

"No, you fucking massive idiot. I mean, you're exhausted and *emotional* and I'm not putting my life in your hands because you're too proud to admit you're not sleeping enough. I've got a kid on the way, remember?"

Well, that took the wind right out of Derek's sails. Nina, Ben's wife, was heavily pregnant and due any day. If he'd had enough sleep, he would have remembered that. But right now, he was running on fumes and adrenaline, and he was pretty sure his emotions were at their all-time basest.

"Yeah," he managed to mumble. "I remember." And then, because it needed saying, he added a much clearer, "I'm sorry."

Crewes snorted. "Forgiven. Now get the fuck in the car. We have a job to do."

Two jobs, Derek thought as he went around to the passenger's side, slamming back the last of the coffee as he went. He was drained, and if this didn't get resolved soon, Alden was going to be out of a job before he'd even had a chance to do it himself.

Crewes pulled out onto the road and put on his siren and lights, zipping toward the neighborhood where the call had come from. Despite the coffee, sitting there motionless was starting to lull Derek to sleep. Ben had been right to take the wheel.

Thank God for competent partners.

"Hey, Brewer." Ben was looking ahead, hands casually resting on the wheel, but something in his voice sounded much more serious than he looked.

"What's up?"

"If you see Alden, tell him to stop poking his nose around down on the Strip. We've got enough trouble there without having to watch over him, too."

Derek frowned. "He was there asking questions about Melanie before he filed the report. He wanted to be sure it was worth filing before—"

"No, man. He was there again yesterday afternoon. Davis had to load him into a car to get him to shove off."

Fucking. Hell. Why hadn't Alden said anything about it this morning? And had he taken Emma with him when he'd gone there? That was beyond foolish. A child had no business being anywhere near that place. Alden knew better than that.

Derek groaned. "I'm sorry. Fuck, I'm sorry." Again. He wouldn't have a chance to call Alden again until he left work at Sentinel, but either way this couldn't happen again. He'd have to apologize to Davis, too, and Donahue, who was Davis's partner. No doubt they'd both been there.

Ben shrugged. "We all understand. But I thought you should know. Okay?"

It was Ben's way of telling him that this time was already forgiven, but he'd better keep an eye on Alden or there'd be complaints.

Derek nodded. "Okay."

He'd call his brother later and tell him that if it happened again, the deal was off. No more pretending to be Alden.

No more seeing Toni.

You can't have her, anyway.

But for the first time since he was a boy, Derek found himself wishing that, when it came to Toni, anyway, he could trade places with Alden forever.

"Goodnight, Toni. I'm heading out."

Doug stopped at Toni's cubicle, his laptop bag slung over a shoulder. She stood, smiling, to say goodbye. He'd stayed later than usual tonight, too, to go over what she'd pulled together so far, and he'd given her some helpful pointers on how to structure her presentation to make sure the execs would support it.

"Have a good night, too. And thanks for all your help." She beamed at him. He really was the best boss she could have hoped for.

"Hey, don't mention it. It was my pleasure. I stand to gain from this, too, after all." He gave a small chuckle and shook his head. "Seriously, though, you've got a great start there. I'm looking forward to seeing your full draft on Friday. See you tomorrow…and don't stay too late!"

She laughed and waved him off, then sat back down to focus again on her work. Everyone else was already gone from the office, but Doug and she were going to do a dry run of the presentation on Friday and another on Monday, so she wanted it to be as solid as possible before then. She'd make some changes tonight based on the input he'd had and then it would be in pretty good shape.

She was still grinning when the familiar whir of a vacuum came close, and she once again stood up in her cubicle with a big smile on her face. But Alden's mouth was drawn tight and he was wearing a strange expression. In fact, he was barely looking at her.

"Hey, Toni."

Even his short greeting had been full of something that felt like—not anger, exactly…more like frustration. Something skating in the between the lines of more righteously defined emotions.

"Are you okay?"

They seemed to be incapable of *not* asking one another that question.

"Fine," he clipped out, his expression turning darker, his mouth moving into a clear-cut frown.

But he wasn't fine. He was very obviously *not fine.* Watching him stomp from desk to desk, picking up trash cans and tossing them like a machine into the large bin, those massive, beautiful shoulders hunched and tight, was too much for her to handle.

She couldn't help the laugh that escaped her.

At the sound, he whipped around, glaring at her, and for a moment she froze, but fear only skated through her for a fraction of a second before his face broke as he joined in her laughter.

It left her breathless and smiling and not even sure why she was so happy.

"Yeah…I guess I *am* feeling a little on edge," he admitted, then turned and started spraying the desks with industrial cleaner, attacking them with a rag with a gusto that screamed *Avoidance Tactic!*

She came out of her cube and approached him, putting a hand on his arm to stop his wild motion.

Oh, that was a mistake.

The feel of his flexing muscles under her fingers nearly made her lose the ability to think coherently. And then he dropped the rag he was holding and turned, twisting his forearm in her grip until they were palm to palm.

Holding hands.

Oh sweet Jesus, don't let me faint from arousal.

"Why are you upset?"

Great. She sounded breathless even to her own ears, and he smirked.

At least he's not glaring at you anymore.

Was it just her, or was he leaning closer? She could smell his deodorant and the subtle, sweet scent of his sweat, and she fought against the urge to close her eyes and let her body drape, press, *rub* against his.

They were still holding hands.

"I didn't say I was *upset*." He reached over and *thunked* the spray bottle back into the caddy of supplies, but he didn't let go of her. She could feel the tension in him practically humming through his skin as he turned back to her.

She rolled her eyes. "Okay, then. Why are you *on edge?*"

He hesitated for a second, then his jaw set and he jerked his chin toward her cubicle. "Who was that guy?" His voice was pitched low, but he didn't sound angry or frustrated or any shade in between.

If she didn't know better, she'd say he sounded aroused.

You do know better. He sounds aroused.

"Which guy?"

You sound aroused, too.

"The one who stopped by your desk a few minutes ago."

He *was* leaning closer. His T-shirt was nearly brushing her blouse—her *breasts*, and he was practically whispering but she could hear him clearly. She lifted her eyes to his, feeling herself sink a little deeper before his question finally registered. She frowned and pulled back, gasping when she realized exactly how *close* they'd been.

She would have kissed him. They'd been about to.

Hadn't they?

God knew she wanted to do it. The desperate desire for Alden was being buoyed and expanded by the growing need for something pleasurable in her life, just for herself. She wanted to kiss Alden Brewer. She wanted…well, she wasn't sure what else. But she'd take anything he gave her.

He was still looking at her expectantly, and she blinked at him, trying to clear away the fog that was filling her mind. "Are you talking about Doug? My *boss?*"

Why would Alden care about Doug? And why would he ask her that in response to her asking if he was upset?

Oh. Wait. Could he—?

"You're *jealous*." The wondering statement was out before she could stop it, but from the way he tensed and looked away, she knew she was right.

Oh my God.

"Alden." She stepped close to him again, and this time she could feel the fabric of their clothes rasping against each other. *So close.* "Doug is my boss. He's in his *fifties*."

"He's not a bad-looking guy." Alden's jaw was clamped so tight she was amazed he'd even gotten semi-decipherable words out.

It made her smile. "You're not a bad-looking guy, either."

This close, though they weren't exactly touching, she felt him soften a little at her words, and the feeling made her bold enough to ask, "Do you—are you *attracted* to me?"

Because I think I am making it more than clear right now that I'm attracted to you.

He didn't respond, though. Just stood there like a stone as though fighting against his own will. *But why?* She had to know.

"Look at me," she murmured, and when he turned to meet her eyes, she took the opportunity to slide up his body and press her lips to his.

Chapter Seven

He shouldn't be doing this.

He shouldn't be letting Toni slide her mouth over his, stroke his lower lip with her tongue until he opened for her, his own tongue darting out to lick over her teeth. He shouldn't be pressing his palm against her lower back to urge her up against his cock, which was straining against his jeans.

But here he was, devouring her kisses and grinding against her like a teenaged boy with no finesse.

She seems to like it, though.

He slowly pivoted, guiding her until her back was against the low wall of the cubicle, and dropped his hands to her waist, stroking and rubbing down her body, down her legs.

She broke the kiss for only a moment to moan with pleasure, the sound urging him to grab two handfuls of fabric and pull them upward, raising her skirt up to bunch around her hips before thrusting one of his denim-clad thighs between her legs at the same moment he met her mouth again in a hot, wet kiss.

She reached up and wound her arms around his neck, pulling him closer, her hips sliding upward so that her panty-covered clit was dragging over his jeans. He could feel the wet heat of her despite the thick fabric between them, and the knowledge of how turned on she was nearly killed him.

She moaned again, and the sound made him even wilder.

He *had* to get inside of her. It felt as though his very survival depended on fucking this woman against a cardboard half wall in the middle of an office building.

Where anyone could see you and have both of you fired.

His hands, which had been moving upward, stopped short of her breasts.

Or arrested. Wouldn't that be entertaining for the guys?

He broke the kiss this time and pulled away from her arms.

And oh yeah—she thinks you're someone else.

He lowered his thigh, slowly moving it away from her to give her time to adjust.

Then he took a step back.

Their harsh, heavy breaths were the only sound on the floor. Her hair was tousled, cheeks flushed, and her lips were even more plump and pink than usual.

Do. Not. Start. Up. Again.

"Toni, I—"

"Whatever you do, don't say you're sorry." Her voice was soft, but he could hear anger in it. *Damn it.* Of course she was angry.

"I'm not sorry," he growled, wishing he could push her smooth, slender legs apart, bury his face between them, and *show* her how not sorry he was.

You're not helping your cause here.

He sucked in a deep breath and let it out slowly in an attempt to calm himself. "I'm not sorry," he repeated, relieved that he sounded much less intense this time. "But we can't do this." The hurt in her eyes at that statement had him rushing on. "I want you. I *like* you. But my life is complicated right now and I don't know when it won't be. I'm not—myself. It's not fair to you to do this."

At least nothing he'd said just now was an outright lie.

And she seemed to accept it, because she gave a tight nod before wrapping her arms around herself and sighing. "At least it's not me this time."

What did that mean?

He wanted to ask, but it felt too intimate after such a raw moment. He shouldn't be digging in deeper with her when he'd only just pulled away.

"Toni, I really am sorry," he murmured.

"Me, too." She looked down at her feet, seeming to steel herself, because in the next moment she brought her head up again, squared her shoulders, and returned to her desk, immediately sitting at her laptop with her back to him.

He'd been dismissed.

He kept cleaning, the both of them studiously ignoring one another.

An hour later, when he came out of the last conference room, Toni was gone and he immediately felt like a jerk for not walking her out. It was dark in the parking lot and she could have used an escort.

She's been fine the past couple of nights. You just want to be near her.

He needed this shit to be over, already. He was through with lying and angry that, even when he was able to stop pretending to be Alden, he could never approach Toni again. She'd hate him for deceiving her, and she might even tell her good-looking boss.

No way was that guy in his fifties. And no way did Doug not have designs on Toni. Or at least fantasies. Derek had seen the way Doug had looked at her earlier.

Fuck, he was so jealous.

Derek slid into his truck after he'd finished up the job and dialed Alden. He'd called his brother right after he'd gotten off work earlier, but there'd been no answer so he'd left an angry voicemail that made it clear what was at stake if Alden went to the Strip again. Then Alden had called him back while he'd been inside Sentinel and hadn't wanted to take the risk of someone listening in and catching on to what he was doing.

Alden picked up immediately. "Derek. Hey. I tried to call you earlier."

"I saw. I was at Sentinel." He headed out of the parking lot.

A rattle of the speaker indicated that Alden had blown out a hard breath. "You went?"

"Yeah." *And I nearly fucked Toni Park on the desk in her cubicle.* Exactly like he'd imagined doing the first night he'd met her.

Goddamn it.

He was going to have to jerk off when he got home. *Needed* to. Sex would be better, but his hand would be more than fine as a substitute for now. Until he got past Toni long enough to stop seeing her face, her body, every time he closed his eyes.

The woman he was casually seeing had texted him last night, but he'd been sleeping and hadn't been able to respond with so much as *I'm sorry, but this is over.* They already hadn't seen each other in over a month, but it felt too callous to do it this morning when he'd woken up and seen the message, so he'd replied with the truth: that he'd missed seeing her text and that they would talk next week.

Once this mess was over and he had the energy to deal with any fallout, he'd officially break it off with her. In the meantime, a good solo job would have to do.

Which he'd take care of as soon as he was home.

He pressed the gas pedal a little harder.

"Oh thank God." Alden sighed the words, pulling Derek out of his ill-timed fantasy, and the obvious relief in Alden's tone had Derek on alert.

"Why did you think I might not go?" He'd left a message for Alden that afternoon, telling him in no uncertain terms that if his brother went poking his nose around in the case again, the deal was off. "Did *you* go to the Strip?" he barked. He was feeling frustrated on so many levels.

"No!" Alden's reply was immediate and indignant-sounding.

His brother was telling the truth, that meant. Derek knew Alden's behavior almost better than he knew his own, especially based on the way he'd been acting lately. Particularly around Toni.

"Then why did you seem to think I was going to bail on your cleaning gig? I told you this morning that it was okay!"

There was a moment of silence before Alden's much calmer voice said, "Because you've been weird lately and…look, I'm sorry. I didn't know. June hadn't gone to work yet and I had a little free time, I thought I'd be able to find her, so I figured I'd ask around again since you got that lead about the john on the Strip. But it was only that once and it won't happen again."

Derek barely heard the rest. He was too focused on Alden's comment that *you've been weird lately.*

"How have I been weird? What are you talking about?"

Another beat of silence. *Alden* was the one acting weird. He never made these meaningful pauses before, but now they were pretty much constant. But before Derek could growl at his brother to mind his own fucking business, Alden spoke again.

"That's exactly what I'm talking about. You've been angry and aggressive lately. That's not like you. What's going on?"

Toni. Toni was what was going on. He wanted her and could never have her because of this stupid farce. But he was not about to confess that to Alden. Derek was better than that. Tonight had been a momentary lapse in judgment that wouldn't happen again.

He was the *good* twin.

He merely sighed. "I'm tired. That's all. Leave it alone."

Fuck those meaningful silences.

"Okay," Alden finally drawled, then thankfully switched topics. "So. Any leads come in today on Melanie?"

Derek turned onto his street, rejoicing that he was almost home. He needed to come and then to sleep. "Nothing yet." He paused. He had to be blunt about this, even if it hurt. "At this point, though, it doesn't look good. When a girl's been missing this long…" He didn't need to fill in the rest, and there was no good reply to that, so Derek went on. "Any progress on finding someone to watch Emma while you're at work? Someone who isn't June?" he added.

He eased his truck into his driveway, feeling his tense muscles relax somewhat. At least here, in his home, he knew who he was.

"Sort of. I've got a woman coming tomorrow to interview. She seems promising and I'm hoping if it works out that she can start by Tuesday, Wednesday at the latest." Fortunately, Alden seemed to be avoiding talk of Melanie as much as Derek was.

He threw the truck into park and cut the engine. "Okay. After Tuesday, I can't cover for you, anyway. I'm working the night shift on Saturday to build back some goodwill, then I'm off on Sunday and work again Monday and Tuesday morning. So you're covered for the rest of this week, then I can swing two days at the start of next, but after that I can't promise anything."

In the meantime, it was going to be torture to keep seeing Toni in the evenings. He *never* should have kissed her. There was almost no doubt she'd be working late again tomorrow, since she'd said her presentation wasn't until Tuesday and she still had to finish it. Now that he knew how she felt, how she tasted, it was going to be even more difficult staying away from her.

"I understand. Thanks for everything, Derek."

Derek tensed at the thanks, but at least this time Alden's voice didn't have that groveling tone to it. His forthright delivery made Derek feel less uncomfortable to hear the words.

"It's all right," he managed to respond, pushing himself out of the car and heading to the front door. "Look, I just got home. I'm beat. I'll talk to you soon."

He disconnected the call at the same time that he unlocked the front door, slipping inside and shutting and locking it behind him before striding to the living room, opening the fly of his jeans and pushing down his underwear along the way.

His cock sprang out, so painfully erect that he knew already this wouldn't take long.

He practically collapsed onto the sofa at the first tug of his hand. Leaning his head against the back, he closed his eyes and thought of the way Toni had felt tonight. The demanding caress of her mouth, the damp heat between her legs…

His hand sped up and he let out a grunt as his balls tightened.

An image popped into his mind of Toni unbuttoning that unequivocally professional shirt to reveal soft, full breasts—in his imagination she never wore a bra. His hips pushed up off the couch, his hand starting to get slick from the fluid leaking from the slit at the tip of his cock. He worked his hand faster, in time to the fantasy of him pushing up her skirt—no underwear, either—spreading her legs, and plunging into her slick channel, working himself in and out in fast, rough strokes as she writhed and moaned beneath him, one of her hands cupping her breast while the other played over her clit. *Faster, faster—*

"*Oh, fuck,*" he rasped, his climax exploding out of him, shaking his body as he came in intense bursts, warm liquid shooting up and over his hand as it made a few last, rough strokes, drawing out as much come as he could before he collapsed back against the cushions.

A few moments later, he stumbled to the bathroom to clean himself up, then fell into bed, where he dreamt that Toni kissed him, fucked him, and called him Derek.

Toni woke up the next morning with a resolution that wouldn't budge as she got dressed, ate breakfast, and drove to work.

She was going to seduce Alden Brewer.

If his only argument for stopping truly was that *he* didn't want to complicate life for *her*…well, she was no stranger to complications. And she believed him when he'd told her that was why he couldn't take things further. She *trusted* him, even if it had been a long time since she'd known his younger, more innocent self.

But she also wasn't going to be like the people who had dropped her as a friend, an acquaintance even, when they'd seen how demanding her own life was. She was going to stick around long enough to slake whatever this attraction was between them, and if they both ended up wanting more despite the complications of both their lives, she could deal with that when they got there.

In the meantime, was it so wrong to think that they could both benefit from having something pleasurable? She *knew* he'd enjoyed it last night, the way he'd responded to her kiss, those blue eyes getting smoky and…

Wow.

Even thinking of it, twelve hours and forty-two minutes after the fact, was making her breath catch and her pulse race. Of course, it had been more than a little kiss between them, but all their clothes had stayed on.

Only because he stopped it.

She wondered if she really would have let him have her right there in the middle of the office. Driving home last night, she'd come to the conclusion that, yes, she would have. But he'd pulled away and it had been so difficult not to cry. It had felt as if the one person she felt a connection with was abandoning her, too. It had hurt so much that when he'd told her he was trying to protect her from things in his own life, she hadn't been able to think it through clearly.

This morning, though, it was different. She was resolved.

In the office, it was difficult to sit in her cube and not imagine what had happened there last night. She managed to make it through her tasks until noon, but at that point she was feeling so turned on and nervous about that evening that she decided to take a walk during her lunch hour, to clear her head and hopefully make it easier to get through the rest of the day.

She headed out of the building and walked toward the main street of downtown Greenbriar, going over possibilities in her mind for what she might say to Alden tonight. *If* she saw him. She was planning to stay late, but hoped he wouldn't avoid her out of some misplaced sense of honor.

She crossed the road at one of the lights and passed by a row of shops along the way to a deli she often visited for lunch. But before she went very far, someone called her name.

"Toni."

She stopped and looked around, her eyes scanning the street. No one seemed to be looking at her, or coming toward her, or even standing still. Had she imagined it?

"Toni!" The voice called her again, and she realized it wasn't actually a shout, like she had initially registered it. It was a loud whisper. Coming from the darkened alley immediately to her left.

She pivoted slightly and peered into the dim, narrow space, making out a shadowy figure standing a few feet back from the street.

"*Sal?*"

He was still alive. Thank God.

He did this from time to time. Showed up in her life out of the blue to ask for something—usually money—before slinking off again and leaving her to wait and wonder. She wanted to tell him about the rehab, but she had a feeling she'd never hear from him again if he thought she would grab him away next time and lock him up somewhere without access to meth.

"Come here," he whispered.

She started to step toward him, but stopped. No way was she going into a dark alley with him, even if he was her brother. She shook her head. "You come here." It was horrible to think about it, but she couldn't see him well enough to trust that he wouldn't hurt her. He could have been holding a knife or a needle or-or—

Whatever. She wasn't going in there.

"I won't," he rasped.

"Why not?"

"Because, you bitch, the light hurts my eyes."

She recoiled slightly. He sounded angry, and when he was angry, he could be violent. It didn't matter that they were related. Arguing with a junkie right outside an alley was stupid. She should leave.

But she didn't. Because despite her logical mind telling her it was pointless, somewhere she registered that he sounded almost lucid. Kind of rough, and maybe there was an undercurrent of pain in his voice, but he didn't sound like he used to when he was high. Raving and fast-talking and sometimes slurring his words.

"What do you want, Sal?" She kept her voice calm and soft, trying to get him to talk across the divide of dark and light.

It hurts him to come out of there.

She thought of Alden and how he must have struggled, too, and her heart squeezed with sympathy and regret.

"I—I wanna get *clean*, Toni." She could hear a strain in his voice, and suddenly she caught a sheen of something on his face.

He was crying.

"Sal." She swallowed hard, pushing back her own sobbing. That wouldn't do either of them any good. She had to seize this opportunity and not let it dissolve under the weight of her own feelings. Sal was depending on her.

"I don't want to die like this. I want to get clean," he whined, and she nodded, knowing he could see her clearly even though she couldn't see him.

"I want you to get clean, too, Sal. I really do." This was the opening she'd been waiting for. She kept her voice soft and patient. "There's a rehab program I—"

"I'm not fucking talking about rehab!" he roared, the explosion sudden and scary, and she jumped, on the verge of running away for fear that he'd burst out of the alley and attack her. But his shadowy figure didn't move. She could only hear the sound of his heavy, labored breaths and see the outline of his fists clenched at his sides.

She made herself stay and listen. Thank God no one seemed to be paying any attention to her, standing there looking for all the world like she was talking to herself. Of course, maybe that was why people seemed to be steering clear of her—because she looked crazy. She nearly giggled at the thought, but managed to hold back. That would probably only make her seem *more* crazy—enough to get noticed—not to mention Sal might think she was laughing at *him*, and who knows what would happen then.

"Get me some vike. That's what's gonna fix me." Sal sounded fervent now, and she could hear that he truly believed it would.

Get him some Vicodin? As what, a replacement? Getting hooked on vike had been his first big addiction—what had put him on this path to begin with. Everything had only ballooned from there. Did he really think he could get clean by retracing his steps back to sobriety?

"Sal, I—"

"Shut up and listen to me," he broke in. "I know it'll help me so don't fucking argue. My friend Boney, he did it. He made it work. The vike is holding back the cravings. He doesn't have enough to give me, though, and I know *you* can get it. Please, Toni. *Please.*"

He knew she could get it?

It was true. She could. But there was only one way.

"What are you asking, exactly?" she hedged, trying to figure out if she could play it dumb and pretend it was completely impossible.

"Don't be a cunt, Toni. You can get it in on the back end and get it into my file. *I know you can.*"

She ignored the insult—it didn't matter when compared to what he was asking her to do—to go into the system at Sentinel and issue him a prescription for Vicodin from the back end. It was beyond illegal. She'd get fired for certain if she got caught and no one from Sentinel would ever give her a reference after that. They might even bring charges against her. It was foolish and risky and there was no way she was going to do it.

She shook her head. "I can't. I—"

"Yes you can!" he hissed. "It's the only way. Don't you see? I'm dying, Toni. I don't wanna die," he whimpered.

Oh, Sal.

What if it *was* possible?

Maybe…maybe it wouldn't be terrible if she did it only once. Or at least looked into it. Once probably wouldn't get noticed. Maybe there was even a way she could do it without anyone realizing it was her.

You're nuts. Are you seriously considering this?

She squinted into the alley. Sal was hunched over now, clutching at his belly and rocking a bit as though trying to comfort himself. He looked so alone and sad. How long had it been since anyone had comforted him? She remembered snuggling next to him in their parents' bed as Mom read them a bedtime story. How solid and warm he'd felt when they were like that, small and innocent and full of love and hope.

Her chest felt suddenly tight and she found herself nodding.

"I'll see what I can do," she breathed. "I'll need a couple of days. I can't get into the system anytime I want. It'll look too suspicious. I…give me a couple of days, okay?"

She needed time to figure out whether it was worth the risk. Her brother's life…

There had to be another way, but the way he'd responded to her suggestion of rehab made it seem like it was going to be a much bigger battle than she'd anticipated. What if he died in the meantime? All this work wouldn't even matter anymore.

A cruel part of her couldn't help but imagine the relief his death would bring, though.

You are a horrible person.

She closed her eyes for a moment, trying to shut her mind off of that trail of thought. When she opened them again, Sal's form had retreated farther into the alley.

"Sal?"

"I'll find you in a few days." His voice carried from a distance and the sound of shuffling steps told her he was backing off.

"I don't doubt it," she muttered, and with that, he was gone, skulking down the alley and disappearing completely into the darkness while she was left to shakily contemplate what had just happened.

Chapter Eight

"Alden."

Derek jerked his head up at the sound. Toni was standing in the doorway to the conference room, an intense look on her face.

A smoldering look, if he had it right. And from the way his body responded immediately, he was pretty sure he had it right.

He thought he'd successfully avoided her tonight. She'd been in the office when he arrived, but had been conveniently away from her cubicle when he'd cleaned on that side of the floor. He'd assumed they'd reached a tacit agreement to simply stay away from one another. It was good, really, because when the real Alden came in to work, if Toni happened to be staying late, hopefully they wouldn't get close enough for her to realize what they'd done.

But he was almost finished with the job and suddenly here she was, looking like a woman on a mission.

She stepped into the room and shut the door.

And flipped off the lights.

Oh, shit. She was on a mission, indeed. He could feel the blood already shooting downward, his body giving up the fight before it had even begun.

A small amount of illumination from the fluorescent lights outside shone in through the window next to the conference room door, and he watched as she slunk toward him. There was no way he could stand up to this. He'd been drowning in fantasies of her and now she was practically trapping him in a darkened room with the last of his crumbling resolve.

"Toni," he began, making a desperate grab for sanity, but

she shushed him.

"I don't care that your life is complicated. Mine is, too."

What was she talking about? His mind went in circles a few times before he remembered what he'd told her last night. That he couldn't get involved with her because his life was too complicated.

That he wasn't who she thought he was.

Which he still couldn't tell her.

Could he?

No. Not now. No woman wants to find out she's been played in the middle of a seduction.

She'd be hurt and humiliated and enraged, which most likely meant she'd tell someone about his and Alden's deception. Now was definitely not the time to spring the truth on her. Of course, telling her *after* they had sex wouldn't exactly be wise, either.

Damn. He should leave. Now. Avoid this whole thing altogether.

He was paralyzed by his thoughts, so much that he didn't bother moving away as she came toward him, and somewhere in the back of his mind it occurred to him that he didn't *want* to move away.

"I want this. I want to do this with you. To give you something and take something for myself." She was whispering the words as she pressed herself close against him and kissed him, her mouth aggressive. Possessive. He tried to think of all the reasons why this shouldn't happen, but he found himself stroking her body instead, going immediately to cup her breast through her thin sweater, reveling in the way she felt in his palm.

He needed more.

You're in a conference room at her work. Alden's work, too. This is wrong.

He should have been fighting her, but instead he moved his hand downward and pushed her top up, and she broke away to pull it off the rest of the way, leaving her clad in only a lacy, silky bra. He reached back and opened the clasp, watching as she let it fall off her body, and he took a moment to stare at her, drinking her in.

Holy hell, she was gorgeous. The sight of her like this was simply too much. He didn't care anymore that they were in a semi-public place. That he was pretending to be *someone else*. He couldn't care because his rational mind was *gone*. Utterly defenseless and unable to resist even if he wanted to. He pulled her close once more and they both groaned at the sensation as she pushed one hand beneath his T-shirt, fingers skating over his muscles.

"God, you have a great body," she rasped, before putting her mouth to the side of his neck, sucking and licking as her hand continued its exploration, rubbing up to his chest and scratching lightly into the smattering of hair he had there.

A moment later, her other hand slid over the front of his jeans to press against his erection and he groaned, long and probably much too loud, but *oh*, that felt so good. She leaned away from his neck, dipping her head and staring at her hand over the thick ridge in his pants as though trying to *think* his clothes off. It should have been an indication of what she was about to do, but he was barely capable of uttering a single coherent word, much less thinking past the desperate need filling every cell of his body.

So when she dropped to her knees and reached up to unbutton and unzip his jeans, a surprise dart of lust had him momentarily frozen in place, his heart stopping long enough for her to push his pants and boxers to his thighs, take his straining cock in hand, and bring it to her mouth.

The second her tongue touched the tip, he could already feel his lower back growing tight.

"I'm not gonna last. Fuck, I'm gonna come so fast," he warned her.

He felt, rather than saw, her lips curving around his cock in a smile, and he thrust into her mouth, making her hum in surprise.

She took the hint and started to suck him in earnest, maintaining the pace he suggested with the push and pull of his shaft across her lips, making sounds of approval and excitement. One of her warm hands gripped him at the base, steadying him as she hollowed her cheeks and took him even deeper, making him groan with the sensation, while the other hand came up to rub and gently squeeze his sac.

"Yes. God. That's it." He was mindless now, feeling a mix of awe at the speed with which his orgasm was rising and a desperate, driving need to finish this now, to come in her mouth and feel her drink him down. Her grip tightened and she began to slide her fist in counterpoint to her mouth, fast and slick and—

"I'm coming. I'm fucking *coming*," he groaned, feeling his cock pulse as his body shuddered with release, his chest heaving as he poured himself into her mouth, jerking harder at the sensation of her throat closing convulsively with her swallows.

It went on like that for what felt like hours, though it was probably no more than two minutes total, until he was limp and dizzy and completely, thoroughly sated.

Her turn now.

He reached down and hooked his palm beneath her arm, using his considerable strength to haul her slender body up against his. He dropped a hard, swift kiss on her nose before pushing her back against the conference table, guiding her to lie down on it before he methodically, swiftly opened her work trousers and yanked them down her legs along with her panties.

She kicked everything to the floor, leaving her totally naked while he was still wearing most of his clothes, only his rapidly re-hardening cock and the tops of his thighs exposed. It made him even more rabid for her. He didn't hesitate before sliding her to the edge of the table, spreading her legs, and kneeling between them.

"*Yes*," he thought he heard her whisper, but he was already busy lapping at the slick entrance to her body, one of his broad thumbs rubbing around her clit through coarse curly hairs. She tasted sweet and he wanted more, plunging his tongue inside of her in his quest to have it.

She cried out, her legs squeezing around his head for a moment, until he curved his free hand around the top of her thigh and gently pushed her back, leaving her whimpering, thrashing, on the table.

She was beautiful like this.

He licked his way up to tongue her clit as his hand that had been playing there walked downward, switching places without preamble, his thick middle finger sliding past her snug entrance to sit itself deep inside.

"So good," she gasped. "So good. I'm so close."

He could feel the truth of her words. Her inner muscles were pulsing around his finger, and he flicked his tongue faster, harder against her clit as he stroked in and out of her body, listening to her moans, coming quicker, her gasps more breathy. *So close.* He could feel the muscles of her thigh trembling beneath his palm.

He slid his finger almost completely out of her, then added a second one when he pushed back in.

That was all it took. One thick, stretching thrust and she shattered, wailing as her body convulsed around him, everything throbbing and tensing for a long, long moment before suddenly going immediately, perfectly lax.

He slowly withdrew his fingers from her body and looked up at her, sprawled on the table, and grinned like a predator who had just feasted on the most delicious prey he'd ever known.

But he should have known the satisfaction wouldn't last.

"Alden," she groaned, her voice guttural and thoroughly sated-sounding.

It killed him to hear his brother's name from her lips, but after a deep, bracing breath, he stood and leaned over her prone body. "Toni."

"Kiss me," she whispered, and of course he obliged. This wasn't supposed to have happened. He was the *good* twin. This shouldn't have happened.

At least kissing her would keep her from saying the wrong name again. After what had just happened, he didn't think he could handle hearing one more reminder of his lies.

"Are you okay?"

Alden's voice was quiet in the dim light as she lay on the conference table with him hovering over her. She half laughed at the question that had come to be a strange tradition between them. He'd kissed her after making her come so hard she felt like she'd left her body for a moment, and now he was looking down at her with a slight furrow between his brows.

She could feel the hard length of his cock against her leg, but he wasn't making a move to do anything about it. Instead, he seemed to be focusing on the way she was feeling emotionally, instead of trying to stick his dick into her the way her past boyfriends probably would have done.

But Alden's not your boyfriend.

The painful truth of it made her do something she hated doing.

She lied.

"I'm great. What about you?"

He flashed a grin at her. "*Great* doesn't begin to describe it, but yeah. I'm great, too."

It had been fast and furious, and she was reminded of the reason why she'd come after him so aggressively in the first place. Sure, she'd resolved to seduce him, but not like this. It was running across Sal today that had added a layer of intensity to it all.

"Can I ask you a question?"

Another grin. "I don't know. *Can* you?"

He reminded her so much of her third-grade English teacher that she rolled her eyes and groaned.

His answering laugh was impossibly delicious. "I'm teasing you. Go ahead."

Go ahead. It wasn't the most pleasant topic at the moment, but she had a feeling if she didn't ask now, she never would. And she wanted to know before she went any further with Sal's request. "Have you ever heard of meth heads breaking the addiction by using vike instead?"

She felt Alden tense above her and there was a moment of charged silence before he spoke. "I've come across a couple cases in recent years." He sounded hesitant, and it was funny, the way his words came out. Like he was speaking as a doctor or some kind of professional instead of a former junkie. It reminded her of the first night they'd met when he'd described her brother.

Something uncomfortable and questioning pushed against the front of her brain for a second.

But then he cocked his head and looked at her sharply, as though pinning her to the table with his gaze. "Why do you ask?"

Uh. Shit. She couldn't exactly tell him the whole truth. Telling him she was considering helping her brother addicted to a replacement substance probably wouldn't sit well with Alden, given his own experience. "I read something in some comment section online about addiction that seemed to suggest it was possible. I was curious if it was an urban myth, or something like that."

Ugh. She was a terrible liar. Even to her own ears, that had come out all stilted and shaky.

For a moment, Alden looked at her strangely, but thankfully he seemed to buy her cover story, because a second later he nodded. "It's not completely unfounded, but it's not a good idea, either. Doing that is illegal, to say the least."

He was tense, though. She could feel disapproval rolling off of him in waves. Definitely not sitting well with him. If the mere suggestion of weaning someone off a drug by using a less damaging drug was making him this upset, she could hardly tell him she was actually considering doing it. Or at least, helping Sal to do it.

Complicated.

It made her curious to know… "How did you get clean?"

His mouth turned downward. "I was never on meth, Toni." He drew away abruptly, pulling himself upright to loom over her.

Wrong question, then.

She shook her head, trying to tamp down the fear that he would abandon her now, spread out naked on the conference room table.

How humiliating.

She swallowed hard and willed herself to keep her voice calm. "I know. I wanted—I mean, apart from that, I was wondering. I'm curious to know more a-about *you*," she said as she sat up, wincing slightly as the hard edge of the table dug into the soft skin at the back of her thighs. She watched him tuck his softening penis back into his boxers and pull up his jeans in tight, jerky movements.

"I know what you're doing," he bit out, making a sharp line of fear lance through her. Had he found her out? But then he clarified, "Don't pin your hopes for Sal on me." He zipped up his jeans and looked at her with a mixture of anger and contempt. "Don't make me the poster child for his future. It's not fair to either—to *any* of us."

Okay, that hurt.

But he'd warned her, hadn't he? He'd told her he had a complicated life. He had a kid, for God's sake. Complicated. And still, she'd failed to recognize that also meant he was a complicated man.

But she had her struggles, too. Ones that she was tired of

carrying alone.

"My parents want me to go back to California," she blurted.

He frowned, but not in anger. More like puzzlement, and she took the opportunity to press on.

"My dad told me to, anyway, because I've sacrificed enough. He said that he's willing to sell the house to pay for Sal's rehab, and if it works, they'll buy something smaller and deal with things as they come." She took a short, desperate breath. "That was yesterday morning. But this afternoon, something happened"—she stopped herself before she could give away too much about Sal's request—"I had a moment when I realized it's actually because they've *already* given up hope for him. They're making plans to break away because they've written him off as a lost cause. His own *mother and father*." She was barely keeping back the tears as she added, "*Someone* has to believe he can still turn it around."

She'd walked back to the office after seeing Sal and it had come to her in a rush. It had made her feel so lost and alone, which in turn had intensified her need for Alden tonight. But she didn't want him to feel like she was using him. She wanted him for himself as much as for the comfort he could bring.

She focused on trying to keep the peace and reached out a hand, so close to touching him but not quite making contact. "Anyway. All this to say…I'm sorry. I won't ask you about it again. I just wanted to know. Not so you can be a poster boy, but to have something for myself that can keep me going a little while longer. Not because I expect you to be his salvation or anything."

He had to realize she meant what she'd said. She wasn't lying about that, at least. Especially not while he was standing, fully clothed, and she was sitting there half-naked and vulnerable and practically begging for him to reach out and take her hand.

After what felt like an eternity, he slowly stepped forward, curling one hand around her shoulder while the other cupped her face right before he kissed her, the contact soft and sweet and much too brief.

He backed away again after that. Though he didn't say anything, it felt like forgiveness.

She dressed quickly, smoothing and straightening her own clothes over her body while he watched in silence. When she was fully clothed again, he took her hand, looked right at her, and said in a low voice, "It's not easy to break an addiction. It requires a lot of determination and a willingness to admit your own mistakes. You have to face your worst demons, your greatest fears, and you have to be brave and tough enough to handle the emotional as well as the physical pain of withdrawal as you become what is essentially a completely different person."

The way he said it seemed almost as though he were realizing it himself for the first time.

He was right. It took a strong person. A strong man.

She squeezed his hand. "It's admirable. I—"

"It's *not* admirable." He cut her off with his sharp tone and a slice of his other hand through the air. "For all the pain that drug abusers put others through, the struggle of coming out of addiction is no less than they deserve. Junkies are—"

"People, too." It was her turn to stop him before he could say something she couldn't bear to hear. "And no person is perfect. We all work through difficult things, and if someone"—she noticed he didn't like to refer to himself and chocked it up to discomfort with his checkered past— "happens to have experienced a less, uh, *savory* challenge than others might, it doesn't mean that his accomplishment in correcting his mistakes is any less worthy of recognition."

They stood in silence, their words settling between them, and she willed him to understand. She might be about to make a huge mistake and, if something went wrong and she found herself having to atone for her crime, she only hoped that someone out there would recognize that her penance was worth something.

She hoped Alden would see her that way.

After a long stretch, he abruptly changed the subject, shattering the growing intensity between them. "Well. I should probably do another pass of cleaning in here before I head out."

She grinned, recognizing the opening for what it was. "I have no idea how it got to be dirty again."

He raised a brow and said in mock-seriousness, "Oh, I have plenty of ideas. I've been thinking about them for a few days."

Oh. Well. That was flattering.

"Honestly?" She had considered teasing him, but found herself wanting to know.

For a second his face shuttered, but then he leaned in close and replied in an utterly serious voice, "Yes. Honestly."

Chapter Nine

Derek was walking across the parking lot when his phone rang. He'd had to spend another half hour finishing up after Toni had left, but it had been worth it. His heart skipped a beat at the irrational thought that it might be her before he realized that she didn't have his phone number.

After what they'd done tonight, though, he consoled himself with the reminder that it was the least irrational thought he'd had all night.

Not that it was much comfort.

What kind of man was he turning into?

The phone rang again, jarring him back to reality, and he fumbled for it in his back pocket, yanking it out and glancing at the screen long enough to see it was Alden before he answered and put it to his ear.

"Alden."

"Hey, are you still at Sentinel?"

"I'm about to leave, actually. I'm heading to my truck now."

"I won't keep you long, then. I'm sure you're tired and I can't thank you enough—" he stopped at the sound of Derek loudly clearing his throat. "Yeah. Well. I wanted to let you know that I hired the woman I interviewed today. She spent some time with Emma while I went outside and walked around the yard. Emma did okay, and we've set up a couple more times for them to get together without me. An hour tomorrow, two hours on Saturday... Anyway, assuming it all works out on those days, too, she'll start officially on Wednesday after Emma gets time to adjust. So I'll only need your help through Tuesday. Not on the weekend, of course. And if that's still okay, I mean."

Hearing the news was like being punched in the stomach. Relief and frustration mixed together nearly bowled him over. He thought about Toni and how much more he still wanted from her, and yet he couldn't have asked for more perfect timing. He couldn't imagine she'd be working late again after her presentation on Tuesday. He could keep this up until then.

You should tell her the truth.

But he couldn't. Not only would that mean putting Alden's job at risk, but she would hate him, especially after what had happened tonight.

Coward. You're supposed to be good.

Okay. Fine. Maybe he'd tell her. But only after Alden picked up the job and it had been a week or two...

"Can you still do the job for a couple days next week? It'll be over after that, I promise." Alden sounded sure of himself. Confident, even. It had been a long time since he'd heard confidence from Alden.

"Yeah. I can do it." Derek got into his truck, sitting back against the seat for a moment and letting his exhaustion ebb out of his body and sink into the leather. He was tired, but he was also more relaxed than he'd been in a long time.

A mind-blowing orgasm will do that to a man, he supposed.

That didn't change the fact that he'd crossed a line tonight with Toni that he'd told himself repeatedly not to. Strangely, though, he didn't actually feel as bad about it as he told himself he should. What was more oddly urgent was the strange compulsion he felt about something Toni had asked earlier.

How did you get clean?

He'd answered her as best he could, trying to be honest without giving away the truth. And in doing so, he'd realized that there were things he'd never asked his brother. He'd said things about Alden-as-himself that had him questioning more than his morals.

"Listen, I'm know you're wiped out so I'll let you go. But this has been—it saved my ass. So thanks. I mean that." Alden's tone brooked no argument.

Derek wasn't in the mood to give him one, anyway. The fatigue was creeping in on him and he needed to head home and sleep. He started the engine and put the phone on speaker.

"Derek?" Alden sounded confused. "Did you fall asleep on me?"

Derek huffed out laugh and started driving. "No. Don't hang up, though. I want to ask you something."

"Okay." Alden sounded wary.

"What made you decide to get clean?"

An odd sound came through the speaker, almost as though Alden had *squeaked* in surprise. Derek grinned at the thought. He wasn't going to let his brother off the hook, though.

A few seconds passed before Alden replied, "I watched someone die."

Derek's head went back in shock.

Well, fuck.

He'd never known.

Because you never asked, dumbass.

He wasn't sure now whether this had been a good idea, but Alden was talking again and Derek was loath to stop him.

"It was a few weeks after Emma was born. Melanie had just reamed me in court and I'd lost custody. That day I was so down about it that I went out to the Warehouse—" Alden named an old, dilapidated building where junkies used to hang out and get high before SWAT had shut it down. Derek had been on that raid, and it had been a strange feeling to go in and recognize some of the addicts his brother had hung around with as they'd purged the building.

Opposite sides of the divide.

"I was high. Like, the highest I'd ever been. I think the dealer we got that batch from had mixed it with something because it wasn't a good kind of high. It felt like I was being poisoned. I could barely move and my gut was twisting in pain…"

He trailed off, obviously disturbed by the memory, and Derek had to hold tight to the steering wheel to keep from veering into another lane out of sheer distraction. When Alden spoke again, his voice was shaky, but strong. "I was sitting against the wall next to this girl Amanda. I mean, she was really a girl. I think she told me she was seventeen or something. I could tell something was wrong with her, too. Her face was all contorted and she was making these quiet distressed sounds. I tried to reach out for her and help her. I don't know what I would have done, really, but I was too far gone to move much. I was too high to sleep, even, so I tried my best to ignore the shitty trip I was having and watch over her, instead."

Derek could feel his heart thudding in his chest. "I was on that call," he rasped. "We got a call one morning that someone had ODed at the Warehouse. Amanda Mason. She was *fifteen*. I was on that call. But you weren't there."

"I'm the one who called 9-1-1." Alden's voice was hollow and distant as if coming through years and not a phone connection. "I watched her die. Slow and agonizing, if her face was anything to go by. After a while, she stopped moving, and when I finally came down after hours of incapacitation, it was too late. She'd been dead a while. I left the Warehouse and called 9-1-1 from a payphone, went home and told Melanie I was done with drugs, and the rest… Well, you know the rest."

Shit. Shit and damn.

The image of that girl's face was forever burned into Derek's brain. He'd helped to process the scene, turned the body over to the coroner. Her young face had been frozen in a mask of pain. At the time, he'd been enraged over how senseless it was, how *stupid* addicts were.

Now, all he could think of what how horrible it must have been for her. For her parents. For his brother, to watch it happen and be helpless to stop it.

Alden might have died that day, too, if they'd been taking

the same stuff.

What was happening to him? Since when did he feel compassion for addicts?

And yet he couldn't bring himself to judge Toni harshly for feeling pity for her brother and wanting to help him. He thought about what she'd asked earlier, about Sal and weaning him off meth by setting him up with his old vike addiction, instead, and he recognized the desperation of a last hope when he saw it. He only hoped she wasn't going to do anything stupid.

Neither he nor Alden had spoken for a while. Derek was almost home by the time he realized. He cleared his throat, feeling an unexpected tightness in it.

"Thanks for telling me, Alden."

There was a pause, and then all Alden said was, "Goodnight, Derek," before the line was disconnected.

Derek pulled into his driveway, headed inside, and was asleep within minutes.

What are you waiting for?

Everyone else was gone from the office. Toni looked at the clock on her computer. Half past six. At least no one would be suspicious that she was staying late tonight, but if she didn't do this now, she probably never would. It had taken most of her courage to get to this point even, and she could feel how close she was to running out.

Not to mention that she still had work to do on her proposal. The dry run of the presentation that she'd done with Doug this morning had gone well, but he wanted some changes that she needed to take care of over the weekend so that she'd be ready for their next practice on Monday.

Do it, already!

She brought up a browser and logged onto the patient

records system then entered "Park" in the search box, but before she could continue, her ears caught at a sound from somewhere nearby. For a second she froze, listening hard.

Someone was vacuuming.

Not just someone. *Alden.*

That only gave her a small window of time in which to do this. She definitely couldn't let him know what she was up to. He'd made it more than clear last night how he felt about it.

She'd better hurry it up before he made it over to this side of the floor. Shaking herself, she turned her attention back to the screen and hit enter, holding her breath as the system pulled up patient records that matched the search term.

She started scanning the results, pausing immediately at the first entry. *Park, Antonia.* Strange. As a higher level employee, surely she *should* have had reason in the past to look up her own information. And yet, she never had, and she'd never thought to do it before. It felt weird to see her name there, as though that line represented a completely different person.

She *wished.*

She wished there were a different Toni Park who was about to do something horribly, terribly illegal that would ruin her life if she ever got caught.

Way to psych yourself out. Remember. You're doing this for Mom and Dad. For Sal. They're worth possibly getting fired over.

Park, David. Park, Hyo. Park, Isabella.

Seeing her parents' names on the list only strengthened her resolve.

Park, Myong. Park, *Salvatore.*

There it was.

She opened up his file and looked at the history. The last entry was three years ago, when he'd gone through that thirty-day detox and the attending doctors had issued him some anti-anxiety pills that he'd turned around and sold as soon as they'd released him from the facility.

Before that, there was a long line of prescriptions issued in various desperate attempts to help him kick his Vicodin habit, but nothing afterward. Once he'd started in with meth, he'd gotten too far off the track to bother with things like that.

Toni dithered, reading through the entries over and over. Maybe it wouldn't seem *too* out of the ordinary to have this prescription show up, but a trained pharmacist might be suspicious of the three-year gap. If that happened—if someone raised questions—it wouldn't be difficult to trace the fake prescription back to her.

But what were the chances of someone raising questions?

Back and forth, Toni debated, until the sound of vacuuming got louder and she knew she was really in a crunch.

Just. Do. It.

She took a deep breath, her hand bringing the mouse pointer to hover over the button to *Modify Patient Record*, and—

Whirrrr!

The loud scream of the vacuum filled her row of cubicles, making her yelp in surprise. She jammed her laptop closed and shot out of her chair, popping out of her cubicle to find Alden looking at her with a slightly amused expression.

He shut off the vacuum and approached her. "That happy to see me, huh?"

"Yes!" It came out as more of a nervous squeak than a seductive caress, though, and she had to flex her fingers for a moment to work out some of her tightly wound fear.

She'd almost been caught. A part of her was relieved that she hadn't gone through with it, either. She *was* glad to see him, for more reasons than he could ever know.

Without another word, she closed the distance between them, wrapped her arms around his neck, and kissed him. By the time she pulled back, she was feeling a different sort of pent-up energy taking over the anxiety of earlier.

"You're shaking." He frowned down at her.

"I want you," she replied. That was part of the reason she was trembling, anyway. A few more minutes of their mouths joined together, his body against hers, it would have been the only reason.

He frowned at her for a second longer, then dropped his forehead to hers. She could feel his breath on her nose, coming fast and hard as though he'd been doing vigorous exercise.

"Toni," he groaned.

She felt the same way. "I want you," she repeated, pressing her palms over the muscles on his chest, wanting more than last time. She wanted to be beneath him, no clothes between them as he thrust inside her.

She could feel the pounding beat of his heart and was sure its pace matched her own.

He closed his eyes for a moment as though considering something, and when he opened them again she could see steely resolve beneath the blue heat of his gaze. "I have to finish the job. Are you going to be around for a while?"

She swallowed hard and nodded.

"We can go to my place after. I'll work fast."

Yes. Thank you. Yes.

He started to pull away, moving toward the vacuum again like a man on a mission.

"Let me help you," she called after him. "It'll get done faster that way."

He looked back at her with a teasing grin. "Don't you have work to do?"

She shrugged. "I can finish it this weekend. I'd rather get out of here as fast as possible."

He regarded her for a split second, then nodded. "Okay, then. Let's get to work."

Chapter Ten

Something was up with Toni.

He wished he didn't want her so much so that he could stop and think for a second, try to figure out what she was hiding that had put the shadow of a lie in her eyes when he'd first seen her tonight.

Like the lie in yours?

But once she kissed him, he'd convinced himself he didn't need to know. That thinking with his dick was okay in this situation, because he wasn't on duty and *for fuck's sake* he wasn't Derek right now. He was Alden. He was allowed to make stupid, uninformed decisions that were solely about pleasure.

He was tired of fighting it. For once in his life, he had the perfect excuse to be bad. He was the bad twin and he was going to take advantage of it while he could.

Sick. You're sick.

He ruthlessly shut his conscience out and focused on cleaning. The sooner this got done, the sooner he could fuck her.

"What do you want me to do?" She was standing close to him—so close her head was tipped back a bit so she could look up at his face. He could feel the heat of her body.

I want you on your knees again. Like last night, but more.

But he knew she didn't mean that. Not now, anyway.

He made himself back up and walk over to the caddy hanging over the trash can on wheels that he pushed around while cleaning. He grabbed a spray bottle and towel and handed them over to her. "If you can get all the desktops, I'll empty wastebaskets and vacuum."

She nodded and started to turn on one daintily heeled foot, but he stopped her.

"Do you want some gloves?"

"Yeah, actually. That would be great."

She set down the spray bottle and towel and took the pair of yellow rubber gloves he offered, sliding them on before holding up her hands and spreading her fingers wide, looking at herself with a giggle.

How did she manage to make even cleaning gloves look sexy?

He grunted. "I think yellow is your color."

Funny, given what they'd been doing last night in the conference room, and what they obviously planned to do after this, that such an innocent remark would make her blush. He could see two little faint spots on her cheeks. Maybe pink was her color, not yellow.

He wondered how pink she was between her legs. It had been too dark to see her clearly last night. He wanted to know whether the color would darken and shine after he'd fucked her the way he wanted to...

"I'll work fast," she told him, a breathlessness to her voice that hadn't been there a second ago.

He realized his pants were too tight again. Stupid, unruly dick leading his thoughts.

But still, she walked off and started spraying and wiping the desks, and he figured it couldn't be all bad if it made her as eager as he was. What did it matter what she was hiding if she was up for getting naked with him? With him pretending to be Alden, no less. Alden could be the kind of guy who didn't care that a woman was keeping secrets.

He started walking down the rows of cubicles, emptying wastebaskets.

"So how long have you been doing cleaning?" Her voice floated over to him from the opposite end.

"Five days," he called back, then grinned. At least he didn't have to lie about that.

There was a lull of silence. He'd probably surprised her. It took her nearly a minute to reply. "What were you doing before this?"

I was someone else.

But now you're Alden.

"Odd jobs," he threw out. "Nothing like this, though."

That was true, anyway. The closest he came to custodial services at the station was throwing away his takeout box after lunch.

She was coming up the row toward him, looking at him with too much curiosity. He didn't feel like answering any more questions that might get him into trouble, so he turned it around and asked as nonchalantly as he could, "What do you do when you're not working late?"

She stopped in mid-stride, and even from several feet away he could see the wash of pink that stole up her neck and into her cheeks. He was starting to think that blush was the most erotic thing he'd ever seen.

"Not much." She didn't meet his eyes. "I hang out at home and read. Do some yoga." She shrugged. "I used to be really into ice skating but I don't have much time for that anymore."

She didn't say anything else and he could tell that it made her uncomfortable to talk about herself.

If he were here as Derek, he'd behave and wouldn't push her. But he was tired of being a gentleman. He was undercover in his own life, and he reveled in the freedom it gave him.

"But you have time to fuck me?" He knew he was being crude, but some insane urge to push her was making him behave abominably. He stared at her, the two of them facing off across the industrial carpet.

While that sexy-as-hell blush went deeper.

Her eyes closed for a moment before she slowly opened them again. He could see heat simmering in those dark orbs.

"To fuck," she echoed, her voice almost a whisper, and the words coming from her made him hard. "I don't, but I want it so bad..." She trailed off and he filled in the rest.

She wanted it—him—so bad that she'd *made* the time.

The confirmation of it inflamed him.

"Hurry," he growled, then turned and got back to work, moving as quickly as he could through the rest of the job. He could see her working furiously, too, practically sprinting from desk to desk.

It was oddly reassuring to see she was as excited and needy as he was, because a part of him didn't like how she made him feel *too much*. He was being reduced to base desires and simple thoughts, and it bothered him as much as it turned him on. Soon enough, though, he'd get her beneath him. He'd have her over and over, fast and furious and hard, and once it was done he'd be able to put this gnawing need to rest. Just for tonight, and then the weekend would separate them and he might not even see her on Monday.

Alden would take over on Wednesday and Derek would be able to put all of it behind him—go back to being the upstanding man he was supposed to be.

It took them not even fifteen minutes to wrap up the rest of the cleaning. She threw the bottle and towel back into the caddy and peeled off those yellow gloves, tossing them after the cleaning supplies with a barely controlled impatience.

If she brought this kind of intensity to bed, chances were good she'd be into what he wanted tonight.

"You want to ride with me?" He didn't care that it sounded dirty. He was focused on logistics right now. Step one, step two—whatever he had to do to get to the end goal.

"I-I have to go home right after, so I'll follow you."

It was agreed upon so quickly that only then did Derek register that *his* place was supposed to be Alden's. He did a quick mental recap of his house, giving silent thanks he'd only bought it about a month ago and most of his things were still in boxes. He had some of his police uniforms in the closet, but he didn't expect there to be any reason for her to go poking around in there. Mail he usually sorted as soon as he got home...he simply wouldn't check the box tonight. There was an extra bedroom that she could assume was Emma's—he wouldn't volunteer any lies, but he'd just have to remember to shut the door before she got a chance to look too closely. And he hadn't unpacked any photos or things like that yet. Only the bare essentials.

"Let's go, then," he replied, and they walked out of the building together, stopping only for him to throw the trash into the dumpster before heading on to her car.

"I'm over there." He jerked his thumb toward his truck, parked in the far back corner of the lot. "I'll get the supplies loaded and be back here in a sec."

She nodded, turning to get into the car, but he grabbed her, pulling her back with a hint of roughness, pushing her against the door. Her eyes went wide, and he stilled for a moment, waiting.

If she was afraid, if she protested...

He'd dial it back for the rest of the night. He wouldn't push this on her, no matter how wild he was feeling.

But she didn't protest. The opposite, in fact. She wrapped her arms around his neck and practically pulled her body up against his, her heels scrabbling against the pavement as she attacked his mouth with hers. Her hips pushed against his, pressing her lower belly against his cock, rubbing and writhing as he licked into her mouth.

It was driving him insane.

"I want to fuck you right here," he rasped. "Up against the car."

She stilled.

Fuck. Had he scared her off?

But then she whispered, "Do you have a condom?"

Did that mean what he thought it meant? That she'd let

him do it?

Not that it was really an option right now. Because...

He shook his head.

No, he didn't have a condom. He wasn't the kind of guy who carried around condoms in case sex fell into his lap. Maybe he should start, though.

She pressed a soft kiss to his lips, clearly trying to tone things down. Smart girl.

"Next time, then," she told him.

Next time. Next time he could have her in the parking lot.

He only had a couple more nights of working here and hadn't planned on anything, but now...

Get through tonight first, dumbass.

Right. He pulled away. "I'll go get my truck. Be right back."

And then he was racing away, too full of excitement to care he was already in deeper than he should have been.

She pulled up right next to Alden's truck, in the driveway of a one-story house in a modest neighborhood. The lights were all off out front, but he got out of his truck and immediately came over to her car door and offered her his hand and she got out.

She slid her palm into his, feeling his fingers curve around it, intentionally holding her hand.

How was it they hadn't touched like this yet?

It did something to her.

Things had gotten a little intense back in the parking lot, and even though she wanted the illicit, almost harsh experience Alden was offering—that she could tell he wanted as badly as she did—she felt comfortable saying yes because of *this*.

The tender way he cradled her hand in his. The consideration he showed when he led her slowly up the sidewalk to his front door, letting her lean on him so she wouldn't stumble on anything in the dark. How he didn't release her hand even when they stopped on the porch and he had to sort through his keys to find the one that unlocked the door.

She might have gotten reacquainted with him only a few days ago, but she felt like she could *trust* him. Like maybe he understood the growing frustration she had with her life and was giving her a safe place where she could let it out.

The safe place being his body.

She wanted it rough. She wanted to struggle. She wanted to fight it out with him, between her legs and in her body, so she wouldn't have to find another outlet for her rage that might end up hurting her parents even more than they'd already suffered.

He opened the door and stuck his free hand inside for a second. A light turned on in a small entryway, and he gestured for her to go ahead.

She stepped inside. In the darkness beyond the tiled floor where she was standing, she could make out stacks of boxes. What looked like a sofa. There was no other furniture she could see. No painting on the walls.

He came in after her and shut the door. Suddenly, the space seemed impossibly small. Her back was to him, and she could feel every inch of his body next to hers even though they weren't touching at all.

She started to turn. To face him. "Did you just—"

He moved so fast she couldn't do anything except let him sweep her up and carry her along. Turning her all the way, his mouth on hers, hands roaming, the bar of his cock pushing relentlessly against her belly.

Before, in the office, she could feel some restraint in him. Before, there was room for pauses. For breath.

Here, there was only *feeling*.

He yanked up her skirt, bunching it around her waist as

cool air hit the back of her thighs through her thin pantyhose. The jolt of cold went straight to her hot, already-wet center, making her moan and arch against him, straining in her heels to get higher so his hard cock would rub against exactly the place she needed it. A little higher. A little—

"Eep!" She let out a startled exclamation against his lips as he pulled his embrace tighter and lifted her straight up, until her feet were dangling a few inches from the floor and her heels simply dropped off onto the tile, clattering down as he started to walk out of the entryway, holding her like that as he went.

Wow, he was strong.

And now that he was carrying her, she was exactly where she wanted to be. She lifted her legs and wrapped them around his waist, murmuring her pleasure when the ridge of his erection settled against her.

He grunted and walked faster, across the living room into a short hallway with a few darkened doorways leading off it. He took her into one of those rooms and then she was being lowered until her back hit a soft mattress, the dim light of the moon shining from an open window the only illumination. He laid her on the bed and drew back to rip off his shirt and push his pants down, and she caught the outline of a long, thick erection right before he laid atop her, naked skin on her proper work clothes.

It was simply too much. They didn't need to take their time right now. They'd been building up to this for several days.

She pushed him away and sat up to tear at her own buttons, nearly ripping her shirt in the process of removing it. He knelt beside her and unhooked her bra as she unzipped her skirt in the back, and when she leaned forward to shimmy out of her skirt and hose and panties, her bra fell off like magic.

And then, suddenly, she felt *very* naked and *very* small next to him, and this time when he covered her with his body, she took her time exploring his bare skin, reveling in the knowledge that, in this moment when she was at her most vulnerable, she was also more powerful than she'd ever been.

He trailed kisses down her neck as one hand came to her breast, kneading and pinching a bit too hard, but she *loved* it. It was exactly what she needed right now.

"Alden," she whispered, bucking up her hips, but instead of intensifying things like she'd expected, he pulled back a bit with a sigh, pressing one hand down hard on her hip as though he were trying to stop her.

Pinned there, she wasn't sure what to do. Had she offended him?

But before she could apologize, he spoke.

"*Toni.*" His voice sounded almost pained in the darkness, but that didn't seem right. She must be misinterpreting. She couldn't see the details of his face, after all. Maybe he simply wanted to take a step back and cool things down so it would last longer. "I have to tell you—to *ask* you—I want to be…" He paused for a second, but she didn't move to fill the silence. Instead, she waited. It sounded like something important. Worth waiting for.

She was right. After another second, he continued. "I want to you so much that I might be—it might get rough. But I don't want to hurt you."

Unlike him, she didn't hesitate with her words. "Yes." She said it loudly. Clearly. Given how reticent he seemed about moving forward with the possibility that he might unintentionally hurt her, she didn't want there to be any question in his mind. It seemed like it would bother him if there were a question, afterward.

She saw his head move in the darkness. Nodding. "Tell me if it's too much, though."

She took a deep breath. "Okay."

Moonlight glinted off his teeth as he bared them in a feral smile.

That was the only warning she got.

Before she could register what he was doing, his free hand

went between her legs, two fingers circling her slick opening—once, twice—before pushing inside, burying them completely in one quick move. His other hand still held her hip, pinning her in place when all she wanted to do was grind against his hand.

"Fuck, you're tight." He sounded like he was gritting his teeth. He rubbed the sides of her entrance with his thumb as the two fingers inside her slid in and out, the tips curling upward on every stroke. "So fucking tight. I don't want to hurt you."

"Yes you do." She laughed as she said it, but the sound came out choppy with arousal. She could feel her upper thighs getting slicker as he played in her body, but he wasn't giving her any pressure on her clit and he wasn't letting her move to get it herself. It was the best kind of torture.

He laughed back, sounding as raw and ragged and she did.

And then he yanked his fingers from her body so fast she winced and whimpered at the loss.

"I'll fuck you soon." He slid off the bed and stood at the edge, then circled her slender wrist with his fingers and tugged. "Come here first."

She slithered onto her belly and came forward, letting him cup her chin with moist fingers and press his thumb into her mouth. The same thumb that had been between her legs a few minutes ago. She sucked on it, tasting her arousal, swirling her tongue over the pad of his finger and gently nibbling the tip.

He squeezed her chin, sliding his thumb out of her mouth, and slowly pulled her forward by her face, until she felt the tip of his cock against her lips.

"Suck it," he hissed, pushing the head into her mouth.

She took it eagerly, angling her head forward to take more of him. She'd already forgotten how big he was, filling her mouth and making her struggle down his shaft. Halfway down, she started to slide her mouth up again, but he groaned, one big hand coming to the top of her head, fingers threading through her hair.

"God, yes. That feels so good," he told her, gently urging her forward again and back down. This time, she relaxed and took him a little deeper.

He made a noise that sounded a little like a man drowning. A gurgling, desperate sigh—but in this case, one of pleasure. She hummed low in her throat, pleased with herself, and he gasped. His fingers tightened in her hair, pulling at her scalp. It hurt, but not enough for her to pull away or to tell him to stop. If anything, it was a signal he liked what she was doing, and his approval spurred her on, urging her to take him deeper, faster, until he was panting, his hands curling around her skull as he thrust into her mouth while she slid up and down his shaft.

It was a reminder of what they'd done last night, and the memory of how he'd licked and fingered her into orgasm only a day ago made her channel ache in anticipation. Giving him pleasure was turning her on even more and she wanted something, anything, that could relieve some of the desperate pressure between her legs.

She bobbed her head again, but this time he pulled out of her mouth with a soft *pop*, his cock so stiff and hard it sprang up and smacked against his stomach.

She wanted that inside of her. Now. He must have wanted the same thing, because he knelt on the bed and gestured to the mattress.

"Lie down and spread your legs," he commanded, and she didn't even think before she obeyed. The lust was blinding her to anything except the pulse point at the juncture of her thighs.

He turned, bending slightly, and slid open a drawer in a table next to the bed. She heard the distinct sounds of a box being ripped open and a packet being torn, and then the snap of rubber as he rolled on a condom.

And then he was moving between her legs, draping her thighs over his and spreading them even wider while he rubbed his sac up against her opening, the base of his impressive cock sliding against her clit too hard, making her cry and try to jerk away.

But he held her in place, keeping up the sharp pressure, and so she held her ground, letting him continue until the pain numbed a bit and her entire channel started to squeeze and clench around an aching emptiness.

More. Every time she'd thought she'd had enough, he showed her how much more there was to want. She could hear the slick sounds of their bodies as he moved against her, the soft, wet sucking sound driving her insane with need. She could feel pleasure rising, an orgasm gathering low in her belly, and she struggled to shift her body so he'd be at exactly the right angle to take her over the edge.

But that, of course, was the moment he decided to move away.

"Fuck you," she growled, gasping as soon as the words were out of her mouth. She never spoke like that. And certainly not while naked and writhing beneath a big, powerful man like Alden Brewer.

But he only laughed and curled one of those big hands around his shaft before guiding the broad head of his cock to her entrance, nudging it up against her enough that she could feel a hint of pressure from his penetration.

"I think it's the other way around," he said, grabbing hold of her thighs and yanking her body all the way onto his entire cock—so large and so jarring that she wailed as her inner muscles convulsed around him in climax, her body coming in endless waves, until she was wrung out and limp from the most intense orgasm she'd ever experienced.

When she came down from her high a few moments later, she realized he hadn't moved at all. She was still fully impaled, her muscles sensitive and sore. She wanted to sink into the bliss of sleep, fully sated, but that was when he started to thrust.

"Oh!" She was immediately panting again, her body protesting but eager at the same time. "I'm too sensitive. You're too big," she whimpered. It was true. He was thick and long and she was so swollen from coming that the sensation was nearly overwhelming.

"Should I stop?" He slowed down, the words coming out as though he were biting them off.

I want to be rough with you.

But I don't want to hurt you.

She trusted him.

"Don't stop," she gasped. "Give me everything."

He groaned and sped up again, shifting so he was fully lying atop her, his cock driving into her as she lay there and panted, until she adjusted enough to bring her legs up to wrap around his waist, his strokes pushing even deeper.

She slid her hands down his back. Curved them over his ass. She pushed him into her as she brought her hips up, rolling them against him, then gasped in surprise at the sensation that shot through her at the contact. She had thought she was too *used* already to come again, but she'd been wrong.

She could feel herself climbing again, seeking out another orgasm.

His breath grew harsh in her ear and she felt a spike of pleasure at the sound.

"Alden," she moaned. "I'm gonna come again. I'm so close."

At her words, though, there was a slight slowing—a hiccup in his movements—as though he wasn't sure how to proceed.

Oh, Alden.

She started to urge him on. "Harder. Faster. *Please*. I want to come again. I *need* to."

He groaned, all hesitation forgotten as he started to pound into her, his pelvis knocking against her mound every time and sending a *zing* of pain-pleasure directly to her core. Oh, God, it was good. It was so good and she was going to—

"I'm coming!" she shouted. "Fuck, I'm *coming!*"

She shrieked the last word as the pleasure hit, harder and more intense than before, and she vaguely registered Alden had finally stopped thrusting and was now groaning and grinding against her as he came, too, his cock pulsing inside of her as she trembled beneath him.

When consciousness finally returned to her body, all she could think was that she'd be sore later, she was sure, but it had been more than worth it.

Alden was starting to get heavy, though.

She pushed at him and he rolled off of her, but pulled her close to him, wrapping one arm around her breasts and cuddling around her.

"That was incredible." The way he spoke reminded her of when he and Sal were younger and would be stoned and slow. Had sex replaced his drug addiction? She selfishly, jealously hoped not. She didn't want to be one woman in a string of many. He sighed. "I—*my God*, Toni. I've never…"

He trailed off, his body sinking into the bed, and she wanted to push him to say more. He'd never what? Felt like that before? She certainly hadn't. It reassured her.

Then again, what if he'd meant he'd never had to work so hard to make a woman come before? Would that make her a failure?

Before she could work out what to ask to get him to complete his thought, a beep sounded from his phone on the table alongside the bed. The side closest to her.

"Do you mind passing me my phone?" He sounded on the verge of sleep, and she almost argued with him that it could wait until tomorrow, but luckily some lingering sense reminded her she wasn't his girlfriend, and she had to get up and go home soon, anyway.

So she grabbed the phone.

But the screen had lit up with the notification and her eyes went to it, taking in the message before she even realized what she was reading.

Someone named Karen in his address book had written: *Want to come over for a quick fuck?*

Then the words actually registered and a bad kind of pain, humiliating and regrettable, sliced into her body. Her arm suddenly felt numb, but she passed the phone to him, anyway, and immediately jumped out of bed, searching in the dark for her clothes without a word.

He must have read it, too, because not even a second later, she heard the phone clatter to the floor and his angry voice saying, "*Shit.*"

She heard him roll off the bed, his feet falling on the floor, and she sped up her search. She already had her shirt and skirt in hand. It was enough. She could go without her underwear and stockings if that's what it came down to.

She started to dress.

But then a light flipped on and she yelped, covering her eyes at the shock of such brightness after so long in the dark.

"Toni, wait. Don't leave like this."

His voice sounded even angrier—like Sal did when he was in one of his meth rages—and for the first time she found herself *scared* of Alden. She was alone in his home and no one knew where she'd gone because she hadn't bothered to tell anyone.

What had she done?

She immediately went into a defensive pose, rolling her shoulders down and trying to protect herself. At least she'd managed to pull on the clothes she'd found. If she had to make a run for it, she'd be somewhat decent and could go to a neighbor's for help.

She uncovered her eyes but kept them averted. She'd adjusted to the light, and she could see one hairy, muscled thigh and long calf out of the corner of her eye.

"This isn't what you think."

She watched his feet walk closer and she hunched even further.

"Toni, I—" But then he stopped suddenly.

He was close enough she could see his limp cock now, too, looking oddly comical hanging between his legs. Still large, though, even when flaccid.

He didn't move.

Neither did she. Still bent forward, still hunched over.

Hiding.

"Are you—are you *afraid* of me?"

He sounded so incredulous she wanted to sob.

She'd reacted out of habit, and now that the tone of his voice had changed and the tension she'd felt earlier had all but disappeared, she felt like a fool.

He'd already shown her he wouldn't hurt her. Not really. How could she have thought he would be like Sal?

She was so messed up. Even if she hadn't seen that text he'd gotten—the one that had proved to her how *un*special she was in his life, this would still be the part where he realized how much baggage she had. How she wasn't worth the trouble.

If he thought he was complicated, he had nothing on her. This was the part where he said goodbye and good luck.

She kept her head down still, not because she was afraid of him anymore, but because now she was ashamed.

But he didn't tell her to get out.

"Toni. I'm going to step back now. Will you please turn around and look at me?" His tone was so soft and gentle he probably could have lured a badger to sleep. "There's nothing to be afraid of. I'm not going to hurt you."

She lifted her head and turned to look at him.

It was the first time she'd actually *seen* him naked. He was so beautiful, she nearly reached out to touch him. Luckily, she caught herself in time.

"Did you think I was going to hurt you?" His eyes were soft and worried.

She shook her head. It was the truth, after all. But years of conditioning were hard to erase, and she wanted him to understand why she'd reacted that way.

"I'm not afraid of you. I wasn't…thinking, really. It was automatic, what I did." She shrugged, not sure how to explain.

"Two years ago, when Sal first got hooked on meth, he was still living at home. We were trying to help him get clean but nothing was working, and we didn't realize at first his drug use had actually gotten worse. He used to turn violent when we least expected it and I learned pretty quickly I couldn't fight back or look threatening in any way. It helped if I turned away and..." she trailed off, unable to finish. Alden had lived amongst users. He probably didn't need her to fill in the details, anyway.

He blew out a breath and ran a hand through his hair, and she observed somewhat detachedly that she liked how he hadn't bothered to cover himself. She enjoyed seeing him naked, and comfortable in his nakedness.

It made everything that had happened between them less regrettable.

"I'm sorry, Toni." He took a step forward, half holding up his arms, as though he wasn't sure whether to give her physical comfort.

Despite the way the evening had taken a turn for the disappointing, she *wanted* the comfort.

She stepped forward, pressing her cheek against his chest and letting him hold her.

That felt *so* good.

Too bad she wasn't the only woman in his life, though.

She could hear his heartbeat against her ear, strong and steady.

"I'm sorry," he repeated. "About Sal. But also about—" he waved a hand in the direction of the floor where his phone lay. "That person—the woman who texted me, we were really casual. I was in the middle of a move and—well, anyway, that's not important. I haven't seen her in over a month. Not even to break it off. But I did—I *do*—think of it as over. Even if it hadn't been over before now, it definitely was the second you and I kissed back at the office. I know I probably don't come across as the most reliable guy, but I don't get involved with more than one woman at a time. I do have *some* honor."

She couldn't help feeling thrilled at the confession it was only her. She had no claim on him. She hadn't even intended to see him again after tonight. But there was something about the way they'd come together that made her want more.

She pulled back and looked up at him. "You say that like I think you had no honor to begin with."

"You think a junkie can be an honorable person? Or even a good one?" He shook his head.

"Of course I do!" She grabbed at his arm, feeling the need to *make him see*. "I said it the other night—addicts are still human beings. And they can be honorable, too. Just because they struggle with drugs doesn't mean they can't do the right thing. You're not even hooked anymore. Those days are over for you, right? And *all* people are more than their superficial appearance, Alden. Not everything is black and white."

His mouth had gone down when she said his name. Maybe he felt like she was lecturing him. But she felt it too keenly, the easy way others judged her for her family's problems. It was hard not to insist *she* was more than what she appeared to be. He'd listened to her tonight. He hadn't shut her out and decided she wasn't worth the trouble. She needed him to understand that she valued him and admired him and thought that he was worthy of so much more than what he seemed to believe.

He'd seen more in her than what she'd seemed on the surface, and she wanted to give the same gift to him. And she wanted to keep seeing him. She wanted *him* to keep seeing *her*. The real her.

He still hadn't said anything, and after a moment she sighed, then rose on tiptoe to brush a gentle kiss against his lips.

Thank God he returned it, taking her mouth in a slow, easy caress this time.

When they finally parted, she was smiling. "I hate to go, but I do have to. It's getting late."

It was either that or call her parents to tell them she'd be even later than usual, and on a Friday night no less. They'd be more than a little curious as to why.

Fortunately, he nodded. "I'll walk you out."

At her car, she kissed him again. "Until next time."

She felt his body tense a second before he asked, "Next time…did you mean what you'd said, earlier?"

She knew what he was referring to. The way he'd told her he wanted to fuck her in the parking lot, and she'd told him *next time*.

She nodded. "I did."

He opened the car door, the light inside turning on and illuminating his face. He looked practically predatory, and even though she probably shouldn't have liked it, Toni was glad he didn't seem to have lost interest in her after she'd gone all weird back inside.

"Then I'll see you Monday night," he said, once she'd settled behind the wheel. "The usual time and place." He gave a low laugh that skittered down her spine and settled above her clit, making it pulse and throb.

She wished she wasn't leaving. She wished he'd asked her out for this weekend.

But at least she had something to look forward to.

"Monday night," she agreed. He shut the door. And she drove away.

Chapter Eleven

Thank *God* for the weekend.

Derek slept in late on Saturday morning, grateful for a day off so he could recover from the double work week. He'd have to go in later for the night shift, but at least he could catch up now and be able to take a real rest tomorrow.

He took his time waking up, sitting at his table and drinking two cups of coffee in his T-shirt and sweatpants before opening up one of the boxes in his dining room.

He laughed when he saw what was inside.

"So that's where I put all the towels."

He'd ended up buying new ones when he moved in because he hadn't been able to find them. No wonder, since they were in a box labeled "DISHES."

He was halfway through the actual box of dishes, loading them into his cupboards, when the doorbell rang and he froze, his heart racing.

Toni.

No. Couldn't be.

It was probably Alden. It was always Alden.

He sighed and headed out of the kitchen toward the door, taking the time to calm himself. There was no way it was Toni. She wouldn't be here. No way.

He opened the door and his heart dropped into his toes.

He hadn't realized how much he'd hoped it would be her until he saw who was standing there, instead.

"Hey, big guy." Karen, his casual hookup, was on the doorstep, smiling seductively at him. But instead of feeling excited and turned on by her obvious intent, he found himself irritated and impatient, instead.

"Karen. This is a surprise." He wished he weren't still wearing the clothes he'd slept in. It didn't quite feel like enough of a barrier between them.

"Yeah, well, you mentioned we should talk later, and…it's later." Her smile widened and he fought the urge to recoil. Even talking to her felt uncomfortably like he was two-timing Toni. Usually it wouldn't be such a big deal, but after what had happened last night, he felt much more protective of her feelings than he had before.

Fuck.

"Aren't you going to invite me in?" Her smile had fallen at his prolonged silence and he could see her starting to register that he wasn't as happy to see her as she'd obviously expected him to be.

"Karen, I'm sorry," he began, but she held up a hand.

"There's someone else, isn't there?"

In more ways than one. There's Toni, and there's me pretending to be someone else…

He nodded.

"I should have known." She huffed, but there was no real anger behind it.

"I'm sorry I didn't tell you sooner. It's pretty new and—"

"You could have texted me," she broke in.

"It didn't feel right to tell you that way," he explained.

To his surprise, she laughed. "You've always been too upstanding for your own good, Derek. *I* would have texted *you.*"

For a moment he was stunned, not at her admission that she would have cut things off with a short message, but at her admonition that he'd *always been too upstanding* for his own good.

What the hell did that mean? He was upstanding. He was good. That was who he was.

Except for the whole fucking-under-false-pretenses thing.

He must have let his frustration with himself show because Karen gave him a strange look. "Well, for what it's worth, good luck. For some reason I feel like you'll need it."

She was still on his doorstep. He hadn't even done the right thing and invited her in.

What was happening to him?

Before he could make a move to fix it, she gave him a small wave. "See you around."

And then she was turning and heading back down the short sidewalk to her car, and all he could do was call after her, "Take care."

She didn't look back.

He didn't want her to.

Too upstanding for your own good.

He did some more unpacking, but soon enough it was time to head in to the station, her words swimming around in his head, mixing in with thoughts of Toni and Alden and making him wonder where the clearly drawn lines of his life had gone.

On Sunday, he and Alden hung out most of the day and Derek found himself constantly filtering his words so as not to reveal how deeply involved he'd gotten with Toni.

He was turning into Alden—the shifty, junkie version of Alden who'd perfected the art of evasion whenever he didn't want to let on that he was high.

Worse, as the day went on, he found it easier to lie, and before he knew it, it was Monday and he was facing down another day of having to be two different people, and he was no longer so sure which of those was his true self.

She couldn't go through with this.

Toni closed the browser in which she had once again

opened access to Sal's medical file and pushed away from her desk, bending her head down to rest between her knees.

She felt like she was going to be ill.

Over the weekend, she'd thought about it and decided to give it one more try this morning in the office.

And oh my God, she'd come so close to issuing the prescription. She'd filled out the record and had been on the verge of saving it and sending it to a pharmacy when she'd panicked, deleted the entire thing, and clicked the window closed.

The irony of it, really, was that it hadn't been thoughts of how disappointed her parents would be, or even of how miserable it would feel to be fired in such disgrace. It had been the image of Alden's disappointed face when he found out what she'd done that had made her decide against it.

She was falling for him, hard enough to make it hurt, and she was tired enough that she couldn't resist her feelings at the moment. She had worked hard on the presentation this weekend, spending long hours on it at home on both Saturday and Sunday, and she was already looking forward to when it would be over.

She was already sick of the project.

But isn't this what you want? You were the one who insisted on this even when Dad offered you an out.

Well, yes. But after two long days of swimming in numbers, graphs, and what felt like trivial data, she felt angry and resentful over how hard she was working when everyone else had abandoned the cause, so to speak. Irrationally, it had made her angry that her parents hadn't pushed her harder to *just give up*.

She had to get out of here. Take a break. Some fresh air would probably do her a lot of good and get her mind off of all the things she couldn't have.

Hopefully she wouldn't run into Sal along the way.

Fifteen minutes later, Toni walked out of the coffee shop,

mug of tea in hand, and headed back toward the office. The walk had done her good. She'd made the right decision, and was relieved she'd figured out that she wasn't going to go through with this illegal prescription. Sal would be angry, but it wasn't worth the risk.

She swung her head around, trying to stay on alert in case Sal was around. He usually got in touch with her by simply showing up wherever she was, like an unwanted puppy looking for drugs.

The image of a puppy asking for vike momentarily made her giggle with exhausted abandon, and she wished Sal could be there with her as his normal, clean self, to laugh along at the idea and make fond insults about her hair.

There had to be a way to help him that wasn't illegal. There had to way to pull him back from the brink of death. But it was like healing the leper in Galilee; it would take a miracle.

And she was no longer sure she had it in her…but Mom and Dad no longer had it in them. What would happen if they *all* gave up on Sal? She couldn't do it.

As she continued walking toward Sentinel, she passed by a large park with a playground at the far end. A child's happy shout caught her attention and she looked across the grass to see a little girl with light brown hair swinging high into the sky. Toni stopped with a smile, listening to the shrieks of joy and watching as the girl swung back down toward her—

"*Alden.*"

There was no way he could hear her from so far away, but she kept her voice to a whisper. Merely seeing him brought back energy to her body, made her blood start pumping and adrenaline rushing. Seeing him made her think of last night and tonight and suddenly, the day didn't seem so long.

That had to be his daughter with him—the girl who was clearly having a lot of fun on the swing. Toni hadn't been thinking last night about how Alden had a daughter. She'd forgotten about that, too wrapped up in her attraction to him to remember even her own name. And he clearly lived alone, though maybe one of those shadowy doorways she'd seen when he'd been carrying her to his bedroom belonged to his daughter.

She wondered if he spent every day with his daughter or if this was a special occasion. But judging from the easy way they interacted, she was willing to bet he was a devoted father who was with his kid often, if not daily. It made her want to know more about him. Had he been as devoted to the mother of his child as he was to the little girl? Did he have a good relationship with his ex now? Was he close with his brother and were his parents still alive?

Most of all, she wondered whether Alden wondered about her. Maybe it was just sex with him. It wasn't as though they'd spent a lot of time together.

But she could have sworn there was something more between them on Friday night.

She watched them for only another minute before continuing on. She didn't want to intrude on his time with his daughter, and she didn't want to put him in the awkward position of having to explain to the little girl who this strange woman was, who had no hold on him.

But she couldn't deny he had a hold on her.

Chapter Twelve

"You feeling all right, Brewer?"

Derek looked up from the computer where he was scrolling through Sal Park's arrest record. James Donahue, golden boy of the department—at least in terms of looks and sheer masculine accomplishments—stood on the other side of his desk, looking down at Derek with narrowed eyes.

It annoyed Derek to no end that Donahue never seemed to have learned staring was impolite. The guy could stare a hole through an iron wall. Right now, those laser blue eyes were focused on Derek, and he didn't like it.

"All good." He managed what he hoped was a carefree smile. "Why do you ask?"

Donahue's eyes didn't so much as flicker. "You look like someone punched you in the face. In both eyes, to be more specific. Why the dark circles?"

Derek was pretty sure his own expression was a mix of fear—at being found out he was moonlighting—and anger that he'd been stupid enough to give himself away. "It was a rough weekend." All those confusing thoughts and lies jostling around in his brain had made it difficult to sleep, though he desperately needed the rest.

"Maybe you should see someone," Donahue offered, a little too nonchalantly.

I am seeing someone.

"Maybe," Derek replied, trying to keep his tone as cool and uncaring as Donahue's, but the thought of the way Toni had felt beneath him as he'd wrapped around her body and rocked them both to pleasure had his temperature rising, making his throat tight and his voice raspy.

Donahue laughed. "All right, man. Have it your way. Although I hope she's worth it."

Derek opened his mouth to protest, but Donahue was already sauntering away, looking for all the world like he didn't give a damn about the way everyone's eyes followed him as he walked…women, men, hookers, and thieves. They were all drawn to Donahue's charisma.

All of them except Derek, that was. Donahue was too observant by half. Derek didn't believe for a second that Donahue thought it was merely a woman keeping Derek up late, but for some reason his fellow officer had let it go at that.

It was actually a relief, too, that Derek hadn't had to outright lie.

He was having a hard time keeping things straight. Even his own identity.

He was going to see her again tonight and he could barely contain his excitement. He'd thought one night with her would be enough, but it wasn't even a fraction of what he wanted now.

Earlier today, when he and Crewes had been out on patrol, they'd stopped on the Strip and he'd tried to talk to some of the hookers and pimps lounging around in their down time, but Crewes had ended up taking over much of the questioning because Derek hadn't been able to focus. His head wasn't in the game. It was too busy reliving Friday night with Toni.

Would she be there tonight? What about Tuesday? And then what?

He wanted more. But if he wanted to continue whatever it was they were doing, he'd have to confess what he'd been doing. He'd have to tell her he wasn't really the guy she thought he was, and he'd merely been playing a part.

She'd probably never speak to him again.

Maybe he could win her over a little more tonight by getting some information on her brother that might help her feel safer. That was why he was looking in the system now. The way she'd reacted to him on Friday night, cowering and hiding, was telling. Even though she blamed it on the way Sal had acted years ago, he didn't believe it was only that. He didn't know when or how she was interacting with Sal, but this kind of behavior had to be ongoing and was probably only going to get more dangerous.

He had to figure out how to protect her without her realizing the guy she thought was Alden was actually a police officer who'd arrested her brother a few times already before. If he could figure out how to locate Sal, there was a state-funded detox program for incarcerated addicts. It might be the only way to save Sal's life.

It was obvious to Derek that no matter how much her brother had hurt her, Toni cared about him.

From across the room, Crewes's voice rang out. "Brewer, heads up! We got a tip in about Melanie."

Fucking fuck. He'd gone off on a Toni tangent again and forgotten he was supposed to be investigating the disappearance of his brother's missing ex. Not to mention all the other work he had piled up on his desk. If he started slacking, Chief would no doubt put him back on traffic patrol and make him work nights, to teach him a lesson.

Chief Travers was a good guy, but he'd come up through the ranks in another precinct run by a guy with an iron fist. It was tough love for the officers here, and most of them stayed out of trouble. Derek always had, too.

He didn't want to start now.

He closed the window on his computer. He'd get to Sal Park some other time. He stood and headed over to Crewes, who hung up the phone as Derek approached his desk.

"They found the driver of the blue car and three witnesses that say he was the one behind the wheel the night Melanie got in and disappeared. They're bringing him in now for questioning and we're working on getting a warrant to search the car. Hopefully we'll have it by two o'clock." Crewes's face was grim. Too grim for the news he'd delivered.

Derek sighed. "Come on, man. How long have we been working together? Give it to me straight."

Crewes looked at him for a second, then shook his head. "The guy denied ever being at the Strip when Officer Serrano picked him up. But we've got three witnesses swearing up and down he's the one who Melanie went with. We've already told him we've got no solicitation charges on him, so why would he lie about that?"

Damn. Crewes was right. More often than not, the guys who lied about their whereabouts despite witness testimony were guilty. It didn't take a master detective to figure that out. And unlike in television crime shows, the suspects were usually just smart enough to avoid arrest for as long as it took them to flee the state.

Things didn't look promising for Melanie. But then, Derek had already had a feeling for a couple of days that she'd met with a bad end. It was impossible to be in this field and not develop a kind of sixth sense about shit like that. Not that he was going to voluntarily share those thoughts with Alden. But if his brother asked, he wasn't going to hide them, either.

"At least Serrano didn't bungle this one," was all he said. Tim Serrano was a young jackass punk who had done well enough at the Academy to get some elevated status, but lacked the experience to handle the responsibility with aplomb. He grated on every senior officer's nerves.

Crewes gave a sardonic grin. "I wouldn't count it a victory yet, Brewer. They're still about fifteen minutes away. Plenty of time for Serrano to fuck things up." He gave a what-can-you-do laugh.

"Great," growled Derek. "That's great."

But before he could turn around and walk away, Crewes leaned forward and said in a low voice, "If I'd said that a week ago, you would have laughed along with me. I don't know what's going on with you, but you need to get a handle on your attitude before Chief Travers starts lasering in on you for some discipline."

Crewes was right. Derek couldn't afford one more pair of eyes scrutinizing him. He'd already put himself at risk with Toni and Donahue. He should have known his partner of five years would have noticed, too. And Crewes was warning him fair and square.

He nodded. "Thanks, man."

Crewes straightened back up and clapped his friend on the back. "Any time, okay? And don't worry about Serrano. He's a dumbass but he's got Wojkowski with him, so at least they won't lose the suspect on the drive in."

Wojkowski was old as the hills, but at least the guy didn't take shit from anyone. He was a good fit for Serrano, who had gone through a few partners before they pulled Wojkowski off desk duty and made him drive the younger officer around. Derek suspected Chief had offered the senior guy a fat incentive package, which Wojkowski could use, what with one daughter back at home with a baby after she'd discovered her ex had been dealing meth to—

Wait.

"What was the name of Wojkowski's daughter's ex? The dealer? It was something Hodges, right?"

Crewes raised a brow. "Gary Hodges, I think. Why?"

"Alden said Melanie knew not to touch meth, but what if she changed her mind. For whatever reason. She would have gone to Hodges, or someone who works for him. He's been out of prison for at least a few months. Maybe more. I can look it up."

Crewes studied him for a second, then nodded. "I'll pull up the file while you finish up that pile of shit on your desk."

Derek blew out a relieved breath. "Thank you."

Crewes shrugged. "It's no problem. It's a good lead. You're a good detective, Brewer."

But not a good twin. Not anymore.

The thought nagged at him as he walked back to his desk.

She didn't have to be here tonight.

Toni tapped her fingers on her laptop keyboard and watched the clock time creep slowly up to half past six. Thank God everyone had left, since until about ten minutes ago, she'd had to work hard at looking busy, like she had a legitimate reason to be there. At least now she didn't have to pretend anymore.

But she was still feeling on edge.

Doug had applauded her presentation in today's dry run and had told her it was perfect. There was no more work to be done on it before tomorrow. But she'd already been apart from Alden for nearly three full days. She'd told him she'd see him tonight.

On the one hand, she couldn't wait.

On the other hand, if she thought too hard about what she'd signed up for—*sex in the parking lot, you bad, bad girl*—she might not go through with it.

Besides, maybe he'd forgotten all about it.

"Toni."

At the sound of his voice, she whipped around in her chair to see him standing right next to her cubicle, looking down at her with such a hot expression that she had to squeeze her legs together to keep them from spreading open in invitation.

She didn't miss the fact that she hadn't heard the vacuum yet, and it was still early. That meant he'd come directly to her before he'd even started cleaning.

Maybe he hadn't forgotten at all.

She blushed. "Alden. Hi. How was your day?"

He came closer, pitching his voice low. "I thought about you."

"Did you?" She felt suddenly breathless with excitement and worry both. *Were you thinking I was too messed up to keep seeing me?* "I thought about you, too." *And I saw you with your daughter.*

Oh, the things people never said.

For a moment, Toni was unable to resist wondering: how many secrets were woven between every sentence ever uttered? How many secrets she had. How many did Alden have? *Was* he keeping secrets of his own?

She was so into him it was ridiculous. She cleared her throat softly. "Listen, about Friday night…"

He was very close now. He bent forward and dropped a kiss on the top of her nose, then slid his mouth down to hers for a long caress. It made her mind go blank and mewling a second before he rocked back and smiled down at her. "It was really great."

Save me. I'm drowning in you.

She concentrated hard on getting her brain back. Screwed up her courage. "It was. Really great. But, um, I was kind of wondering…do you have any other jobs after this? I was thinking, maybe we could go grab a drink? Or something? I mean, if you don't drink we can still go out somewhere. After…"

She was too embarrassed to say *After we have sex in the parking lot*. She was already babbling. Sounding like an idiot.

Save me. I'm drowning.

But she'd done it, no matter how clumsily, and she was glad of that. She didn't want to be like the woman who had texted him last night, who didn't even merit an in-person conclusion to their relationship. She wanted their relationship to be about more than that, and it was worth a shot.

Save me.

She ignored the little voice that kept whispering strange words in her mind, and waited nervously.

Heaven must have thought she could use a little karmic reward, though, because Alden didn't seem turned off by her question. Instead, he looked at her with a serious expression and nodded. "Yeah. I'd like that."

They locked gazes, and for a long moment stood there in

silence, looking at one another, until he broke away, saying, "I'd better get through the cleaning first, though."

"I, um, I can help you. I just need to pack up." She gestured to the laptop and notebooks still out on her desk.

He flashed her a grin and headed off to start cleaning. A moment later, Toni heard the vacuum start up. She quickly shut down her computer and packed up her things, then moved out from her cubicle and wandered to where Alden had left the bin on wheels. This time, she didn't bother to ask him what to do, but simply grabbed the supplies she'd used the day before and started working alongside him so naturally it was almost as though they'd been doing this together for a long time.

He nodded in acknowledgment but didn't stop. She didn't blame him, if he was as eager as she was to spend time together. But she watched him as surreptitiously as she could. Now she knew what those muscles looked like beneath his shirt. How the scrape of his leg hair felt against her smooth thighs. The heavy weight of him as he lay on top of her. His cock stretching her open as he fucked into her body.

"You okay?"

She startled at the feel of a hand on her back. Alden was looking at her with equal parts amusement and concern, and she blushed hotly. "Getting lost in memories."

His eyes darkened, and she knew he was thinking about Friday night, too. He didn't say anything before he went back to work, but his movements were less controlled now, and he'd picked up the pace a little.

But she wanted to talk, too. The sex was…well, incredible. She didn't want to give that up. But the whole point of asking him out was to get to know him better. She may as well use the time they had now as well—in case they lost themselves in passion again tonight and didn't end up talking any more.

Think of something light. Conversational.

"I-I saw you today with your daughter," she blurted.

That was so not conversational. But A-plus for creepy and intense.

Alden stilled for a second, then made a weird movement with his head that might have been a nod and said, "Emma."

At least he hadn't told her to get out of his sight. Toni smiled. "I was passing by Rogers Park and saw you guys from far away on the swings. She's really cute. How old is she?"

He seemed to relax when she explained where and how she'd seen them, and a smile spread across his face as he talked. "She's three. Smart kid, though. Brilliant, in fact. But she's also really sensitive. I think the combination sometimes causes problems."

"I can see that. But it seems like the two of you have a great relationship. I saw the way she looked at you in the park this morning."

He shrugged. "She's definitely a daddy's girl."

It was funny how Alden sometimes answered questions. He didn't say, *She's my girl* or *We have a special bond*. Sometimes it was almost like he was talking about someone else. But maybe that was a result of his years of addiction. Sal sometimes did that—tried to distance himself from blame. She wondered if it was the same when accepting compliments or positive associations. Maybe the distance became ingrained.

Or maybe she was projecting her own feelings onto his behavior.

The realization shook her for a second. *Did* she feel distanced from her own life? Her own experiences?

But now was not the time to explore the answer to that question. She'd already behaved oddly enough with Alden, and he had dealt with it nicely. But she didn't want to risk alienating him again.

She wiped down a desk and asked, "Where is Emma now? Is she with her mother?"

He shook his head. "Actually…her mother ran off about a week ago and hasn't come back. My ex's family is pitching in a lot, but my gut tells me Melanie—Emma's mom—is never going to return."

He said it so casually it took Toni a second to register his meaning, and then her jaw dropped. "Oh. *Wow*. Alden, I'm so sorry. I—that must be awful."

He shrugged. "That's the life of a junkie."

But it was still sad. She wondered if he really believed it to be as inconsequential as his shrug suggested. He'd been a junkie, after all…no matter how many times they'd already discussed it, she had a hard time believing that he would truly dismiss that part of himself as something—some*one*—that didn't matter. And yet it was almost as though he had put down a dividing line between addicts and non-addicts, and only one group was worth caring about. Black and white. Good and bad. No room for the *humanness* that might blur that line.

All she could think was, his dividing line was more like a protective wall, not a true belief system. Like, as long as he stayed on the right side of the line, he couldn't get hurt anymore. She wished she could make him see how lonely and isolating his view was. She didn't say anything in response, though. He didn't seem the type to need reassurances or condolences or any of what she could offer him in words.

He'd said Melanie's family was helping. Were they not letting him have Emma more? From the glimpse she'd seen of Alden with his daughter at the playground, she couldn't imagine him not wanting to be involved. Toni wanted to know, but it felt too intrusive to ask. Their relationship was still new enough that it didn't seem right to dive deeper into what was likely a very painful story.

They worked on, and she managed to come up with some truly conversational topics, like how her parents had met in grad school and her dad's family had objected to him marrying someone who wasn't Korean, but had finally reconciled when Sal was born, and the grandparents she'd known had been loving, kind people. She waxed eloquent about spicy dumplings, her favorite comfort food, and he laughed at her passion for something so simple. She focused on happy things, and any time she talked about Sal, it was about his life before he got into drugs.

Alden told her about going camping with his brother in their backyard and the fort they'd built out of rocks and tree branches. Everything he'd shared had been happy or funny, and she noticed he didn't talk about his years on drugs, either.

By the time they closed up the office and headed out to pack the cleaning supplies into his truck, it was well past eight o'clock. They'd slowed down quite a bit while they'd been talking, but it was worth it. It had been almost like a date.

He'd parked in the far corner of the lot, away from the big lights that lit up the rest of the pavement. She could barely make out the outline of his truck in the isolated darkness.

A thrill rolled through her. A perfect place for doing something illicit. But he'd been parked here on Friday night, too, when she'd followed him home, and it seemed like a routine thing for him, rather than a special choice for tonight.

"Why do you park so far away when the place is deserted? Seems like a lot of effort."

He chuckled and hit the button to unlock the truck. "Habit, I guess. I'm used to trying to keep out of sight. Low light, no cameras reach this part of the lot. Maybe that'll change with time, but for now it's more comfortable than parking close to the building."

She supposed he meant because of the times when he'd been doing drugs. He'd probably met a dealer in places like this, hidden out of sight. Even now, she could see how it would appeal. Here, he was nothing more than a big shadow in the night.

Darkness and light. Black and white.

She wondered which one she was to him.

Alden opened the door to the truck and the cab light came on, making her blink. The light illuminated the more prominent features of his face, casting the other parts in shadow. It was a compelling image, and she couldn't tear her gaze away as he worked, putting most of the cleaning equipment into the backseat. It was a big vehicle, with an extended cab, shiny and black. It suited him, and yet—it didn't.

"Nice truck," she murmured.

He shut the door. "Thanks." He went around to the rear of the truck, carrying the vacuum along with him, and opened up the tailgate. He lifted the vacuum with ease and slid it into the bed, but he didn't shut the gate again. Instead, he turned and pulled her to him for a kiss.

A hot, needy kiss. As frantic as last week's kisses had been, but this time with the experience of their night together at his house between them, it was even hotter. All she could think about was the way he'd taken her so completely, and her arousal nearly exploded into a moan.

Nearly. She managed to keep quiet by letting him explore her mouth with his tongue, thrusting and licking and driving her crazy.

She brought one hand down his chest, stroking hard over his ribs and pushing her fingers into his hip before she slipped her fingers between their bodies and rubbed his erection through his jeans.

He groaned into her mouth.

She loved the way he felt through his clothes, his hard length confined by the thick fabric. It made her think of a caged animal that would spring on her the second she let it loose. It made her think of how much she *wanted* to release him so he could do exactly that.

But she was so rarely the instigator of anything. She wasn't quite sure how to start with him. And then she remembered—

"Did you bring a condom this time?" she whispered it against his lips, glad of the darkness hiding her blush.

His hips jerked in surprise, and he separated from her just enough she could see his eyes blinking down at her. "Yeah. I did. But…are you sure?"

She nodded.

"Then say it," he demanded. "Say what you want."

"I want—" she began, but had to stop to gather her courage.

He waited.

"I want you to fuck me right here. Right now."

But he still waited, and she thought about the way he'd handled her the last time—their first time really together. How he'd been so needy, had known how intense it was going to be, enough to ask first and make sure...

"Give it to me rough," she added.

And then he was on her before she could even take her next breath.

Chapter Thirteen

This two-timing gig was making him crazy.

That was the only explanation for how out of control Derek had gotten.

It was getting dangerous. Toni had told him she'd seen the real Alden from afar this morning—thank God she hadn't gone over to him—and there was no way she wouldn't realize if she got close enough.

And yet, he couldn't seem to put an end to it, to cut things off with her. He was playing the part of Alden too well. Illicit and wild and *bad*.

He didn't really *think* about what he was doing as soon as she'd given him permission to have her in a public place, and now he was going to take what he wanted. He turned her to face the bed of the truck, and with a push on her upper back, bent her forward, all the way down, until her belly was pressed against the cool metal gate.

For such a delicate woman, she could really take a good fucking. Probably because she liked it so much. He could tell by the way she smelled when he lifted her skirt up to her waist. Even through the tights she was wearing beneath it, he caught the scent of arousal wafting up, and his cock throbbed in response.

"Don't let me hurt you. I don't want to hurt you," he insisted, grateful that some still-good part of himself had inserted himself and insisted on keeping her protected.

From him.

He didn't want to think about how he'd become a man who a woman needed to protect herself from. He didn't think about how he wasn't really talking about the way he had sex with her. He didn't want to hurt her in any way, and yet he was bound to cause her pain eventually.

He didn't want to be like Alden. But he *was* Alden.

"I need you," she whispered, and his focus shifted, lasered in on the woman in front of him, laid out like a gift.

I don't deserve this.

But he was going to take it, anyway.

He kept one hand on the small of her back, and with the other he curled his fingers around the waistband of her tights, then yanked them down to her mid-thigh, trapping her legs together while exposing her sex.

She moaned the second he bared her to the night.

"You're not wearing panties." His eyes had adjusted well enough to see the two pale globes of her ass and the dark outline of her sex. Even in the low light he could make out moisture gathered there, glistening in the moonlight.

She lifted her head a little off the bed of the truck and shook it side to side, her silky black hair sliding over her shoulders. He stroked his hand up her back, through her beautiful hair, then wound a thick strand around his palm and gave it a soft tug.

Her back arched, making her ass rise higher in the air.

Seeing her like this—well, fuck, it might kill him, but at least he'd die a happy man.

Hold up…did that mean he hadn't been happy before?

He shook away the question. He didn't feel like thinking about that right now. All that mattered was he was happy, in this moment, with this woman.

Toni.

His curved his other hand around her hip and stroked lightly over her body, bringing his fingers between her folds and immediately groaning with agonized arousal. "Fuck, you're *so* wet." He pushed one finger into her body and her inner muscles immediately squeezed him tight as she made soft sounds of pleasure. "So warm and tight," he murmured. "I couldn't stop thinking about you all weekend. How good you felt coming around my cock."

"*Alden.*"

He ignored the name itself and instead focused on the way she said it, so breathless and pleading, and it made him smile. He pulled her hair a little harder and pushed another finger into her wet heat.

"*Oh.*" The word was little more than a puff of breath on a soft sound, but she wriggled and arched, her movements saying as much as words.

He slowly withdrew his fingers from her and grabbed the condom packet from his back pocket. He'd slipped it in there before he'd gone into the office tonight because he, who'd always been the one everyone else could count on, had been counting on *her.*

And that, more than anything else—even more than the lust breaking him down cell by cell—rocketed him forward.

He had to let go of her hair to get it open and slide on the condom, but the second he finished rolling the rubber sheath all the way down, he took a fistful of those gorgeous sleek strands and tugged her head back, slowly enough that she could protest if need be.

She didn't protest.

So he didn't hesitate. He positioned the tip of his cock against her opening and pushed, using his body weight to breach her, groaning as he felt her give way. He didn't stop until every last inch of him was sunk deep. And then he stopped cold, trying not to come from the simple sheer pleasure of being completely engulfed by *this woman.* In this position, with her legs pushed together, he was packed so tightly into her body the pressure was almost unbearable.

He pulled her hair tighter and leaned a little harder against her body, and she gasped and fidgeted beneath him. The rounded edge of the tailgate had to be pressing against the tops of her thighs, but he wondered whether the discomfort of it was something she actually enjoyed. She *seemed* to enjoy it.

He pulled out slowly, torturously so, and she whimpered—

And then he slid in again, deeper than before, stretching her open. This time, she moaned, the sound echoing through the empty parking lot.

He wasn't going to last. There was no way he could last, seeing her like this, bent over the back of his truck and making those animal sounds while he fucked her. He managed only a few more hard thrusts, his hips banging against her body, driving her against the metal of the truck, before he had to pull out. He didn't want to lose control and finish too soon. She had to come, too. He wasn't *that* horrible of a person.

He turned her around and guided her to lie down in the bed, her legs dangling over the edge of the tailgate, and grabbed her tights by the center seam. "These have got to go." He ripped them right down the middle before pushing her legs wide and thrusting so hard that she inched up the truck bed. Another thrust, and her body moved higher up the slick metal surface, so he kneeled on the gate between her thighs, wrapped her legs around his waist, and started to stroke, in and out in slow movements that made her pant and whimper. The truck dipped and rose every time, adding something to the illicit pleasure that pushed his arousal too high, too fast.

He brought one hand to her mound and started to rub right above her clit with the heel, with enough pressure meant to make her come as quickly as possible, because he didn't have time to tease. He wanted her screaming. He wanted to come.

And he could feel it now. Her muscles were starting to clench and she was arching up against him, meeting him with her hips every time he pushed into her. He was thrusting harder and rougher now, his knees biting into the cold metal of the gate with every slam of his body into hers.

She started to curl up toward him. "Oh, yes. I'm *coming*. *Alden*."

I'm not Alden, for fuck's sake!

He wanted to shout it, to push away the intrusion of his brother on this moment, but her body started squeezing hard around him and all other thoughts fell away. It was pure sensation, the intense bliss of being milked to orgasm by a woman who was letting him fuck her in public on a chilly night.

He came with a groan, grabbing her knees and using them to brace himself as he collapsed forward, his hips jerking as wave after wave of climax rolled through him. It felt like his entire soul was being pumped out of his body, and if he were a spiritual man, he might even have said that was the moment he was reborn.

But who was he now?

Toni lay in the bed of the truck and struggled to breathe. That orgasm had knocked the breath right out of her, and Alden's weight wasn't helping much. She pushed at him and he grinned, pressed a sloppy kiss to her cheek, then grabbed the condom and yanked his jeans back up before rolling off, landing on his back in the bed next to her.

Her heart skipped a beat. She wanted so much more from this man. More attention, more time, more sex…just *more*. Now that they'd gotten the sex out of the way, would he refuse to go out with her like he'd agreed to do earlier this evening?

She might not recover from the wound if he turned her down.

Maybe she shouldn't even ask.

But in that moment, lying beside her, Alden brought his hand to her wrist, then skimmed his fingers downward to wind them through hers.

And then neither of them moved.

They were lying under the stars, holding hands in the darkness.

The silence stretched, but it wasn't uncomfortable. Still, after a minute, he slowly pushed himself onto one elbow and looked down at her. "So. Where to now?"

He'd remembered. Initiated, even. She couldn't stop herself from grinning that he wasn't putting himself to rights and saying goodnight, leaving her alone in the parking lot. "How about Eagan's?" It was a local pub where some of her coworkers liked to go for lunch, and at night it had the same kind of restaurant atmosphere, but it was casual and cozy, too.

He hesitated for a second, but before she could suggest something else, he nodded. "Eagan's it is."

Why had he hesitated? Maybe he was worried about it being too expensive. He'd said this was his first contract and he'd only been doing odd jobs before. And with a daughter to support on top of everything else. She should have thought of all that beforehand.

Of course she'd pay, but she didn't say that. She'd simply insist on it when the bill came. At least his hesitation made sense now.

She scooched to the edge of the tailgate and started to strip off her ruined tights. At least the jacket she had in her car would make her warm, enough that she'd be fine with bare legs, anyway.

"Why don't you drive with me? I can bring you back here afterward." He'd sat up, too, his face so close that when she turned to look at him, their noses brushed.

He caught her lips in a sweet kiss that nearly destroyed her. She wanted *more*.

But when he pulled back, all she did was nod and say, "Okay. I'll grab my jacket and then let's go."

Chapter Fourteen

The second they walked into Eagan's, Derek knew it had been made a mistake.

Eagan's was a police hangout. Even though he, Crewes, Davis, and Donahue always went to a dive bar called the Clipper, most of the other officers preferred Eagan's. When Toni had suggested it, he'd nearly said no, but that fucking hopeful look she'd given him...

He'd let it lead him into making a mistake.

A group of guys from the station were at the bar, including Serrano, the little punk. But there was nothing to do now except brazen it out. At least most of them knew he had a twin, so with some luck and the low lighting, he'd get away with it.

He guided Toni to a corner booth, keeping his back to the guys, and they managed to settle in without being noticed.

"So you come here a lot?" he asked.

She shook her head. "Not as much as some of my coworkers. I tend to grab my meals on the fly. Usually I'll only eat away from my desk if there's a going away lunch or something like that."

"What exactly do you *do*, anyway?" He grinned. "I heard about this big presentation, but I don't actually know what your job is. Seems like something I should know."

She laughed softly. "I'm an operations manager for our insurance offerings. I make sure patients can enroll easily, that they can sign up for the right services, claims get paid, doctors get their money...it's pretty boring but it's a good position. Better than I'd expected to get, in fact."

Hmm. That was surprising. She had what sounded like such

an involved and maybe even important job, but she seemed to view it as settling. Timid in certain situations, wild and abandoned in others.

He could spend a lifetime unraveling this woman.

It shocked him for a moment, the realization he might *want* to.

He floundered past that punch to the gut and managed to ask, "Why do you do it if you think it's boring?"

She shrugged, but didn't answer right away. Instead, she fiddled with her coaster and turned her head to the side and studied a framed print of a beer bottle.

Real classy joint you brought her to, man.

"I do it for Sal."

She said it so softly he almost didn't hear her. But he could have guessed, anyway. The way she clearly held out hope for her brother, how she talked about him when she was trying to explain why her body reacted in fear to certain situations—maybe she was afraid of Sal, and maybe she no longer even loved him the way a sister *should* love a brother. But she was sacrificing a lot for the hope of saving him.

Or maybe Derek was living vicariously through her. But he didn't think so. When you had a brother like Alden used to be, like Sal was now, you equal parts hated them and were willing to move heaven and Earth for them if only they would be free from the grip of addiction.

On impulse, he reached across the table and took her hand in his. She had such a delicate hand. Small, with long slender fingers and smooth skin. No scars. The opposite of Alden's hands. The real Alden, anyway. But even against Toni's palm, Derek's looked like the hand of a monster. He looked away, bringing his gaze back to her face. She was looking at him again, too.

She opened her mouth. "I—" But she stopped suddenly, her focus shifting to something right behind him.

Or rather, someone.

Fuck. He already knew who it was. From where he was sitting, he could see the guy's boots.

Serrano.

Derek turned his head and angled it up, giving a cursory glance at Serrano before turning back and asking Toni, "Ready to order?"

She nodded. "Yes. I'll have—"

"Is this a joke?" Serrano's voice was good-humored, but Derek could detect an undertone of annoyance. "Brewer, I didn't know you were coming out tonight. Why don't you bring your friend over to join us?"

Toni was looking from Serrano to Derek in confusion. He had to get this right. He turned back to face Serrano, full-on this time. Their eyes locked, and Derek did his damnedest to keep his expression neutral.

"I'm sorry. Do I know you?" He barely resisted the urge to lean forward a little when he asked it, which was a default behavior he knew he had—they'd had to analyze their own tells when he'd been going through training to become a detective, and he'd been surprised to see how identifiable he was.

"Okay. It's not funny anymore. Never was." Serrano was scowling.

Derek blinked and shook his head slowly. On purpose. He squinted up at Serrano. "I get it. You think I'm Derek."

"You're fucking right I think you're—"

"Hey, Alden." Another officer—Kian Howard—had come up behind Serrano. He must have heard Derek talking to Serrano. "Been a long time. How's it going?"

Howard held out a hand and Derek shook it, trying not to cringe in shame. Serrano was one thing, but Howard was actually a good person whom Derek respected. He didn't like lying to the guy. But luckily, Howard had met Alden only once, and that had been a couple of years ago.

When he'd booked Alden for possession.

That had been really fucking embarrassing for Derek.

How do you think Alden would be feeling now if he was the one who was really here?

The question threw Derek for a loop. He'd never really thought about it that way. He'd never really looked at it from Alden's point of view, because why would he value the opinion of a junkie?

"It's all right," he made himself say, even though his mind was reeling.

But Howard must have mistaken Derek's distraction for embarrassment, too, because he added, "I'm Kian Howard. I booked—" Howard's eyes flicked over to where Toni was sitting, then back at Derek. "We met a couple of years ago, so you probably don't remember me. I work with your brother, so I see him every day. Was easy to recognize you."

"Of course. Officer Howard. I remember."

Serrano huffed. "He's a twin? *Two* of that—"

Howard's lifted eyebrows had Serrano stopping mid-sentence. Derek made a mental note to praise Howard at the station more often.

"Let's let these two get back to their conversation, man. Sorry to interrupt. Good to see you again." Howard grabbed Serrano by the arm and walked off.

Howard good, Serrano bad.

The *basicness* of that thought had Derek frowning as he shifted again to face Toni.

Not everything is black and white.

Was that really the way he thought about people? Probably. But only lately he was starting to be bothered by it.

"That guy was a jerk. I'm really sorry." Her face looked sympathetic. Damn, she must think his frown meant his feelings had gotten hurt. Not that he was going to correct her. If he admitted that, *No, actually, I'm enraged*, she'd probably think he had an anger problem. Then he'd be no good in her eyes and she'd leave him.

He no longer felt surprise at how much he didn't want her

to leave him.

He shrugged, making a show of being relaxed, and made himself smile. "It's all right. Happens all the time."

Her eyes widened slightly. "I don't know how you do it. Being an identical twin, I mean. I think it would drive me crazy if people were constantly mistaking me for someone else. I have enough to deal with from my brother."

Derek's smile grew tight. He really hated lying to her about who he was. He hated having her think Serrano was wrong—okay, maybe he didn't hate that part because it was Serrano, who could stand to be wrong often—and he hated what it meant for the future. It didn't matter how much he wanted to keep seeing her. After what she was going through with her brother, there was no way she'd stick around for Derek once he revealed he'd been lying to her all this time.

Fucking Alden. Look what you've gotten me into.

He pushed the focus off of him, not wanting to feel the rage rising again.

"So. You were saying you do your boring job for Sal." He tried to keep his voice light and a little teasing, and thank God it worked.

She let out a small laugh. "I think I was being melodramatic. It's a good job. It's good for my resume. It'll help me a lot when I—" She stopped and shook her head.

When I move on. He knew that's what she was going to say.

"You want to leave again once Sal is better?"

Even though Derek was pretty sure the next stop for Sal was six feet under.

Toni nodded. Didn't say anything.

"That's why you said you're doing it for him. You want to save him, huh?"

Even in the low light, he could see she was blushing. But she didn't deny it. In fact, this time she actually said the words. "Yes. I do. My parents tried, but now they're more scared than hopeful. I think they've given up, but they haven't accepted that yet themselves. I'm all he has left."

Derek shook his head slowly. "That's not true."

She leaned forward and her grip on his hand tightened. It surprised him to realize neither of them had let go in all this time. "It is true. My parents have pulled away, he doesn't have any friends, he—"

"He has himself." He couldn't take it anymore, the blind faith she had in her brother. He hated the way it made him feel. When Alden had been hooked, Derek had done his best to separate himself from his twin. He'd become the opposite in every way.

Bad and good. Black and white.

It had been the only way to survive the agony.

"It has to come from him, Toni," he continued. "You can't save him unless he's willing to be saved. I've seen too much of this shit, time and time again, to believe another person's faith alone is enough. He has to want to be his own savior."

He stopped talking and she was quiet for a while, looking at him. Could she see the secrets he was hiding? Did she have faith in *him* even though they'd known each other only a handful of days?

He found himself hoping so.

When she finally spoke again, it nearly knocked the breath out of him.

"I like you, Alden Brewer," was what she said.

And before he could stop them, the words were spilling out of his mouth. "I like you, too."

Toni nearly squealed with happiness when Alden told her he liked her, too.

She'd told him about Sal and about how she'd sacrificed a

life for her brother and Alden hadn't run screaming in the other direction like the few men before him had. She was out having fun and he wasn't grilling her for the gritty details of life as a junkie, like some of her girlfriends used to do—finding titillation in her brother's suffering.

She liked him, and he liked her. It was refreshingly honest. He was the kind of guy she could put her faith into. Already had, in fact. It felt good to believe in someone like him. And the way he'd acted earlier with that guy who'd mistaken him for Derek…she'd been impressed by how calm and laid back Alden had been about it.

Their waitress arrived and took their drink orders, but before they could get back to talking, Alden thrust his hand into his jeans pocket and pulled out his phone, which was lit up and buzzing.

He looked at the screen and grimaced. "I'm sorry. I have to take this."

Before she registered what was happening, he'd slid out of the booth and stepped outside, phone pressed to his ear.

Well.

She fought the fear it might be that woman who'd texted him the other night. She had to believe him when he'd told her it was over. She believed in him. A guy who stood by her and was interested in who she was, instead of the sordid details of life with her brother? He wouldn't lie to her.

Alden had been gone for all of thirty seconds when the waitress dropped off their drinks. Toni wanted to wait for him, to toast to…well, whatever they were doing, so she sat back and tried to relax until he returned. That was when the jerk from earlier came sauntering back over. Toni barely refrained from rolling her eyes at the cowardly way he was approaching, waiting until Alden had left.

"Evening, ma'am," he said, stopping by the table. He didn't sit. Was he waiting for an invitation? She wasn't going to extend one.

"We meet again," was what she managed to say.

He gave an *Aw, shucks* laugh that sounded completely manufactured. "I regret we didn't *actually* meet earlier. I'm Tim Serrano, Greenbriar PD." He held out his hand.

She reluctantly took it, intending to give him a brief, polite shake, but he held her fingers for a bit too long. A bit too familiarly. She practically yanked her hand away.

"I'm Toni," she replied. "Nice to meet you."

But not really.

"I saw your date leave and wanted to come make sure everything was okay." Serrano stared at her like he was trying to will some secret message into her mind. Or maybe he was trying to come onto her but didn't realize how creepy his intensity was.

Either way, she wished Alden would come back right *now*.

She nodded. "Thanks, but I'm fine. He got a phone call and had to step outside for a moment. He'll be back any second."

"Yeah…" Serrano gave a practiced shrug. "Although I feel I should caution you that you can't always count on guys like that. I have sisters, and I'd want someone to warn them of this, too, but the man you're with is a drug addict. He might not be trustworthy."

What a dick. Right after Toni had been thinking just *how* trustworthy Alden was. Serrano wasn't doing a good job of making his case.

"He's not an addict," she told him, her irritation rising.

He didn't seem to notice the anger in her voice, though. "Not to be rude, ma'am, but I'm a police officer and I know—"

"He is a *former* addict, but he's not anymore," she snapped.

He finally seemed to register that he was pissing her off, because he blinked. Paused for a second. Then apparently decided she was stupid, because he actually tried convincing her again.

"All the same, I'd advise you to watch out. You're a

delicate thing and I'd hate to see you hurt. Alden's a big guy and he's here in a bar. *Drinking*. That isn't a good thing for a recovering addict."

She sighed. "Former addict. Last I checked, drinking wasn't illegal, and it happens in bars all over the world. Are you implying there are drugs in our drinks? Did *you* put drugs in our drinks?"

Serrano's face turned red and splotchy, and Toni had a hard time suppressing a smile. "No! I didn't—I would never—"

"Did you see someone *else* put drugs into our drinks?" she asked.

He shook his head, his jaw tight and his face thunderous.

"Then I suggest you get back to your friends and let us worry about our own safety," came a voice from behind Serrano.

Alden had come back.

Thank God.

Serrano's jaw went tight but he didn't argue. The two men did an odd little squaring off as Serrano turned to walk away and Alden moved to slide back into the booth, but otherwise there was no drama.

That was another thing she liked about Alden. No drama. He gave things to her straight, whether it was about how he wanted to fuck her, his involvement—or lack thereof—with other women, his struggle to get work—she could trust him.

"Sorry about that," Alden said after she'd left. His mouth was twisted down. "About the call and that guy. I didn't mean to leave you open and vulnerable."

She didn't like the way he seemed to take the responsibility on himself. She gave him a seductive smile and played with her finger around the rim of her glass, looking up at him through her lashes. "I thought you liked me open and vulnerable."

From the way he sucked in a breath, she was pretty sure she'd managed to shift his mood, which had been her initial goal. But now that she could see how her words had affected him, she wanted something else. She wanted to go back to his place and let him strip her down and ride her into pleasure.

Which was why it was more than a little disappointing when he blew out a hard breath and said, "Sorry, Toni, but that call was urgent, and I have to leave."

Chapter Fifteen

This twin business was brutal.

Things had been going well enough so far that Derek hadn't expected to get such a call tonight. The suspect in Melanie's disappearance—the man they'd brought in earlier—kept messing up on his story about where he'd been the first night Melanie hadn't returned. Derek had put him in a holding cell for the night. If nothing came out of the search of his car once they got the warrant, he'd have to be let go.

But something had come out of it.

The warrant had finally come in shortly after his shift ended, so another detective had taken on the search. The call had been to tell Derek they'd found bloodstains in the car. Spots consistent with spatter, in the door behind the window gasket, some between the seats. A cleanup job that hadn't been thorough enough. They were doing an analysis on it to determine blood type, and they were towing the car in for full dismantling, to see if they could find anything else like hair or belongings.

It didn't look good.

He had to get to the station and look things over, then go to Alden's place and talk to his brother about it. To prepare him, in case what Derek already believed was true...was true. Truth fucking sucked sometimes. But telling it had been his responsibility and his cross to bear for the past few decades, and he couldn't break the habit of a lifetime after a few days of playacting.

Except it didn't feel like playacting. More and more, it was starting to feel like who he'd been pretending at these past few days was actually who he was.

He really had to get out of here. He took a deep breath. "Really. I'm sorry. It's kind of an emergency and—"

She shook her head. "It's no problem. I understand. I hope everything's okay."

He gave her a tight nod, then pulled some cash out of his wallet and threw it down on the table. He liked that she didn't prod him to tell her what was going on, but he could tell she was unnerved and maybe a little hurt by it. Hell, he was unnerved by the situation. He only hoped that the other officers at Eagan's wouldn't make the connection between Derek getting called in and Alden leaving the bar suddenly.

They drove back to the office in silence, and he could practically feel her confusion hanging in the air between them, but he didn't try to explain. It was better this way, to let her think he was too shady, or making excuses or something, so she wouldn't want more. She would be the one to sever their connection, because God knew he wasn't doing a good job at resisting when it came to her.

But when he pulled up next to her car, he blurted out, "Can I get a raincheck on tonight?" Like a compulsive, impulsive fool.

Like a junkie.

Being Alden was taking over his mind.

But her answering smile was worth it.

"I'd like that. Maybe, um, maybe we can trade phone numbers."

He gave a self-deprecating laugh. "I think we're doing this all wrong. Phone numbers are supposed to come first. Not after…" he trailed off. He had been about to say, *Not after we've gone at it like animals*. But that wasn't the message he was going for, really.

Fortunately, she ignored his fumble and laughed. "It's not the wrong way. I don't think there's a wrong or a right for this." She looked at him shyly. "It's *our* way."

She said it so convincingly it seemed unreasonable not to

believe her.

When they'd plugged each other's number into their respective phones and he'd made sure she got safely into her car and driven away, he sat behind the wheel of his truck in the parking lot and called Alden.

His brother picked up on the first ring. "Hey, man. How did it go tonight? How you feeling? One more day and it'll be over. Any news from the guy they brought in today?"

Derek closed his eyes for a moment, not sure which question to answer first. But in the end, he settled on the most important one.

"Yeah. There's some news on that front. Nothing definite, but I'm coming over to talk to you about it."

There was a long pause before Alden replied. "Sounds good. I'll see you soon."

This really sucked.

Derek said his goodbye, then hung up and started to drive, thoughts of Toni the only thing that kept the weight of doing the right thing from crushing him flat.

The presentation was over.

She'd gotten the promotion.

Toni shook the last executive's hand as they filed out of the conference room, heading toward another office to visit with the team there. Doug was going with them, but he was the last one out, and he stopped to congratulate her.

"Amazing work, Toni. You deserve it. I wish I could take you out to lunch to celebrate, but I have to go with these guys. Later this week, okay?"

She grinned. "Yes, of course. And I'm the one who owes you. I should be buying you lunch."

But he only shook his head and laughed, walking out the

door with a friendly, "Don't stay late tonight. Go out and celebrate!"

His words swirled around in the empty conference room. Staying late…celebrating…Alden…

She wanted to share this with him. Their date last night had been cut short, but she'd had a good time before then. Pulling out her phone, she texted him.

I got the promotion!

Congratulations. I knew you would.

The reply came almost immediately, and Toni was so pleasantly surprised that she couldn't resist a shout of triumph and a punch of her fist into the air. It was the first time she'd contacted him this way and she hadn't been sure what to expect.

Are you free to celebrate with me tonight? If you have Emma or some other plans, we can take another raincheck.

I don't have Emma. No other plans. As soon as I finish work, I'm all yours.

She stared at the message, feeling a goofy smile stretching her mouth. *All yours.*

She wished, anyway. As much as she wanted him to be hers, Alden Brewer wasn't easy to pin down.

She texted him a final, *I'll see you here later*, then gave a little squeal of joy before dialing her parents. Mom picked up immediately.

"So? Did you get it?"

"Yes!" Toni couldn't resist shouting into the phone. "I got it."

"Oh, sweetheart, congratulations! I am so proud of you! How about we take you out to dinner tonight?"

That brought her up short. "Oh. I—well, I was planning to go out with, uh, with a coworker."

That wasn't quite a lie. Alden did work in the Sentinel office, anyway.

Luckily, her mother didn't seem upset about Toni's plans at all. "A coworker? Oh, Toni. I'm so happy. That's-that's wonderful and of course you should go out with your friends. Really, I—we can take you out this weekend, instead."

The obvious joy Mom had over Toni going out with "friends" made Toni realize how worried about her social life Mom had been. Maybe this night out with Alden was beneficial on many levels.

"Okay. I'll be home a little later than usual, so don't wait up." She didn't want her parents to worry, after all.

They said their goodbyes and Toni disconnected the call with a smile. This day was going so well, she was going to take *herself* to lunch.

After her solo celebratory lunch, she was walking down the path that wound around the lake in the middle of the city. Full of pride and excitement over her promotion, she allowed herself to indulge in a hot, heavy daydream of Alden peeling off his T-shirt to reveal his taut, hard stomach. Alden, bracing his body over hers as he kissed her—

"Where are my fucking pills, Toni?"

Toni yelped in surprise as someone fell into step right behind her on the path. *Sal.* Where had he come from? She tried to turn around, but before she could, a hand pushed at her back, making her stumble forward on the gravel path, and she barely managed to keep herself from falling as his rasping voice behind her demanded, "Answer me!"

Goodness. Had daydreams of Alden really made her tune out someone as dangerous as Sal?

Toni whirled around to face her brother and had to stifle a gasp.

He looked *awful.* His face was practically skeletal and covered in horrific scabs. She'd read about how the drug made users' skin feel itchy and crawling, and many of them were constantly scratching at their bodies. His hair had thinned and his eyes were sunken, and the sight of her big brother like that—

It was too much. This was *Sal*, after all. The boy who had taught her to climb a tree and shuffle a deck of cards. The big brother who had scooped her up and carried her all the way home after she'd fallen from her bicycle and skinned her knee. And now…she didn't know who else he'd become, but he was still her brother. He was still worth saving if only because he was a part of her.

He wanted to know where his pills were and now she had to tell him that she wasn't going to issue any prescriptions in an underhanded way. He needed help, and she was going to *talk* to him about getting it.

Her hands shook as she reached out to touch him, to try to grab hold of some sense of connection still between them.

"Sal—"

But he lashed out, knocking her hands away with such force it made her yelp in pain as his elbow connected with her wrist. She immediately recoiled, clutching her hand to her chest, and he feinted to the side, as though her movements were some kind of attack, or—or God knows what. She'd heard the drug made meth heads paranoid on top of everything else, but did he really believe she was trying to hurt him?

He looked wild. *Oh, God.* Was he going to hurt her even more? He had a few inches on her—and probably ten pounds at least, despite his thinned out appearance. Not to mention the power of irrational rage.

He stepped toward her. Lifted his hand—

"Hey!"

A shout from somewhere to her right reached her ears as Sal jumped, pulling his hand back right before he turned and took off down the street, racing away faster than she'd ever seen him run before. She whipped her head around to see two uniformed men running toward them from across the street and she couldn't suppress a gasp of surprise.

Alden. It was *Alden* running across the street.

One of the men split off and went after Sal, while Alden

made a beeline for her. He reached her side in a few more strides and frowned down at her.

Why was he frowning? And why was he wearing a policeman's uniform?

Not that she was complaining about that, really. If she'd found him attractive in dark jeans and a T-shirt, seeing him in a uniform like this—all hard metal and black fabric—was like throwing a match into a tank of nitrous oxide. Explosive hot.

She could feel her pulse under her fingers where she was still holding her wrist. The throbbing pain gave way to something even more intense, pushing outward, burning.

"Alden?"

"Are you all right, ma'am?"

They spoke at the same time, and of course, as soon as his name left her lips, she wanted to cringe and hide. It came out so breathy, so *needy.*

But to her surprise, he didn't give her that same, liquid smile he had last night. Instead, his gorgeous lips flattened out and a crease appeared between his brows. He looked between her face and her wrist, as though debating whether to address her or her injury. After a moment, he finally asked, "Do I know you? You a friend of Alden?"

"I'm sorry, I—" Toni started almost automatically but then paused, confused. *What's going on?* This was Alden. She knew it. She knew *him.* "I don't understand. Is this a prank?"

His face softened then and it was all she could do not to put a finger to those lips to trace them as he gave a soft exhale. What was it about this man that got to her like this?

If he was really Alden, of course. He *was* Alden. He had to be.

"Sorry, ma'am, but I'm Derek. Derek Brewer, Greenbriar PD."

Okay...not Alden. And of course she should have realized it sooner. The fear from Sal's attack had scrambled her brain for a moment.

It shouldn't have been surprising that she'd thought it was Alden despite the knowledge that he had a twin who was a policeman. The officers last night at the bar had made the same mistake. The level of her attraction to both brothers, though, was causing its own confusion in her body. It felt wrong to her to be so emotionally and sexually affected, so easily, that she couldn't tell the difference between two different men.

"Are you okay?"

Derek's voice sounded like it was coming from far away, but she still noticed that he was speaking too normally, as though Toni wasn't reeling from the revelation there were two men in the world who looked exactly alike, sounded exactly alike, and gave her the exact same feelings of arousal and need.

Are you okay?

That was *Alden's* question. Alden's voice. But it wasn't Alden and she was having a hard time processing how this man—Derek—made her feel *exactly as good* when he asked it.

And suddenly it felt oddly…disappointing. Whenever she'd read books in the past in which a woman fell in love with a brother who had a twin, the heroine was invariably able to tell the twins apart, even when the rest of the world couldn't.

Not that she was in love with Alden. Not yet. But she certainly felt *something* for him.

Apparently, she felt it for his brother, too.

She wanted to say, *No, I'm not all right.* But that would probably send Derek after Sal with an assault charge, and she didn't want that for her brother. She was supposed to be helping Sal, not getting him into even more trouble.

She shook off the fog of confusion and lust. Her reaction to Derek was probably just adrenaline-based from what had happened with Sal. She likely merely *thought* she might feel more for him and for Alden than she really did. These brothers probably made women fall all over themselves with a mere look. Both were tall and muscled, with dark hair and soulful eyes that—

That happened to be staring at her expectantly.

Damn it. He'd asked her if she was okay about six hours ago.

She nodded. "Uh. Yes. I'm fine." She forced herself to pull her hand from her wrist. It didn't hurt anymore, but as her hands swung to her sides, she immediately regretting losing that small measure of protection between her body and Derek's.

The way he made her feel… Hot. Bothered. Exactly like his brother had made her feel.

You are sick.

Toni closed her eyes.

Strong fingers curled around her upper arm. "Steady there. Let's get you to a bench or something." His voice was soft and solicitous in her ear.

Please keep talking.

Except—he'd only taken hold of her when she'd closed her eyes. He must think she'd been about to faint or something. He walked her to a nearby bench and helped her sit down. She probably should have insisted she could do it on her own, but a perverse part of her didn't want to lose the contact of his fingers on her arm.

As soon as she settled on the bench, the other officer who had been with Derek earlier came jogging up, shaking his head.

"I can't believe I lost him. That guy was *fast.*" He nodded toward her, panting only a little. "Ma'am, did he accost you?"

The "ma'am" thing was starting to get to her.

She watched the officer's eyes flick over her. Years with Sal had taught her to be hypersensitive to even the tiniest changes in expression, so she didn't think she was imagining things when she saw his eyes widen ever so slightly at the sight of Derek's hand on her arm.

What's that about? Were officers not allowed to touch people they were helping, or something? She liked it, but she didn't want to get Derek in trouble. As gently as possible, she pulled her arm from his grasp. For the barest second, his fingers tightened, but then he released her and straightened.

"This is Officer Ben Crewes." Derek gestured toward the other cop. "Ben, this is T—er—terrific timing, as I was about to talk to Miss…" He trailed off and looked expectantly at her.

Weird. A moment ago, she'd thought he'd been about to say *Toni*, even though he couldn't possibly know her name. But he'd said *terrific* instead.

What kind of a cop said stuff like that?

"Miss Park. My name is Toni Park. You can call me Toni." *Not ma'am.* It bothered her, the way that address put distance between her and Derek.

The other officer—Crewes, he'd said—was also a good-looking guy who was wearing a wedding ring, and it made her eyes cut to Derek's left hand. No ring. So neither he nor Alden wore one, but that didn't necessarily mean anything. Some married men didn't wear them.

She hated that she'd looked.

Officer Crewes had a more elegant attractiveness about him than Derek, but she preferred Derek's sort of rough, rude looks—though his behavior toward her had been gentle and kind. He was smiling now, too, looking like he wasn't affected in the least by how close their knees were to touching.

"Miss Park," be began.

"Toni," she insisted.

He nodded, but he didn't seem to have really heard her. "Was that man known to you?"

Sal, holding her hand as they walked to school. Sal, sitting on the kitchen floor and trading Halloween candy with her…

She turned her head away and took a deep breath. "He's my brother."

Officer Crewes pulled a pad of paper from his back pocket and opened it up. As he started writing, he asked, "Would you like to file an incident report?"

She swung her head over to look at Derek and shook her head at him, even though his partner had asked the question.

155

"No. He's my *brother.*" She knew she must sound emotional—probably too emotional for them to believe she was thinking straight right now—but she couldn't help it. She was supposed to be getting help for him, not feeding him to the wolves.

Officer Crewes snapped the pad shut. "I understand he's your brother, Miss Park. But—"

"Fair enough," Derek broke in, cutting off whatever Officer Crewes was about to say. She still hadn't pulled her gaze from his, and he wasn't looking away, either. "If you change your mind, come down to the Greenbriar Central Station. You can ask for either of us and we'll help you with the paperwork."

He understood.

Of course. Alden is his brother. Alden used to be a junkie, too.

She nodded, her throat feeling tight. She wondered if Derek felt the same way about Alden as she did about Sal, whether he both hated and would be willing to die for his brother at the same time. She wondered if Alden had ever cost Derek relationships like Sal cost her. It hadn't been clear from his statement about being Alden's twin whether he and his brother actually still talked.

She found herself wanting to ask, but she didn't feel right asking Derek in front of another officer—not to mention she'd only met him for the first time a few minutes ago. But she felt she already knew him, because of Alden. They really did look uncannily alike.

"Would you like us to escort you somewhere, Miss Park?" Officer Crewes asked.

She shook her head. "No, thank you. I'll be all right. I appreciate your help, though."

He nodded.

Derek touched his fingers to his cap. "Stay safe."

"*Terrifically* safe." Officer Crewes was smirking when he spoke, but he seemed to be directing it toward Derek, who appeared not even to have noticed the sardonic note in his partner's voice.

So it had been an odd thing for Derek to say.

Why did she keep thinking of him as *Derek* and not Officer Brewer?

And then they were walking away, leaving Toni feeling more unsettled than ever. She wished Derek would come back and comfort her again. Or was it Alden she preferred?

Alden, definitely. He was the one who knew her—inside and out. That *terrific* Derek had said earlier had left her slightly uneasy about him, though it had been nice to lean against him for a while and feel like she was anchored to another human being. Especially one that reminded her of Alden. Practically *was* him, in fact.

A flash of heat hit her at the thought of how Alden had pinned her down and *anchored* himself in her body.

Tonight she would see him again. Tonight she would let herself surrender to the pleasure and forget about everything else, including *both* these brothers.

Chapter Sixteen

It had been really jarring to see her this afternoon as himself.

Derek looked at the clock, relieved that it was time to head out of work and go over to Sentinel. He couldn't take the stress anymore of wondering when he was going to slip up and expose his lies to everyone.

He'd almost said her name when he'd introduced her to Ben. That would have really fucked things up. Thank God he'd managed to save it, although he couldn't say he was particularly happy to be known down at the station as the guy who said "terrific" on any regular basis. At all, really. Crewes had given him so much shit for that as they'd walked away from Toni this afternoon, though Derek had to admit he preferred Crewes's easygoing teasing to Donahue's eagle-eyed observation and pointed remarks. If he wanted to avoid getting caught at moonlighting, it was Donahue he had to stay away from.

And then there'd been the chat he'd had last night with Alden that was weighing on him.

We found blood spatterings. A sample was sent to the lab and we're just waiting to hear back. But the guy's got a record. A few assault charges. He didn't do time because of technicalities, but I don't doubt for a second that he isn't guilty of those. I wanted you to know.

And then, of course that had to be the time Alden had finally screwed up his courage enough to ask, *I have to know what you think. What's your hunch? Is Melanie...do you think she's dead?*

Derek fucking hated questions like that. Because how could he know for sure? And in this profession...you didn't play around with death. Privately, yeah, if he had to guess, based on everything he'd seen before...it had been well over forty-eight hours, she wasn't answering her phone, she hadn't come back to check on her daughter. Maybe she'd had enough and simply skipped town, and that blood belonged to someone else—which would end up being its own case—but Derek doubted it.

He'd been too tired of all the lies to keep telling them, even to Alden.

Yeah, man. I do.

Alden had bowed his head and nodded once, then looked back up and said, *Okay.* That was it. No arguing, no *Are you sure?* Just...okay. Acceptance.

He was exhausted. Tired of working nonstop. Tired of having to get his brother through something so fucked up. Tired of lying.

At least this was the last night.

But then again...this was the last night. The only thing he wasn't tired of was Toni.

Where did they go from here, though? Nowhere, probably. No matter what, he was only going to lose her eventually.

He parked in the Sentinel lot and grabbed his cleaning supplies, wondering if she'd be at her desk tonight. But when he stepped off the elevator, she was waiting in the hallway for him.

As soon as she saw him, a smile broke across her face. "Alden. *Hey.*" She was standing in the entryway on the opposite side of the corridor, wearing her proper little work skirt and sheer blouse and eating him up with her eyes.

She was here for him. That smile was for him. And he was going to do everything in his power to keep her. Even if he had to maintain the lie for longer than he wanted to.

It was as though that realization broke down any remaining resistance he had about getting Toni beneath him again tonight, because all at once, what felt like thousands of images of him rucking up that fabric and slipping a hand between her thighs ran rampant through his mind.

He gave her a slow smile.

"Hey, Toni. Good to see you again." He was already panting. Already thinking, *I want to bend you over one of these chairs and slick up my cock between your legs.*

"You, too." She must have felt the incendiary connection between them, because she rasped out the words and the hoarseness of her voice made him even harder.

"Congratulations again," he murmured, taking a step forward, reducing the distance between them to slightly less than polite.

Through his pants, the line of his hard dick was clearly visible because she sucked in an audible breath, staring down at it. "Alden…"

That was it. Just his brother's name before she trailed off, her mouth parting in a perfect O. Damn, she had beautiful lips. Ones that had kissed him, sucked him, told him things that made him want her even more.

He forced himself to stay calm. Act like nothing was out of the ordinary. Not because he thought he could pretend he didn't have a massive hard-on between them, but because it was *fun* to mess with her a little.

"Yes, Toni?" He put a little amusement into his voice, and he could tell it caught at her, because slowly, her eyes migrated away from his crotch and traveled upward, almost dragging over his body until her gaze landed somewhere around his chin.

She was blushing so hard, almost her entire face was pink. "I, uh, I met your brother today."

That brought him up short. He hadn't expected her to say that. Sure, he'd hoped she'd mention it eventually, because of course *he* already knew and he didn't want her keeping things from him, but it wasn't as though he could ask her if she had decided not to tell him.

Fuck this complicated setup.

"How did you meet him?" he asked carefully.

She blushed. "*My* brother, um, sort of accosted me outside."

"What?" He hoped he came across as surprised.

"Yeah, um. He was coming after me because he wanted—"

She stopped, and Derek watched her take a deep breath before continuing.

"A week ago, he asked me to do something really bad for him."

He looked at her through hooded eyes. "Issue him a fake prescription for vike?"

Her jaw dropped. "H-how did you know?"

"I didn't know for sure until a second ago. But you'd asked me last week about using it as a transitional drug and now you're telling me he had asked you something and was coming after you, so I figured it was a pretty safe guess."

A blush rose on her cheeks and she nodded jerkily. "Yeah. Well."

"So did you do it?" Maybe he was being too aggressive with his questioning, but he had to know. It mattered.

To his relief, she shook her head immediately. "I couldn't. I considered it. I even went so far as to write out the draft of the script."

Damn, she'd come close.

"But right before I saved the record, I thought about you." She turned to him, eyes full of something he couldn't quite decipher, but that burned hot and intense into what felt like the very heart of him. "I imagined how disappointed you would be in me and how angry I would be with myself if I did something to lose your regard. I admire you, Alden. You came out of a bad situation and turned it into something wonderful. *You* are wonderful. I admire you and I like you and I *trust* you. It was your honesty with me, telling me what I could expect from you and admitting up front that you weren't perfect, that made me want to be worthy of you and do the right thing."

Fuck him to hell and back.

She *trusted* him. He'd inspired her with his *honesty*.

161

And if he read between the lines, he imagined that she might even think herself a little bit in love with him. A man who'd been lying to her from the moment they met.

There was nothing honest he could say in reply, so he did the only other thing he could think of.

He kissed her.

Lips. Teeth. Tongue.

Toni's mind was being blown apart by this kiss. It was as though each time they kissed, some new side of him showed up that surprised and aroused her even more than before. This time, the kiss started off slow and easy, but Alden built it up by degrees until it felt like he was pouring his very soul into her mouth.

She liked it so much. *No.* Loved it. She could feel herself being turned inside out, melting into nothing, breaking apart...

He wasn't *kissing* her. He was consuming her. Everything she'd lived for the past twenty-six years, every pain, every joy— it all belonged to him in this moment, and pretty soon there would be nothing left of her except a slick residue of what had been her life—sole testament that something incredibly hot and needy had taken place in this spot before she'd simply gone up in flames.

She brought her hands up to his shoulders and stroked over the muscle there, reveling in the sculpted hardness for a moment before her palms rubbed downward over his arms, over his sleeves and then onto warm, firm skin where his T-shirt ended. The short hairs on his forearms were soft beneath her touch, and she curled her fingers around a few of them before gently tugging.

He was pushed against her, having backed her to the wall, and his cock seemed to grow and pulse harder before he pulled away on a soft groan, nudging his erection against her body one last time before drawing his hips away.

"Toni. God. *Toni.* I want you."

Such a simple statement, but the way it shot a bolt of arousal directly to the heart of her made her knees actually quiver. Thank God his arms were still holding her. Holding her up.

Wow, he was strong. She wanted all that strength wrapped around her again. Inside her.

"I want you, too," she whispered, but he didn't kiss her again like she wanted him to. After a fraction of a second, he took a step back, his hands moving up her body until they were bracketing her upper arms like bindings. Keeping her at arm's length.

He took a deep breath and shook his head. "I have to finish this job first. Then we celebrate."

She liked how earnest he was about it. How seriously he took his responsibility.

She nodded again. "We'll do it together."

He leaned in and dropped a rough, close-mouthed kiss on her lips, then pulled away fast. "Good girl."

No. She wasn't a good girl. Seducing a man she hadn't seen in years, lusting after him, doing naughty things in her *office*, ditching her parents for *sex*...

It's not just sex.

No. It wasn't. She wasn't going to lie about that. This thing with Alden had given her back so much that she'd lost over the years. He made her feel like she mattered simply because she was herself. He made her feel like she was someone to be treasured. That she was *worth* something.

Their relationship might not last, but she was going to make it as honest as she could. Given the way he was honest with her, it was no less than he deserved.

Chapter Seventeen

He didn't take her home with him.

He wanted to, but as he worked alongside her, he thought about what she'd managed to accomplish today, and how much he wanted to truly celebrate that. She deserved a little recognition for what she'd done, and he wanted to be the one to give it to her.

Besides, if this was the last time they saw one another, he wanted to be sure she got a real date out of whatever they'd had. He texted his friend Kuli while she was scrubbing desks, and when they left, he drove them in his truck, first to a quick pit stop at Kuli's place, in and out in five minutes before his friend could ask any pointed questions, then on to a place far enough away from his house that he wouldn't be tempted to take her their afterward.

And she rolled with the whole thing. Her easy acceptance of whatever mysterious surprise he had planned made him so crazy for her that, when they'd finally parked at the top of the cliff that overlooked Greenbriar, the lights of the city stretching out before them as they sat in the darkness of his truck, alone except for grass and trees and rocks around them, he couldn't help but lean over and kiss her in a long, slow exploration that somehow ended up with him sitting in the passenger's seat with Toni straddling him, grinding down against his erection through the layers of their clothes.

"Toni." He groaned her name as she angled her hips up, rubbing over his length.

"So good," she murmured, her neck arching back, making her breasts push into his chest.

"Toni," he said it again, this time more forcefully, and she tipped her head forward to look at him in question, slowing her movements but not stopping completely.

"What is it?"

"This isn't what I brought you here for." He was sweating and the windows were already fogged up, so he probably looked like a complete idiot, but she had to know.

"Do you want to stop?" She stopped then, sinking down on his lap and stilling, making him grunt at the feel of her soft weight atop his straining cock.

God, no. But he wanted her to know that he wanted her for more than this.

"I got us dinner," he said instead.

"That's very sweet of you. I figured it was food because it smells delicious. But that doesn't answer my question." Even in the low light, he could see her frown. "Do you want to stop?" She leaned close, kissing the tip of his nose before pulling back and looking him in the eyes. "I want you to tell me honestly."

How could he resist a direct request like that? He wanted to be honest with her, too.

"No," he murmured, leaning up to capture her mouth again as his grabbed her hips and pulled her hard against him.

"Good." She smiled against his lips. "In that case, we can eat *after.*"

Thank God he'd remembered to pack a condom in his pocket again. By the time they were ready to eat, most of their clothes had been kicked to the floor, the truck felt like a sauna, and they were ravenous.

"Spicy dumplings!" she squealed, when he presented her with the box he'd picked up from Kuli. "I can't believe you remembered these are my favorite." She grew quiet for a second, looking at him like he hung the moon, then whispered, "This is the nicest thing anyone has done for me in a long time."

The heartfelt appreciation he'd heard in her voice tore at his conscience. Would she still believe in how wonderful she was when she found out he'd lied? He didn't want to take that away from her.

So don't tell her yet.

Instead, he kissed her and teased her back into a lighthearted mood.

The appetite they'd worked up before then might have been part of the reason she proclaimed it the best meal she'd ever eaten, as they sat back and had dinner while watching the city lights through the part of the glass that he'd rubbed clear with his discarded T-shirt, but he still felt like he'd accomplished his mission to give her something special.

When Alden had walked her to her car at the Sentinel parking lot, she kissed him goodbye and drove home with the radio on full volume, grinning from ear to ear.

But when she turned onto her street, she already knew something was wrong before she pulled into the driveway of her parents' house. Every light in the house was on, and the place even *felt* like it was brimming with action—like energy was pouring out of it. It was only a few minutes past nine o'clock, but the level of activity she could sense from inside was aberrant.

What the hell?

She parked and grabbed her phone—two missed calls from her parents—before practically running to the front door, digging out her house key as she went. By the time she unlocked and opened the door, she was on the verge of panic.

"Mom? Dad?" She stepped into the foyer, calling for them.

"In the dining room," came Mom's voice in reply. "Thank God you're home."

She sounded urgent. Something was definitely wrong. Toni hesitated only long enough to lock the front door behind her before rushing into the dining room, what she found there had her heart rate rising again. Her parents were standing in front of a suitcase that had been laid out on the large mahogany table, wearing identical frowns and packing clothes from folded piles into the case.

"What's going on in here?" She looked at the mounds of clothing still on the table and back to her parents.

Mom came around the table and hugged her, and Toni could feel the tension in her mother's body.

"Oh, Toni. I'm glad you're here. We called you a couple of times but there was no answer and we didn't want to disturb you anymore until we absolutely had to. We were talking about whether to call you again now or wait until the packing is done. But now that you're home, you can grab your bag and join us. We need enough for a few nights, we think. You have to hurry, though."

Toni shook her head, confused. What was her mother talking about? And so rapid-fire that it made her speech even more difficult to understand.

Dad came around the table then, too, and stood next to Mom. "Isabella." He put a hand on Mom's arm, and Toni watched her mother visibly relax. "Toni…Sal called us about twenty minutes ago."

Uh-oh.

"He was raving. Honestly, I'm surprised he was lucid enough to remember the home phone number, much less dial it successfully. After a lot of angry rambling, he made some threats and hung up. Your mother and I thought it was best to take his threats seriously and leave. We're going to go to a hotel for a couple of nights."

For a second, all Toni could do was close her eyes and try to fight the rising tide of guilt.

If only I'd gotten him the drugs he wanted. If only I'd tried harder to help him.

"Toni? Honey, I'm sure it will be okay. We're being extra careful, that's all. We don't know where he was calling from or even if he'll remember—"

Toni snapped her eyes open. "I'm going to the police. I'm going to tell them about this and file a report at the least."

Mom blinked at her. "The police...I..."

Why was Mom being so hesitant? It wasn't as though running away could keep them safe forever. They'd seemed ready to walk away from Sal for some time now. What difference would telling the police make?

"Mom, we *have* to," Toni whispered, wanting to cry at the sight of her mother's face crumpling. She rushed forward to wrap her arms around her mom. "I don't mean we wish him dead and gone or any of that. I don't mean we haven't been trying hard to help him, or we should deny him help if he needs it. But we can't go on like this. The two of you have barely lived for the past couple of years and I—"

I've sacrificed myself on the altar of someone who doesn't want to be saved.

Alden was right. She wasn't going to be Sal's savior. None of them were. It was time to face the truth. She couldn't allow her big brother to continue terrorizing them like this. Maybe there was still hope for him, and maybe there wasn't, but they couldn't force him to be the man they wanted him to be.

Over her mother's shoulder, Toni looked at her dad. "What did he say, anyway?"

He met his daughter's eyes. "He said he was tired of us shutting him out, and so instead he would lock *us* all *in*, then burn down the house with you, me, and your mother inside."

God. Her poor parents. Dealing with that kind of fear from one of their own children while the other one had been off sneaking around with a guy. A tiny crumb of attention from a man and she'd abandoned her most important responsibility.

"I'm sorry I wasn't here. I should have been." She stepped back and looked at both of her parents in turn. "Mom, Dad, I didn't tell you right away, but earlier today Sal came up to me while I was walking on the path around the lake and nearly attacked me. A couple of officers saw him and chased him off. I didn't want you to worry so I didn't say anything. But it's clear he's growing more dangerous every day, no matter how much we love him. We have to let the police know. They might even be able to help us."

Dad nodded. "I think you're right. I *know* you're right." He sighed. "But it's hard to actually accept it, even though I've told myself time and again not to get my hopes up and that Sal probably isn't going to come home healthy."

They all heard what her father was really saying. Forget healthy. Sal probably wouldn't come home alive.

Mom sighed heavily, but finally nodded. "I feel the same way. That I thought I'd be ready for this day. I know we've done everything we can. But now that it's here, I don't know if I can call the police. Can we at least give it until tomorrow? I just need a little more time to come to terms with…"

She trailed off, and Toni opened her mouth to argue, but Mom shook her head and took a deep breath before nodding as though she'd come to a decision. "Just for the night. We'll be in a hotel, anyway. He can't hurt us if he comes here. *Please.*"

Toni hated hearing her mother beg. She nodded. "Yes, okay. Of course. I'll go in the morning."

Then her mother turned to her father and leaned her head against his shoulder, letting him support her weight. Toni found herself wishing Alden was there with them so she could do the same thing—to lean on him for support. To let him save her a little bit of heartbreak.

But the only reason she knew Alden in the first place was because of how irresponsible she'd been with him. They'd gotten more deeply involved than she'd intended, but she couldn't keep this up and end up putting him and possibly even his daughter in danger.

"I'm sorry, honey."

For a second, Toni thought Mom had read her mind and was expressing her regrets over Toni not being able to be with Alden. But no…her parents had no idea. She looked at her mom in question. "For what?"

"For...failing. Failing you, failing Sal. Not being a success as a mother. I never meant to hurt you. And the worst part is, I thought I was doing everything right. I thought I was doing what moms are supposed to do. But Sal...well, I was wrong and I don't even know how or why."

"Mom, no." She couldn't stand hearing those words from her mother. "You and Dad both did your best. No one's perfect, and Sal made his fair share of mistakes. But anyway, this isn't about right or wrong. It just *is*."

I don't think there's a wrong or a right for this. It's our way.

Damn it. Everything seemed destined to remind her of Alden. But she doubted she would have had the understanding to even say such a thing to her mother in the first place if it hadn't been for her experience with him.

With the reminder of him came his words, too. "We can't save him if he doesn't want to be saved," she whispered, and the pain of it nearly knocked her breathless. Pain, because she finally saw it for the truth.

And the realization that it was time for her to save *herself*.

Chapter Eighteen

The next afternoon, Derek had just come in for his shift and was standing in the break room, stirring his coffee and thinking of Toni, when Serrano sauntered in.

"I ran into your brother the other night." He walked to the coffeepot and poured a mug. "Looks exactly like you."

"Yeah, well, that's usually what *identical twins* means." Derek didn't bother checking his derisive laughter. Not after the way Serrano had acted that night at Eagan's.

"Funny." Serrano leaned against the opposite counter. "He was with a really hot chick. She was way too into him. Got an attitude problem, though. She was mouthing off to me, and not in a good way."

Derek raised a brow at the other man. "Watch the way you talk about her."

"Okay, okay, sorry." Serrano bent backward a little bit and Derek had to remind himself to dial back some of the aggression. He'd actually taken a step toward Serrano, like he wouldn't have hesitated to put a fist in the kid's face.

Toni had looked way too into him? The observation filled him with equal parts pride and annoyance. Why would having a girl like her be into his brother be "too" anything? Stupid Serrano, putting Alden down before he knew him.

Isn't that what you've been doing, though? Acting out the worst parts of who you think Alden is because you think it fits his image better than the good twin?

He turned away to pull the wooden stir stick from his mug and toss it in the garbage.

"Why do you bother stirring that shit when you drink it

black?" Serrano was frowning.

Derek tried not to let it get it to him. The younger officer had taken the hint and dropped his smack talking about Toni and Alden. It was Derek's own thoughts making him angry now. He didn't feel like dealing with Serrano. With any of it.

He was too goddamn tired, that was all. That was why he was being oversensitive about everything. But he was done with the cleaning gig. No more of that. He had Toni's number, she wasn't going to work late anymore, and he could keep seeing her for a while on his own time.

Just not as himself.

"What, now you're giving me the silent treatment?" Serrano's voice intruded on Derek's reverie and he jumped out of reflex, sloshing the hot coffee over his hand.

"Motherfu—"

"Brewer. Someone here to see you."

Thank God Donahue chose that moment to poke his head into the break room, before Derek could totally lose his shit and punch the immature little sonofabitch. Or worse yet—have Serrano go tattling that something was *wrong* with Derek.

Nothing was ever wrong with him.

Probably would have served him right, though, for being sloppy enough to call attention to himself when what he most needed right now was to fly under the radar. Only for a couple more days.

Donahue stepped farther into the room, eyes narrowing when he saw Serrano. "Get out."

The younger officer left immediately without another word.

Donahue grinned. "That was fun."

Derek blew out a breath. "You're twisted, man." But he was relieved.

Donahue smirked. "Yes. But I also saved you from having to make a choice in which either option would have resulted in trouble for you."

"I don't know what you're talking about."

Fucking Donahue. His power of observation sometimes had Derek suspecting he was psychic or something like that. It would certainly explain his prowess with women. Donahue could walk into a bar and leave five minutes later with the hottest woman on his arm, take her home for a one-night stand and never call her again, and still have her think she was lucky to have known him.

Although, fine, maybe Derek was a *little* grateful for the interruption. Although he didn't like the way his brain had drawn the connection between him and Donahue's string of women.

"Yes, you do. You think your brother wasted his life and you resent him for it, but you can't accept anyone *else* saying a harsh word about him. But you weren't going to defend him because you're also hiding something that has to do with the same woman who gave you dark circles under your eyes."

Derek set down his mug and brought a hand up to pinch the bridge of his nose. His fingers smelled like coffee.

"Why aren't you a detective, Donahue?"

The blond man shrugged. "Because I don't want to be."

"But it's the next logical step on the path to—"

"There's no one path, Brewer. No dividing line." Donahue sounded very suddenly almost angry. Almost like he was taking Derek's words *too* personally. It was so rare for the guy to get upset or to reveal anything about himself that didn't have to do with the women he dated for a few hours that Derek was shocked into temporary silence.

Donahue gave a little shake of his head, almost like he was trying to dislodge a pesky gnat. "Like I said, someone's here to see you. But I have a feeling you'll enjoy this visitor, even though she's only here to file a police report."

Derek stiffened. *She?* It was Toni. He knew it in his gut.

Donahue's eyes flicked over him. "I'm always here if you need to talk. I'll keep your secrets."

No doubt he would. Donahue was practically *made* of secrets. Derek wasn't ready to confide in anyone—he was hoping he'd never had to—but he appreciated the offer.

So he merely nodded, then walked out the door, bracing himself to face her and hoping he wouldn't give himself away as a liar and a fraud.

While another part of him desperately hoped she would know him anywhere.

Every cell in her body seemed to expand when he walked into the room, making her feel excited and giddy and impossibly horny.

For the wrong man.

Was it always like this with twins? Did individuality really not matter? She hated thinking she was shallow enough to base the majority of her attraction to Alden on looks, but seeing Derek, feeling this way with *him*, too—it seemed the most likely explanation.

Don't flirt with him.

"Miss Park. Good to see you again." He walked forward and held out his hand.

She let him grasp hers and tried to ignore the arousal that rolled through her at his touch. They even had the exact same hands. Hands that had been all over her body. Gripping her punishingly tight. Probing deep inside of her and—

"What can I do for you today, Miss Park?" He sounded completely unaffected, while she was practically a puddle of feeling. She couldn't bring herself to look him in the eye, afraid that all the need she was experiencing would be too obvious.

"Toni, please. And I came because I wanted to file a police report on what happened yesterday afternoon. With my brother, I mean. But it wasn't just that. He threatened me again last night. He threatened my parents, actually. He called while I was…out. Told my mom and dad he would barricade all three of us in the house and burn it down."

The horrible words reminded her of the long, fretful night she'd spent in the hotel bed, how she'd sat across from her parents this morning in the hotel restaurant and everyone had avoided suggesting they drive by their house to see if it was still standing. The recent memories quelled the arousal in her, and this time she was able to lift her eyes and look at him.

Okay, nope. That was a mistake.

Because Derek's eyes were Alden's eyes, and she found herself wishing Alden were here so he could hold her. Not for sex. But for comfort. The way he'd talked to her and made her feel like she was worth getting to know, like her burdens were worth bearing for the positive things she brought to his life…the way he got her, and the lesson he'd taught her about salvation for her brother…it had only been a few days, but he had already built a connection with her soul that she couldn't seem to cut loose.

"Why didn't you call me?" he asked, but then shook his head slightly and blinked. "I mean, phone the station? Why did you wait you until today? If he'd followed through—"

"But he didn't," she insisted, because a part of her still felt like a traitor for doing this. "We stayed at a hotel last night, to be safe, and I went by my house this morning. It's fine." She'd had to know. "Besides, I promised my mom I'd wait until today. So here I am." She opened her arms for a second, making a show of herself before she realized, then quickly dropped them back to her sides.

But she'd caught the way his eyes had raked over her body when she'd called attention to it, and she recognized the heat that flared.

Alden wore the same expression when he looked at her.

This is so fucked up.

But Derek simply nodded. "I understand. If you'll follow me, I'll get you a copy of the report form and you're welcome to fill it out here. And I'll need to ask you a few more questions about both incidents, if you don't mind."

"I don't mind."

She followed him to a desk near a row of offices at the end of a big room. He pulled out a chair for her and gestured for her to sit, and she complied immediately. There was something about a good-looking, muscled man in uniform that made her mindless. Especially a man who looked exactly like her lover.

Lover.

What a strange word. It had *love* in it, but was that what she felt for Alden?

No. Not yet, anyway. But she was close, and she could certainly see herself falling that way eventually. Sooner rather than later, in fact.

She watched Derek out of the corner of her eye. He strode to a filing cabinet behind his desk, opened the top drawer, and started sifting his fingers through a row of folders. The black pants and button-down shirt of his uniform fit him perfectly, and she couldn't help but appreciate the way the fabric hugged his ass.

She needed to say something to get her mind off of Derek's sexiness. It wasn't right to lust after *both* brothers, no matter how attracted she was to Derek.

"I, um, I've been seeing a lot of your brother recently," was what she ended up blurting out.

Oh, God. At least she had "creepy" down pat.

He stopped in the middle of pulling a folder out and jerked his head around to stare at her. She wished she could crawl under the chair and disappear.

But after a second, he finished taking out the folder and nodded. "He mentioned you work at Sentinel."

He had?

Derek shut the cabinet drawer and walked back toward her, dropping the folder on the desk. His uniform shirt was short-sleeved, and she enjoyed watching the way the tendons in his forearms flexed.

"Alden's a good guy," she said.

Stop talking now.

Derek was staring at her again—that same, startled stare he'd given her a moment ago. Almost like disbelief. Almost like he didn't understand the words she was saying, about his brother being *good*.

You think a junkie can be an honorable person? Or even a good one?

Alden had said that the other night.

Something tight and uncomfortable gripped her in the throat, but before she could break through the barrier and give voice to the crazy thing that had popped into her mind, Derek spoke.

"Yeah. He is a good guy."

The pressure in her throat subsided.

She chided herself for being such an idiot, trying to foist her own feelings of guilt onto Derek. She'd been crazy to think maybe her attraction to both of them was because they were actually the same person.

She wanted to see Alden again. *Had* to see him. As soon as she was finished here, she was going to text him and see what happened next.

Chapter Nineteen

This morning had been torture.

For the half hour Toni had been at the station, sitting at Derek's desk an arm's length away from him, he'd had to fight the urge to reach out and haul her into his lap, to kiss away the regret he could see in her eyes.

How was it possible that the people who were supposed to love you the most were also the ones who too often tore you apart?

And then she'd left, and he'd had to shove his phone into his desk drawer and lock it to keep himself from texting her to ask if she was okay. He didn't want her to think the guy she knew as both Derek and Alden were gossiping about her.

Or…something like that. Shit, even he was getting confused now about who he was.

Luckily, though, he hadn't had to torture himself for too long. She'd texted him about an hour after she'd left the station.

Feel like getting together after you work tonight? I can't stay late but I can come over.

He was surprised he didn't break the phone in his rush to reply. Those things weren't really made for someone with hands as big as his.

Now he was heading home after finishing his shift, trying not to drive too fast in his eagerness. It was later than he usually finished at Sentinel, since he'd been on a later shift at the station today, but she hadn't questioned it.

She was going to meet him at his place. He'd offered to take her out somewhere else, since he would have been happy to simply sit across from her and talk. Of course, he also would have wanted to take her home after that, but it didn't matter, anyway, since she'd insisted that they didn't need to go out.

When he pulled into his driveway, she was already parked there. She got out of her car as he cut the engine, and she walked around the front of his truck to meet him. Tonight she was wearing jeans and some kind of slip-on sandal things with a soft-looking button-down, so faded it was nearly see-through even in the low light coming from the truck's cab. It was a different look from what he was used to, having so far seen her only in her work clothes.

And naked. You've seen her naked.

"Toni." He stepped out of the truck and shut the door. In the time it took for his eyes to adjust to the darkness, she brought her body up against his, her head tipped back so their lips were almost touching.

"Alden," she whispered in reply, then kissed him.

There was a lot of feeling in that kiss.

And she tasted like apples.

He hated how she called him Alden.

He put a hand on her waist but pulled his mouth from hers. "Everything okay?" he murmured.

Would she tell him about what had happened with Sal? He wondered if she'd even tell him she'd filed a police report today and had seen the man she thought was his brother.

She took a step back, and there was too much distance between them. "I'm okay."

So she wasn't going to tell him. The realization stung probably more than it should have, considering the only reason he knew she was hiding something from him was because he was lying to her about who he was.

You have no right to be upset.

That was why he let go of his tension with a long exhale, then led her to the front door, unlocked it, and walked inside with her while holding her hand as gently as he could.

But before he could ask her anything else about her day, to at least see if she'd mention she was staying in a hotel temporarily, she stepped close and slid her arms around his neck, kissing him deeply.

No matter how much he wanted her to open up to him, he couldn't resist her touch.

He slowly backed her up until she was pressed against the wall of the foyer and he held her there, kissing her like it was the only thing he knew how to do, that he might die if he couldn't do it for hours. Forever. He ran his fingers through her hair and skimmed a touch down her arm, but he didn't take it any further.

Tonight, he wanted to be himself as much as he could.

She slid her mouth to his jaw and trailed a line of kisses along his hair-roughened skin. "Alden," she whispered, and he tensed, trying to resist the urge to correct her. But fuck, he wanted to. Right on the heels of that thought about him wanting to be himself and the confession was trying to claw its way out of his mouth.

But he couldn't tell her yet. She'd hate him. She'd leave him. Maybe next week, when she'd stopped associating him with the cleaning guy.

Or maybe in another week after that, in case she decided she never wanted to see his lying face again.

So he didn't say anything. Instead, he kissed her again, trying to make sure she would know him by his touch, *damn it*, even if not by name.

She stepped out of her shoes, losing an inch of height, and he curved his neck and back to follow her mouth, which made her laugh and push him away. But then she took his hand and led them down the short hallway toward his bedroom, toward his king-sized bed he'd never really thought too hard about before—even the first time he'd brought her here—but seeing it now, a neatly made comforter waiting to be mussed, had him thinking how glad he was he'd bought a big bed. All that space was meant for rolling around in with *her*.

She stopped at the edge of the bed and turned back to face him, tipping her head up for another kiss. This time, he ran a hand slowly down the front of her blouse and she shuddered, arching into his touch, trying to push her breasts against his fingers. He happily obliged her unspoken request, palming one sweet, soft globe through her shirt and the lacy fabric of her bra, feeling her peaked nipple under his fingertip. He tried to lightly pinch it between his fingers, but there were too many layers in the way, and she made a frustrated noise into his mouth, her fingers going to the buttons on her shirt.

No. He gently moved her hands away. He wanted to do it. He wanted to be the one who stripped her bare.

Slowly, he unbuttoned her shirt, pressing a kiss to her beautiful skin each time he slipped a button free. The place right below her throat, where the skin was tight and flat…the space between her breasts, which smelled of something floral mixed with soap…right below the band of her bra…

And then he was swirling his tongue around her navel, making her gasp and giggle, as he pulled the sides of the shirt completely open, making it slide off her shoulders and onto the floor. He retraced the path upward by licking over the line that joined her navel with her throat, until he was standing fully upright again and devouring her mouth, reveling in the sweet taste of her.

Her hands grabbed the hem of his T-shirt and yanked it up, but she wasn't tall enough, her arms not long enough, to get it past his ribs.

He broke away to help her, sweeping his shirt over his head in one fluid stroke then flinging it across the room.

She'd taken off her bra while he'd been stripping his shirt, and while a part of him wanted to protest that he'd wanted that particular pleasure, he was too turned on by the sight of her beautiful breasts to really care. He pulled her close again, letting the soft globes rub against his chest, enjoying how her nipples hardened with sensation until he could feel them poking into his skin.

He dropped to his knees and took one into his mouth, scraping his teeth gently over the surrounding areola, and her hands went to his shoulders as she arched and moaned. "That feels so good."

He switched to the other breast.

"*So* good. So so…oh…so good."

He smiled. Her words were so simple, almost innocent, but they were making him impossibly hard. How she got so mindless with pleasure—how *he* had the power to make her that way—was the hottest thing of all.

He continued to play with her breasts with his mouth while his hands went to the front of her jeans, unbuttoning and unzipping, until he was able to bring both his hands to the waistband at her back and slide them beneath the elastic of her panties. Oh, fuck, her body felt good. He cupped her ass and kneaded the firm flesh with so much focused arousal he had to take his mouth away from her breasts. His forehead rested against her stomach, his nose pushed into the hollow of her navel, and the scent of her…

"I want you," she panted, her words floating down to him like a benediction.

Thank God.

He was more than ready. He pushed the rest of her clothes to the floor and stood up, bringing his hands to the placket of his jeans.

But she stopped him by covering his hands with hers, then pushing his gently away, like he'd done earlier with her shirt. He wondered if she felt the same way he did—that she wanted to be the one to own his pleasure.

She already did. He would tell her gladly, if she would only ask. But she didn't. Instead, she worked open his button and slid down his zipper, then pushed his jeans and underwear far enough that his cock sprang out, so hard and ready that drops of fluid were already gathered at the tip.

She made a low humming sound and curled her fingers

around the shaft.

He had to jerk his gaze away and shut his eyes for second so he wouldn't come right then. Her hand was so slender and delicate that his cock looked monstrous in her grip. He knew it shouldn't matter. She liked sex with him and he sure as hell loved it with her. But there was something about seeing his dick like that…it shot directly at something overwhelmingly intense inside of him.

She gripped him gently and stroked him, up and down, only once before he stopped her with a shake of his head and a hand on her shoulder, pushing her back onto the bed. She was the sexiest woman he'd ever seen. Laid out like that, naked and a little flushed, her legs moving restlessly over the expanse of dark blue comforter, she was everything he wanted.

He pulled a condom from the nightstand and had it opened and rolled on in seconds before joining her on the bed. But he didn't push her legs apart and plunge into her body this time. Instead, he stretched out on his side and leaned over her to kiss her, one hand on the mattress near his head while the other played over her mound, teasing at her clit and making her roll her hips upward, seeking more pressure. She grabbed at his shoulders, trying to pull him on top of her, but he resisted enough until she grew tired. Complacent.

At least, she played along with her complacency. He wanted to believe she understood that tonight was about the real him. The nice twin. He wasn't going to hurt her, even in pleasure.

After several minutes of kissing and petting her, she started to make soft, keening sounds. Needy sounds. Her hips were rising so high off the bed now she was making the mattress bounce every time she brought them down, and the throbbing in his cock was starting to get painful. So he shifted his body until he was on top of her, brought her hands up so he could thread his fingers through hers, and slowly nudged himself into her body, feeling himself grow harder with every audible, desperate breath she took.

She was wet and hot and her body beneath his was practically vibrating as he went deeper inside of her. When he was finally fully seated, she let out a long, low moan and squeezed his hands with hers.

He kissed her, the rest of his body held still, and felt her clench around his cock.

He couldn't wait any longer. He had to move.

He began to stroke in slow, deep-reaching waves, continuing to kiss her while he worked in and out, her limbs relaxing and her body opening to take him. Soft and receiving and everything sweet and easy...

Until it wasn't. Until she started to whimper and strain and he could feel her getting tighter, her climax building, and he was so turned on he couldn't hold back his own. He tore his mouth from hers and sped up his thrusts, grunting like an animal every time he pushed against her, and within seconds her body was arching up, a scream escaping her as she shattered around him, and then he was finished, too, his orgasm shaking loose and exploding out of him, rendering him mindless and empty and completely, utterly *hers.*

Earlier that day, she'd wanted to get lost in his arms. But now that she was here, wrapped up in him, she wanted even more.

After they'd both finished shuddering and shaking out their pleasure, Alden had dragged himself off of her, stepped out of the room for a second—presumably to get rid of the condom, since he came back without it on—and then gotten them both under his sheets and laid down with his front to her back. Cradling her, almost, in the length of his body.

"So. Did you have a good day?" His voice was sleepy-sounding with a hint of amusement.

She smiled. First sex, then talking. They really did have it backward. But it worked for them, and she was letting herself hope this might end up being more than a passing fling. But that meant no hiding. She had to be as open and honest with him as he'd been with her.

"I saw your brother again today, actually."

She paused for a second, waiting for his reaction, but all he said was, "Oh?" But he sounded a lot more awake than he had a moment ago. And oddly, he sounded almost… happy to hear it.

"Yeah. Um…because I went to the police station."

Was it just her, or was Alden tensing up a bit? His arm felt tighter and heavier across her ribs. But she had to tell him, so if he was going to run off when finally confronted with the reality of all her problems, he could do it now. Before she fell even deeper into him.

"After Sal tried to hurt me yesterday and Derek stopped him—well, Derek and another officer. Crewes, or something. Maybe you know him. Anyway, after that, Derek asked me if I wanted to file a report and I said no, but then last night after I got home, I found my parents packing up because Sal had called and threatened them. All three of us. We had to move to a hotel for a little bit. That's where I stayed last night. I have to go back there soon so my parents don't worry, too. But first thing this morning I filed a police report…that's why I saw your brother."

It occurred to her only when the words left her mouth that, in a small way, she felt like she was confessing, as though she'd been *cheating* on Alden. But she hadn't done anything.

You thought about it, though.

Right. And that's what had left her feeling so guilty. But she'd told him. She was with Alden now. He had to know he was important to her. Even if it had only been a short time, he'd given her more understanding than most people had in her life to this point.

She swallowed against the sudden lump in her throat. "Anyway, um. Derek said they'd try to get some patrols to go by the house a few times a day, to make sure it's safe. He said we could stay at the hotel for another couple nights and probably it would be safe to return. Safe enough, anyway." She sighed. "I wish I hadn't given up on *my* brother like that. But I have to accept—like you said—I can't save him. I need help. *He* needs help."

And then she was crying, soft tears that rolled down her cheeks in silence. No great sobs or wrenching wails—there were the tears of resignation and regret.

Alden pulled her a little closer and dropped a kiss into her hair. "I'm sorry, Toni. I really…I do understand, but I know that doesn't make it better."

Of course he understood. He'd been an addict, after all, and his brother had probably felt the same way—more so, even, because Derek was a police officer. Having a brother who stood on the opposite side from you in an *official* capacity likely made it all worse.

The opposite side.

Again, Toni was struck with the sense something wasn't quite right, but at the moment she couldn't move her thoughts beyond the feeling itself. And then Alden spoke again and the feeling subsided.

"So you said you had to get back to the hotel so your parents don't worry. I'm assuming they don't know about us…or are they going to show up on my doorstep accusing me of corrupting you?"

It could have been an accusation, a question about why she hadn't told her parents about him, but she could hear the smile in his voice. It seemed like he understood why she was keeping it a secret and was teasing her about it. She laughed, the mirth stopping up her tears. She wasn't sure why she found it so funny, but something in her shifted in that moment— gratitude, possibly, to him for making her laugh when she needed to, and she actually felt her heart move from *like* into *love.*

Deeper into Alden.

"No, they don't know," she admitted, then immediately

hurried to clarify, "not because I'm ashamed or anything. I think it would add to their worries, that's all."

She could feel him breathing behind her, measured and even, and she relaxed slightly.

"Hey, I understand. It's okay. I wasn't trying to push anything on you."

She turned and dropped a sweet kiss on the corner of her mouth. "Thank you," she whispered.

"So…what are you doing on Saturday?" he asked.

The sudden change of subject didn't stop her excitement at his question, and she fought to keep her voice calm. "No plans at the moment. Why do you ask?"

"I was thinking we could go out. I want to make good on that raincheck from the other night."

"I thought we did that last night. And tonight, too." She was teasing him a little.

"You call this a date? You didn't even buy me dinner," he teased back.

She sighed and relaxed even deeper into him. "I'd love to go out with you on Saturday. But what about Emma? Aren't you with her during the days?"

She wished she knew more about his relationship with his daughter, and even his daughter's mother—had she shown up again after being missing for so long, after all?—but she didn't think now was a good time to ask. They'd just gotten out of a serious mood and she didn't want to plunge them back into a somber discussion. He'd tell her if it was important.

Wouldn't he?

At her question she felt his body tense—it was definite this time—and he was quiet for a bit before he finally said, "I don't always see Emma on the weekends."

Poor Alden. That tension must mean he didn't like whatever arrangement he had going on there. It must be a painful subject for him. Definitely not time to discuss any further.

She nodded, her hair making a scraping sound as it moved against his chest. "Saturday it is, then."

They lay like that for a few more minutes, until she could feel herself growing too sleepy to stay, so she kissed him goodbye and headed out, already eager for Saturday to come.

Chapter Twenty

That Saturday, Derek drove to the botanical gardens, where he'd wanted to take Toni. He'd offered to pick her up at the hotel where she and her parents had been staying, or her house or even her office, but she'd texted him that she'd meet him at the front entrance to the gardens. She hadn't seemed open to negotiation, and the most important thing was that he was going to see her again, so he didn't fight her on it.

Derek left the house and jumped in his truck, pulling out of his driveway to go meet Toni. A couple minutes later, his phone rang.

Shit. He hoped that wasn't her, calling to cancel. He pulled it from the center console and quickly glanced at the screen.

Alden.

He answered and put it on speaker. "Hey, Alden. I'm in the car. What's up?"

"Morning, Derek. Where you heading out to?"

He debated whether to tell Alden, then decided against it. "Meeting a friend." His discomfort made his tone a little more clipped than usual, and of course Alden picked up on it.

"Are you all right? You sound pissed. I'm sorry I haven't been in touch. Between Emma and actually doing the Sentinel job now it's been—"

"I'm not angry." He knew it wasn't polite to cut off his brother's apology, but he didn't want to hear it. Not when he was still capitalizing on Alden's identity to get with a woman he had no business continuing to see.

He was turning into the bad twin.

There was a heavy silence for a moment. Alden's voice

189

finally came slowly through the phone. "All right. Well, hey. I was calling to see if you wanted to come hang out with me and Emma. She wants me to take her to the zoo, or maybe the botanical gardens."

No. No no no. Don't come here. Whatever you do, don't come here.

"I can't today. But if you hold off, I'll join you for the zoo or the gardens tomorrow. Maybe today you can bring her to a movie or something."

He tried to use the Force through the phone, willing his brother to agree. *You don't want to go to the gardens today. You want to stay away from this area.*

"Oh, hey, that's great if you can join us tomorrow. Okay, I'll think of something else to do today. It'll be good to see you, man. I—uh—I miss you."

Knife. Knife to the fucking heart.

Derek hadn't been expecting that one.

"Yeah," he agreed. "It'll be good to see you, too. And Emma. Of course."

Another silence fell and Derek wondered whether Alden expected him to say it back. *I miss you.* But Derek had been missing his brother for years. It didn't feel special anymore. It was simply the norm.

He couldn't say it. Not yet.

Alden cleared his throat. "Anyway, I'll let you get to it. But before I go, is there any update on Mel?"

The initial processing of the blood samples from the suspect's car had come back yesterday afternoon as human. Type A.

Melanie's blood type.

But that wasn't all. They'd been able to lift a print off the rear windshield, and when they'd run it through the system, the print had come up with a match.

Melanie.

Derek had been almost relieved that Melanie had been booked in the past and so her prints were in the system. Now they knew she'd been in that car even though the suspect had said he hadn't been anywhere near the Strip the night Melanie disappeared and had never seen her before. Because of that, they'd extended the guy's stay in jail and raised his bail. Meanwhile, the blood samples were sent off to the lab for DNA testing and the guys at the impound lot had started dismantling the backseat of the car, but Derek hadn't heard anything further. He'd called and left a message for Alden to call him, but by then Alden would have already been at Sentinel.

"No, not yet. I'm off today, but if anything comes in, the guys know to call me. And to call you. You might even hear before I do."

"Cool. Okay, well. Have a good one. I'll see you tomorrow?"

Derek didn't miss the worry and the hope both in Alden's voice.

"Yeah," he replied. "You can count on me."

He hated the way it sounded like a lie to his ears.

She'd never had a date at the botanical gardens. It had never occurred to her as a particularly romantic place to go.

But here she was, strolling hand in hand with Alden through displays of lush plants and flowers, beautifully sculpted beds, and the occasional cascading waterfall. Turned out, it was one of the most romantic places she'd seen.

He'd met her at the gates and had already paid for her entry fee, despite her protests that she was happy to pay her own way. She had to be earning a lot more money than he was, but a part of her did appreciate how chivalrous he was. She'd always thought of herself as an independent woman who could take care of herself—and everyone else in her family—but it was nice, in a way, to be treated so delicately.

Except for the times when Alden was slamming into her body hard enough to make her teeth snap together.

She liked that, too, though.

She blushed, thinking of it, and of course that was the moment he chose to glance over at her. The look he gave her made her even hotter.

But to his credit, he didn't stop to kiss her like she wished he would. He seemed to be treating this like a real date that shouldn't result in racing back to his place five minutes after it had begun. She resolved to do the same.

Hopefully she wouldn't perish of desire before it was over and she could have him inside of her again.

He turned his eyes back to the path ahead and asked out of the side of his mouth, "How is your hotel stay? Still the same?"

He'd texted her yesterday about it and she'd told him she was enjoying ordering room service but couldn't get used to the way the sheets felt nor the impersonal smell of her hotel room. Her sleep last night had been fraught with horrible dreams, of Alden on fire, screaming to her to save him, but she'd refused. In the nightmare, she'd been angry with him. She'd sneered and told him to save himself, and she'd awoken this morning with her fists clenched—not with rage, but from holding herself in check so she wouldn't jump atop him and use herself as a human dousing blanket.

The message had seemed clear. She wasn't going to sacrifice herself for anyone. Not even Alden. And yet, there had to have been another way to save him...why had she refused?

It was only a dream.

She shook her head. "Actually, we checked out this morning. The house has been safe all this time, so we all agreed going back made sense, especially with the police cruisers going by every few hours. Your brother was true to his word."

"Yeah." Alden gave a tight nod. "I guess he tries, anyway."

It was a weird thing to say, but he seemed to think it made

sense, so she let it go. "After we checked out, Mom and Dad went back home and I came here. It's been years since I went to the gardens. I think the last time was when I was in grade school. I didn't remember it being like this. Do you come here a lot?"

"Not a lot, really. But once every couple of months. I don't have a particularly green thumb. I'm a by-the-book kind of guy and plants don't always do what they're supposed to, so I'd rather appreciate someone else's efforts than get frustrated trying to recreate this myself in my yard at home." He paused for a moment, stopping them in front of a Zen garden with beautifully raked sand and polished rocks. "I'm still moving in, though. Gotta take care of the inside of my place first before I can think about anything on the outside, so maybe I'll change my mind eventually. Is it okay?"

For a second, she frowned, thinking he was asking her whether it was okay for him to work on his interior before the exterior. But then she realized he was talking about being at the gardens for their date.

She nodded. "It's perfect."

They studied the Zen garden for a while.

"So you're a by-the-book kind of guy, huh? You've certainly fooled me." She thought about the way he'd pressed her into the tailgate of his truck and wondered what kind of book he thought he was following.

He laughed, but it sounded strange. "I guess I've managed to surprise even myself these past couple weeks."

They turned away from the Zen garden, and right before they started to walk again, she replied, "Then that makes two of us, because I've surprised myself, too."

Chapter Twenty-One

Eight days had gone by.

Eight more fucking days since their date at the botanical gardens, and she still thought he was Alden. After their visit to the gardens, he'd taken her to lunch, and they'd spent a couple more hours sipping wine, eating, and talking. She'd told him about how much she'd loved being away at college because she enjoyed school—was good at it—and because it allowed her the freedom to not think about her older brother.

He'd told her about how he hadn't gone to college and had always regretted it. He wasn't sure Alden felt that way, but he—Derek—did. He tried to be as honest as he could, and if she asked him something that required him to lie, he did his best to shape the answer into something more generic. As truthful as deceit could be.

He'd driven her back to where she'd left her car in the botanical gardens parking lot, given her a relatively tame kiss goodbye—seeing as they'd been in public in the daytime—and then driven home. He hadn't even *tried* to seduce her. Well, not much, anyway. Because he'd wanted her to be sure she liked him enough to keep seeing him.

And maybe that would allow her to forgive him when he finally told her the truth.

A by-the-book kind of guy? You've certainly fooled me.

Fuck, he really had. She was going to hate him.

He'd gone with Alden and Emma to the zoo on Sunday and prayed Toni wouldn't have a sudden, inexplicable desire to look at elephants. When she'd come over to his house that night, he'd pinned her to the bed and made her come so many times, over and over, that she finally begged him to stop and still somehow made it sound like the only thing she wanted for the rest of her life was for him to come inside of her.

So he did stop, but only after he brought her to orgasm one last time. Punishment and reward.

Punishment for trusting him.

Reward...for trusting him.

He was turning into a monster.

He saw her again almost every night during the past week, except for the one day he had to work a graveyard shift. Today—Sunday—they'd gone to a movie and afterward to a coffee shop, where she'd teased him about still not having unpacked any more boxes.

He'd replied as honestly as he could that every available moment he had, he had wanted to spend it with her, not unpacking. He didn't tell her it was because he was trying to cram himself full of her before their relationship came to its inevitable end. Her eyes had softened and she'd leaned across the café table and kissed him, and that had started everything.

And now here they were, half an hour later crashing through his front door, tearing at one another's clothes.

They didn't even make it to the bedroom, but practically wrestled one another to the tiled floor, the push-pull of their excitement overwhelming them like a tidal wave. She wrapped her fingers around his cock and pumped it with strong, quick strokes, until he could see drops of fluid slowly leaking from the opening on his head, making the tip glisten like a beacon as her slim hand shuttled up and down.

Enough.

"I've gotta get a condom," he gritted out, trying to sit up so he could go to the bedroom and get one, but she surprised him by pushing him back down, then grabbing her purse from the floor nearby and taking out a foil packet.

I love you.

The thought caught him off guard long enough for her to open the packet and roll the condom down his length before straddling him and sinking deep.

He let her ride him for barely a minute before flipping her over, crossing his arms beneath her head to protect it. His left thigh tried to push between hers, to open her legs so he could fuck her the way he wanted to, but she was squeezing them tightly closed against him.

Two weeks together and she already knew him so well.

You shouldn't be turned on by this. You shouldn't be enjoying this.

But she was enjoying it, too. She pulled him down by his hair and kissed him roughly before yanking her mouth away. "More," was all she said, and then she *bit* him on the lower lip, hard enough to sting.

He shoved one arm between their bodies, sliding his hand downward to play with her clit. She was so wet that she was slippery even on top of her mound, the moisture spreading everywhere.

Christ. He had to get in her.

Her thighs began to tremble with the effort of holding them closed, so he half rolled onto his side and brought her up with him, her legs relaxing enough in the movement for him to jam his body between her thighs. This time, when the head of his cock came up against her entrance, he didn't hesitate. She was so slick with arousal he went almost fully inside on a single thrust.

He couldn't stop from shouting in triumph.

The feeling of her was unbelievable. The way they'd played around was almost like what he did in close-combat training, sparring and grappling on the floor. Did she realize he'd been taught to do this? Did it even register with her that he was a professional?

See me. Understand me.

It was insanity to want such a thing. It would mean the end. He didn't want this to end.

And in the meantime, her hips kept pushing him up, writhing against him, half fighting, half fucking as he drove into her hard, his wide, hard chest crushing against her sweet, soft breasts.

She clawed at his back and pushed her mouth against his, fighting but not, playing at struggle. He could feel her legs flexing, and after a few minutes, she brought one knee up, jamming it into his stomach to push him off of her. The surprise of it—that she'd actually managed to overpower him—was what had made it possible. She never would have stood a chance against his strength otherwise. And they were rolling together again, out of the hallway, until his back was on the living room carpet.

He grunted as she pushed his arms down to his sides and set her knees atop his wrists, pinning him in a lock he could have easily gotten out of, but the fight—God, the twisted, horrible part of him loved the fight. It made him feel so…*alive.*

He tried to thrust up into her, but she didn't let him. Instead, she dipped her hips and pushed her clit against his sac, pressing hard against it, getting herself off as the coarse hairs snagged and pulled with every pass of her body over his. Pain and pleasure rolled into one.

But now he was so turned on that he *had* to jerk his hands free and bring them to her waist, manipulating her like a toy, pulling her up the length of his cock, letting the wetness of her body coat his shaft before he brought her back down, this time fully impaled on his dick. He'd held her tight, thumb tips digging into the soft skin of her belly, and pistoned his hips up fast and hard, until he was groaning and shuddering with his climax, until she was arching back and grabbing at his thighs for balance as her own body gave way to release.

Toni told herself she needed to stop smiling before people at work started getting nosy, but she couldn't keep the grin off her face. Ever since she'd left Alden's house yesterday with a kiss and a promise to see him again tonight, she hadn't stopped smiling.

She couldn't believe things were going this well.

And she'd finally accepted that maybe, for once, they might stay that way.

Alden liked her. She knew he did. Even though she lived with her parents, even though she did a job she didn't really like for the sake of a brother who wanted to kill her—a brother who had gone strangely quiet in the past week—Alden liked her. He'd stuck around and didn't seem to be going anywhere, and even if it had only been two weeks since they'd met each other again, it felt like the beginning of a lifetime.

Which was why, when the text showed up on her phone at lunchtime, it was more than a little disappointing.

Something came up. I can't make tonight. Raincheck?

She tried not to let it worry her. She hoped something hadn't happened to Emma. She hoped if it had, he would tell her. Or at least know he could call on her to help. She hoped she'd meet his daughter someday.

Everything okay? she texted back.

The answer was immediate, but brief. *It will be. I'll be in touch tomorrow.*

It was difficult not to get upset that he was being so vague. She wanted to know what was going on. She had to remind herself Alden had always been responsible with her feelings, and having to cancel plans was bound to happen sooner or later, as a matter of course. They happened to have had an accelerated timeline too—it made sense he couldn't make this one time. But it seemed strange that he wouldn't elaborate.

Maybe it was something with Emma, after all. He tended to get cagey and clipped whenever she asked about the little girl, which she attributed to him being protective of his daughter. She was trying to respect that, to remember they'd only known each other a short time, even if it felt like so much more than that.

Definitely a raincheck. She sent the message and didn't expect him to reply, so she was surprised when she got one shortly afterward.

I'm thinking about you.

She let herself smile at that. No big deal that he was being a bit secretive. She *trusted* him.

Besides, they'd been spending so much time together that she could probably stand to be apart from him for twenty-four hours.

What could possibly happen in that time?

Chapter Twenty-Two

He was going to remember this Monday as the day everything fell apart.

Derek stared down at the lab results Crewes had brought over. Crewes, Davis, and Donahue were standing in a row in front of his desk, forming a human wall, blocking him from view of the other officers in the station.

He should have already known from that, because "human barricade" wasn't exactly a good sign around here.

But looking down and taking in what was on that paper still managed to suck the life right out of him.

Melanie was dead.

Not simply a gut feeling any more, or a hunch, or whatever the fuck it was called. Confirmed, printed out in black on white. No body, but they had the fingerprint match and enough of her blood—and they knew it was her blood because the DNA confirmation had come back from the lab, too—found in the floorboards and scrubbed out of the backseat carpets, there was no way she could have survived.

He wasn't sure how he was going to tell Alden.

"Hey. You okay?" Davis was looking at him with concern.

Derek's mouth felt dry. He tried to swallow, but his tongue got stuck and he coughed instead. Donahue produced a paper cup of water seemingly from nowhere and pushed it at him.

Fucking psychic golden boy was starting to give him the creeps.

Derek knocked back the water and crumpled the cup. "Did he confess yet?"

Crewes shook his head. "Not yet, but he's getting close.

We only got the results back a few minutes ago, so it's possible once we bring this in, it'll be enough to push him over the edge."

Derek blew out a breath. "I guess I should call Alden."

It pissed him off that he was the one who had to do it. That Alden's choices in life had put Derek into this position of having to be the strong one. The one who delivered the bad news and cleaned up the mess…

You've cleaned up for Alden, literally.

He couldn't keep a wry laugh from escaping.

Crewes frowned. "Maybe you should take the afternoon off," he began, but Derek waved a hand at him, cutting him off.

Donahue was smirking at him.

"What the hell is going on over here? You're not getting paid to have a circle jerk in the corner, gentlemen!" A booming voice rang out from behind the guys, and all of them turned to see Chief Travers standing a few feet away, glaring at them.

"We—" Crewes began, but Travers held up a hand.

"I don't really fucking care, Crewes. Now get back to work." He glared at Crewes, Davis, and Donahue until they dispersed, Crewes heading back to his desk and Davis and Donahue going out to start their shift on patrol.

Travers approached and Derek stood, watching the chief as he drew near.

"Serrano says you're off your game lately and the other guys have been picking up your slack and hiding it from me."

The little shit.

Derek opened his mouth to reply, but Chief Travers huffed. "But none of your cases have slipped as far as I can see, and I can't stand whiny tattletales, so I sent him down on parking patrol for a week to teach him to keep his yammering baby mouth shut unless he has something useful to say."

Derek couldn't resist a small smile.

"But I'm watching you just the same, Brewer. If you're up

to no good, I will come down on you so hard you'll wish you'd never set foot into this station. Do you understand?"

Derek nodded. "I understand."

Travers straightened his shoulders. "Good." But then his face softened a bit, and he added. "I'm sorry about your niece's mother."

Derek made himself straighten as well. He would not let his emotions take over now. He would *not* crumple in front of his fellow officers. "Thank you, sir," he rasped out.

The chief eyed him for a moment, then barked, "I want you to go inform the next of kin in person. Immediately." And just before he turned to walk away, he added, "And take the rest of the day off, for fuck's sake."

Derek nodded at the man's back as Travers headed to his office. He wasn't looking forward to what lay ahead, but no matter the struggles between them, he would be there for Alden now.

But shit—he was going to have to postpone tonight with Toni. Even though Derek was pretty sure Alden would take the news with a hefty dose of stoicism, there was still June to worry about. Melanie had been her only child, and June was hard-working, but not a particularly strong woman.

He pulled out his phone and texted Toni to let her know he wouldn't be able to make it, but he asked for a raincheck. Her reply came quickly, and she asked if everything was okay. He typed in a reply.

It will be. I'll be in touch tomorrow.

One more reply from her and he couldn't resist a final text.

I'm thinking about you.

He sent it, then slipped his cell phone back into his pocket, then returned to his desk and dialed Alden from the station line.

His brother picked up after several rings. "Derek?"

There was a sound of static, almost like a breeze blowing through the receiver.

"Yeah, it's me. Where are you?" He'd have to pay Alden an official police visit, and he preferred it to be somewhere relatively private.

"I'm at the park." Alden sounded strange, almost as though he were drawing out his words from uncertainty. Could he tell that Derek was calling with bad news?

"Is Emma there with you?"

"Yeah, and—" Alden stopped abruptly and there was a pause—*fuck those pauses*—before he continued, "We just got here."

That didn't sound like what he'd been about to say. It was almost as though he were going to name someone else but had chosen not to. A liar by omission, or something like that.

Takes one to know one, Terrific.

He didn't press it.

"Listen, can you meet me at your house in half an hour? Maybe give Emma some TV or something to keep her busy?"

"Sure. Yeah, okay." Alden sounded nervous. Maybe it was simply that he suspected what Derek was going to say and he was preparing himself for the worst.

Derek hung up, rose from his desk, and headed out to deliver the news that the whole mystery that had started the double life he was living had finally been solved.

It felt like he was walking toward the end.

After Alden's text, Toni decided to take a break and go for a walk. She'd been more disappointed not to see him tonight than she'd expected. Things like this happened and it wasn't a big deal. She knew she was overreacting by continuing to feel so disappointed, and thought maybe getting out would help her regain her sense of equilibrium.

She walked for a few minutes, passing by the far side of the park where she'd seen Alden a couple weeks ago with his daughter. To her surprise, as she came upon the edge of the field and looked over to the playscape, she spied a familiar figure in the distance.

Alden.

He was there again, holding his phone to his ear as he stood next to a big structure with steps and slides, peering up onto a bridge where a little girl was jumping up and down. It was still too far away to make out the girl's features, but the girl had to be Emma.

But that wasn't what really caught Toni's eye.

This time, there was a woman standing next to Alden, much closer than a mere friend or acquaintance might stand.

Toni couldn't stop staring.

Alden and the woman were in semi-profile to her—neither of them saw her, she knew. And she knew because he never would have done what he did next if he'd realized Toni was watching. Not even half a minute later, Alden hung up the phone, slid it into his back pocket like he always did, said something to the woman next to him, and then…

Leaned over and kissed her.

Right in front of his daughter. In front of *Toni.*

Even from this far away, she could see that it wasn't a kiss between just friends. It was *sexual.* So blatantly, obviously lusty despite its short duration and public venue. She could see it in the way he leaned in, the way the woman's hand fluttered up and came to rest on Alden's shoulder.

Toni's heart dropped into her stomach.

Oh my God.

So this was why he had to take a raincheck. He was probably planning to be with this other woman tonight.

How long had this been going on? Was this the woman who had texted him that first night Toni was at his house?

Had he planned to tell her, ever?

My God, it hurt. It hurt so much that she couldn't breathe for fear of making the pain even greater by simply existing—

respirating—for one more second.

Of course, her traitorous involuntary reflexes kicked in, and eventually she sucked in a deep, sobbing breath, her limbs shaking from the effort of holding her feelings in check. She stood, riveted to the spot, as the woman gave a wave, then slowly sauntered off in one direction while Alden raised his hands up and lowered Emma to the ground, then walked the opposite way.

Toward Toni.

A second realization hit—he probably had avoided talking about Emma out of a sense of guilt, not protectiveness. He probably hadn't wanted to introduce Toni to Emma in case his daughter blurted out his secret, either.

No. No, she couldn't handle this—confrontation—right now. It would no doubt be a confrontation, too, given how she was feeling, and she wouldn't do that in front of a child.

Gasping, she turned on her heel and fled, racing all the way back to the office and into a bathroom stall.

Only then did she allow the tears to finally fall.

Chapter Twenty-Three

Derek pulled up in front of Alden's place and took a second to pull his thoughts together before getting out of the truck and heading to the front door.

Alden must have seen him approaching because he pulled the door open as Derek reached the front porch. "Hey, Derek. We just got home. Come on in."

Derek stepped inside to find Emma playing on the floor with a puzzle. He walked over and dropped a kiss on her head, and she laughed his name in greeting.

"Hey, Emma. How was the park?"

She dropped the puzzle pieces she'd been holding and stood. "Daddy met a lady and they kissed, and I went down the slide and there was a bird that made a funny sound."

Daddy met a lady and they kissed.

Derek whipped his head around to look at Alden in shocked surprise. "You were on a *date?*"

On a date while Derek had been working to find Melanie, to cover for Alden, to make sure he didn't get into trouble...and Alden was off playing?

His brother wouldn't look him in the eye. Alden's eyes were off to the side—the same, shifty look he'd worn every goddamn time he'd stolen money to get high—and it took every last ounce of control Derek had not to smash his fist into his brother's face. Emma would never forgive him for hitting her daddy. He'd never forgive *himself* for losing control like that. He was here as Derek. He was here to be responsible and deliver shitty news that he wanted someone else to take responsibility for.

"Emma, do you want to watch a show while I talk to Uncle Derek?" At least Alden wasn't completely oblivious. He settled his daughter in front of the TV and brought Derek into the kitchen, where they stood leaning against opposite countertops.

"I'm sorry, Derek," Alden sighed. "I didn't plan meeting up with Georgia—the woman I saw today. I'd been dating her casually right when I first got sober, but then she went on a long-term consulting assignment in Virginia and we lost touch. She texted me yesterday and I didn't really—"

"I don't care." Derek growled the words before he could stop them, before he could even verify in his mind what his emotions had made him say. No, he didn't care. He'd been surprised, but whatever. Alden could date. Alden could kiss someone. Alden could do whatever the fuck he wanted because that's who Alden was.

"What's going on?" Alden's question sounded tentative. Scared, almost.

Here goes nothing. "It's Melanie." Derek forced himself to hold his brother's gaze as he spoke the next words. "The suspect confessed to killing her after we showed him the DNA test results that confirmed the blood in his car is Melanie's. We're working on the next steps—finding her remains—but he seems like he's telling the truth. His account is too detailed for it to be a ruse."

At first, all Alden did was stare, not even blinking. Just…staring at Derek as though he'd been speaking another language and nothing was processing.

But a heartbeat before Derek was about to close the distance between them, grab his brother by the shoulders, and shake him back into lucidity, Alden blinked, cleared his throat, and said in a somber, monotone voice, "So that's it, then. She'd dead."

Derek released a long, resigned breath. "Yeah. She—I'm sorry, Alden." And with that, he finally did close the distance, but this time wrapped Alden in a rough hug. "I'm really sorry."

They stood like that for a long moment, before some unspoken agreement had them pulling apart. Alden nodded as if confirming something—Derek didn't know what it was, but at least Alden wasn't crying or screaming or anything like that.

"Derek." Alden sucked in a long, ragged breath. "You've done a lot for me already and I really appreciate it. And that's why I hate to ask this, but—"

"I'll cover for you at Sentinel tonight," Derek said, before Alden could even ask. Thoughts of Toni flashed into his mind, but he pushed them away. That wasn't why he was volunteering to fill in.

Alden nodded again. "Thanks, man. June will need me. Emma will, too, but I don't think it'll really register with her."

"If you need more time—" Derek began, but Alden shook his head.

"I need to keep things normal for a while. Try to, anyway. I've had enough upheaval. Work is… It'll be good to have it."

It was Derek's turn to nod. "Got it. I'll be there tonight. Do you need me to stick around now, wait with you for June?"

"I'll do it on my own. But thanks."

"Okay, man." He leaned in and caught up Alden in another quick, fierce hug, releasing him with a strong squeeze of his shoulder. "Good luck." Alden needed all the luck he could get at this point.

But Derek couldn't help thinking, as he exited the apartment and walked toward his car, that somehow it felt like his own luck was about to run out.

Toni still hadn't heard from Alden.

It was getting close to eight o'clock on Tuesday evening and she hadn't received a single word from him since yesterday when he'd texted to cancel their date. She'd checked her phone so many times during the day today that the act of picking up the device and turning on the screen was permanently ingrained in her muscle memory.

Not that she wanted to see him again. But she deserved to hear it from him that they were over. She wanted the satisfaction of being able to give him her anger, and the longer the silence stretched, the angrier she became. She'd considered staying late on Monday to see him and confront him then about what she'd seen, but ultimately she decided against it. She shouldn't have to be the one to reach out to him. It should be *his* responsibility to man up and end things the right way, not her job to pursue her own heartbreak.

But if he never contacted her…if this was his way of breaking things off without actually confronting her…well, it wouldn't be the first time it had happened.

Her friends in the past, all the people she'd known since coming back here, had done it like that, too. Once they got involved deeply enough to see how complicated her life was, they backed off—or went completely silent, like Alden was doing now. He hadn't seemed like that kind of guy, and a small part of her rather humiliatingly hoped there was a reasonable explanation for what she'd seen.

You are a fool.

She was worried and angry and hurt and hopeful all at the same time, and she tried not to let the feelings take her over, but it had been well over a day since she'd seen him with that woman and the silence was pulling her further into her pain.

"Are you all right, sweetheart?" Mom looked over at Toni as they sat on opposite ends of the couch, Mom reading and Toni pretending to read.

Toni made herself smile and nod. "Fine. I think I'm a little tired, though. Maybe I'll go to sleep early tonight."

"You have been out late quite a bit lately. Is it still work or something else going on?" Her mother's studied casualness— the respectful way she tried not to make it obvious she was prying a little—made Toni want to lean on Mom's shoulder and cry for a while.

But then she'd have to admit she might have been used and abandoned by a guy, and she didn't think she'd be able to survive that particular humiliation. Not yet, anyway. If Alden called tomorrow and she had a chance to get her anger out of her system by ranting at him, maybe she'd get over it all the faster.

Maybe Alden wasn't who she thought he was, but she was grateful to him for one thing: he'd reminded her that she was worth more than she'd allowed herself to believe for too long.

She was strong, capable, and worthy of love. Even if not from Alden, she had to remember what she was worth. This temporary hurt *would* heal and she *would* go on.

Or at least, she had to believe that much was possible.

"I've been busy, is all," she said, trying to avoid the question entirely. "I think I'll go up to bed, in fact. I might have to work late tomorrow so it's probably good to rest up tonight."

If Alden didn't call tomorrow, she was going to wait for him to show up at the office and she was going to give him a piece of her mind then.

And then she could nurse her heartbreak in private, and get on with her life.

Chapter Twenty-Four

Derek had let the day get away from him again.

It was already past six o'clock on Wednesday and he still sat at his desk after having hung up the phone with the coroner. After the suspect confessed the other day, they'd taken cadaver dogs to one of the forests outside of town and, after a couple of hours of searching, had found Melanie's body. The coroner had conducted the autopsy today and the results were finally in, confirming everything they'd already known.

After slogging through countless official procedures and a mountain of paperwork, most of Derek's official work was over. The suspect would still need to stand trial, but as far as Derek was concerned, all the critical pieces were now complete.

By the time he'd rolled into his driveway last night, it had been almost midnight. Too late to text Toni. And then this morning, he'd meant to do it on the drive into work, but Alden had called, wanting to talk. Derek couldn't hang up on his brother.

Excuses...

He'd meant to call her right after that, but Chief Travers had walked by and wanted to see the case files on a string of murders that had gone cold years ago—some local reporter was digging shit up—and Derek had ended up sitting with the journalist for over two hours, going over crimes that had long been forgotten.

Next time he saw Nina—Crewes's wife and the anchorwoman on the morning news show they ran out of Greenbriar's largest media station—he was going to let her know what he thought about that.

And then he and Crewes got a call and had to leave

immediately.

You're stalling. You know it's time to tell her the truth and you're stalling.

Goddamn it.

He never thought he'd be in this position, but Derek found he actually wanted a few more days as Alden.

But if he texted Toni now as Alden and pretended he'd simply forgotten to call her, she'd probably leave him for being an insensitive jerk who discounted her feelings. If he told her what happened with Melanie, she was going to think it was *his* daughter's mom who had been murdered, and he couldn't take the lie that far. He'd have to tell her truth then—that he'd been busy working that case, not mourning the woman.

And then she'd leave him.

But he couldn't keep pretending to be Alden. With Melanie confirmed dead, any horrible, flimsy justification he had for continuing to lie to Toni was gone. He *had* to tell her who he really was.

And then she'd leave him.

Damned if you do…

But that wasn't quite right. He'd been damned from the beginning, when he agreed to switch places with Alden in the first place. He knew whose shoes he was stepping into and he'd done it willingly.

And now, no matter what he did, he was going to lose.

Which was why he did nothing.

Toni was waiting at her desk at half past six that night.

He should be there soon.

This morning, she'd woken up to…more nothing. No contact from Alden.

And she'd told herself she needed to start accepting the

truth that he was happier with that other woman, who probably didn't have an addict for a brother, and now he was simply bowing out of her life.

But then she'd been browsing the news right around lunchtime and the story had caught her eye and she'd actually gasped loudly in the middle of the office and put a hand to her mouth when she read the words.

Body of a woman found yesterday in the Landlocked Forest. Identified as Melanie Dickinson, 28 years old, of Greenbriar…Leaves behind mother June Dickinson and three-year-old daughter Emma Brewer.

Emma Brewer. Alden's daughter. The woman's body that had been found was Alden's ex.

Oh God. Oh *God*. Alden.

Maybe things between her and him were over, but that didn't stop her from feeling a surge of compassion for what he was probably going through right now with the loss of his daughter's mother. Presumably, he'd once loved her. Maybe even still did. And poor Emma, losing her mother at such a young age.

She couldn't stay angry at him, but she did realize in that moment that it was time to get the closure they *both* needed. Instead of calling him, though, she had resolved to stay late and wait, in case he came to work tonight. She could see it being something he did, to push past the grief and get to work. And if she saw him, she would comfort him, not confront him.

If he came tonight, she would offer her condolences in person, the way he deserved to hear them. Maybe they'd never again be lovers, but she wouldn't abandon him to his troubles when confronted with the mess of his life, like so many people had done to her in the past.

Like he had done to her.

She was going to be more than that, for her own sake.

A couple minutes later, from over the cubicle walls, she heard footsteps and the sound of someone knocking a wastebasket into a larger bin. She took a deep breath, stood…

The smile on her face died instantly. The realization was already there, even if she couldn't articulate it.

That came to her more slowly, in bits and pieces.

His back wasn't as broad.

His face looked more haggard—not by much, but under the fluorescent lights it wasn't hard to see.

His clothes didn't fit the same.

And his hands…those weren't the hands that had been on her body. Inside her body.

But most of all, this man didn't make her feel the same, immediate, gnawing need for him. Yes, he was good looking, but he didn't fire her every nerve ending.

This man resembled Alden. Could pass for Alden's twin, in fact. But it wasn't Alden.

An image of Derek at the police station flashed behind her eyes.

Or rather, this had to be Alden…and she'd been played. This was Alden, and Derek had been pretending to be his brother for whatever godforsaken reason. Derek had lied to her.

While she'd opened herself in every way.

Oh, God.

This man—the real Alden—looked exactly like *Derek* if seen from far enough away. The real Alden would have been the one with his daughter, that day at the park. The real Alden had kissed that woman. Derek had probably been at work, at the job he'd been talking about when he'd said he loved what he did, which wasn't a custodian and *oh my God, I am so stupid*.

Two weeks ago, she'd thought she was a fool, or deficient, or something *not good* for not being able to tell the difference between them. Now she realized it was because it had been the same man. She knew Derek's walk, strong and purposeful and not as loose as Alden's. She knew the slightly more pronounced arch of his right eyebrow, while Alden's were slightly flatter. She knew his lips and his hands and his heavy weight inside of her.

She knew him and she missed him so desperately.

She was still a fool.

But the thought didn't give her as much comfort as she'd hoped. Instead, it only made her think about how she should have chased that hunch she'd had about the impossible sameness of the two brothers. It made her think about how often she'd found his choice of words to be very odd, but she hadn't said anything about it.

She was a *fool*.

She'd never believed in the idea that tragedy could make time feel like it was moving in slow motion, but all those thoughts happened in the tick of a clock, and the next thing she knew she was crying and Alden—*the real Alden*—was walking toward her with a look of concern on his face.

And if the man she'd fallen for wasn't Alden and there was no other woman, why hadn't he—why hadn't *Derek* gotten in touch with her?

Oh, God. Maybe it was her, after all. He was fading out of her life because she wasn't worth going through the tough things for.

The possibility cut deep.

No. I am worth more than that.

"Toni Park?" he asked softly, and the fact that there was uncertainty in his voice, when she was used to Derek's caressing surety, made her cry even harder.

He reached the entrance to her cubicle and held up a hand. "Oh, man. I mean, of course you're Toni. We met the first night I was cleaning. Sorry, I—"

"Don't." She sobbed. He sounded like he was reminding himself of something someone else had told him. Something Derek had told him. "Don't lie about this. Not anything that has to do with me or-or *Derek*." She whispered his name.

"You know." Alden breathed out the words, and his face was so full of regret and compassion that Toni's tears calmed.

This man had just lost someone close to him. Toni wasn't sure he and Melanie had still cared for each other, but she'd been taken too soon and left a child behind. She'd promised herself she would do the right thing tonight to a man she'd thought had caused her pain, and here was a man who'd done nothing wrong to her, getting only her tears.

That wasn't right.

She shook her head. "I only realized when I saw you. It's-it's a shock. But I'll get over it. I want to say—I need to say that *I'm* sorry for *your* loss. I read about it in the paper and that's why I'm here tonight. I thought I should say something to you. I mean, I guess I thought I'd be talking to Derek…" She trailed off. She wasn't sure anymore who or what she was rambling about now, destroying even more of her pride.

Understanding lit Alden's face, and he closed his eyes for a second and muttered, "Fucking Derek."

At least she didn't have to explain anymore.

Then he opened them again and looked right at her, and Toni was struck for a second that, despite their other differences, the brothers' eyes were the same.

Alden took a deep breath. "This is all my fault. I never— Toni, I'm sorry. I asked Derek to fill in for me the first week because that was when Melanie first went missing. I shouldn't have done it, but I felt desperate and—well, the truth is, I'm so used to falling back on him, you know? He was always stepping in to rescue me when we were younger, and being a twin sort of made him the default choice for this gig."

He huffed out a wry laugh. "That's why it's such a surprise…well, look, I don't know the details, but I can tell he fucked up pretty big with you. But he's the most focused, dependable, loyal guy I know. And he's got a good attitude, even though I'm pretty sure he hates me a little. Shit. I hate me, too. But he did it, and he did it because of me. So whatever happened is my fault and…I'm sorry."

It was hard to argue that Derek shouldn't have filled in for Alden. Not with the sad, desperate way Alden was looking at her. But still. "He didn't have to *keep* lying to me," she whispered. "After his part was over, he still didn't tell me. I still thought he was Alden until I saw you tonight."

For some reason, Alden smiled when she said that. "Derek is an upstanding guy. Almost *too* upstanding. I've never known someone who was so adamant about drawing the line between good and bad."

People are more than their superficial appearance. Not everything is black and white.

He'd seemed even then to be struggling, that first week.

Alden continued. "If he carried the lie on for this long, he must be desperately afraid of something bad happening if he tells the truth. But I don't know for sure. If you want to know, you'll have to ask Derek." He shrugged. "I'm a poor stand-in for him."

"No, you're not," Toni protested. "You told me the truth. He didn't."

Alden's eyes were intense now, practically boring into her. "I did, but not because I'm brave or upstanding. I did it because I had nothing to lose. And until he met you, Derek always told the truth, too."

The unspoken words hung in the air between them.

Because he doesn't want to lose you.

But by lying, he already had.

Chapter Twenty-Five

The text came in while Derek was unpacking boxes. He'd come home from work and practically attacked them, using the task as a way to expend his frustrated energy.

He wanted it to be Toni, even though she hadn't called or texted him since Monday. Before that night, he hadn't questioned her silence much, but now that the case was mostly wrapped up, it occurred to him how strange it was that she hadn't reached out.

Of course, he hadn't been in touch with her, either. She was probably annoyed with him over it.

Or maybe she'd simply been trying to give him a little space and felt like it was okay to message him now. Either way, he wanted it to be her.

Please let it be Toni.

He picked up his phone and checked the message. Not Toni. Alden.

Disappointment cut deep.

We need to talk. Very important. Can you come over now?

Derek sighed and texted back that he'd be over in half an hour. He probably wouldn't have unpacked much more tonight, anyway, now that he was feeling so deflated. He couldn't blow off Alden, though. June had taken the news well enough, but they were all still living *too* normally. It was bound to fall apart sooner rather than later. It wouldn't be right to avoid his brother at this point, just in case.

Still, Derek dawdled enough that it wasn't until an hour later that he was finally stepping over the threshold and into Alden's place. Derek waved to June, who was in the living room, watching a video with headphones in her ears.

Forced normalcy.

"Let's go into the kitchen. I don't want Emma to wake up," Alden told him. "She's sleeping in the bedroom."

Emma's room was right off the living room but at the opposite end of the apartment from the kitchen, so they turned that way, Derek standing so rigidly that it made Alden's cramped kitchen seem even smaller.

"How are you, Derek?" Alden's voice was loaded with...something.

"Fine," he clipped out, not wanting to give his mood away but pretty sure it was too late for that. But Alden seemed okay, not broken up or needy, and it put Derek on alert. It almost seemed as though he was trying to get *information* out of Derek, though it wasn't clear for what purpose.

Better to keep things as close to his chest as possible until he figured out what was happening. Maybe this was some strange effect of grief that he didn't know about. The department shrink might have some ideas if he could suss out Alden's thoughts a little further.

"I see." Alden looked down at his mug and then back up at Derek. "And how's Toni?"

It was stronger now, that something in his voice. In made Derek's skin draw tight. Afraid.

Alden was asking about Toni.

He didn't wait for an answer, though. He delivered the news like a knife to the heart. "You know, she was at the office tonight when I came in to clean. She knew right away."

Fucking...

Derek's face must have gone all weird, or maybe pale, or—whatever, because Alden's eyes went big a second before he crossed the kitchen and pushed Derek into one of the rickety, too-small chairs at the kitchen table.

"Sit," he barked after Derek was already sunk into the seat, which would have been amusing if Derek hadn't felt so shocked. Alden immediately went to the stove and turned on the flame beneath the kettle, boiling water like they did in movies when someone was about to deliver an emergency baby at home.

Or in this case, like someone was about to deliver a reckoning. Which, Derek supposed, he deserved.

Toni knew.

And she'd found out in a way that she never should have had to experience.

Derek had a feeling he was going to hurt more tonight than he had in years. A lifetime, even.

And it was all his fault. He never should have been so cowardly as to avoid the truth for so long. He should have told her well before tonight.

Goddamn it.

A couple minutes later, Alden set two mugs of tea on the table and crammed himself into the chair opposite Derek, folded his hands together, and leaned back all casual-like, as though he hadn't just blown up Derek's world.

"You're in love with her."

He said it so matter-of-factly Derek felt the need to protest immediately. "I am not!"

Alden raised a brow and rolled his eyes at the same time, and Derek sighed.

"I *like* her. I think she's really cool and I like talking to her and—" he managed to stop himself before he said *having sex with her*, but Alden had obviously gotten the gist. He snorted in response.

Now it was Derek's turn to roll his eyes. "Look, I do really like her. I'll admit that. She's easy to be with. Yeah. I like her. I mean, she doesn't push me but I like telling her things anyway and…" He sighed. "Fuck. Yeah, maybe I'm in love with her. Maybe."

Alden laughed.

"But it's only been a couple weeks," Derek protested. "I

thought it, you know. I've already thought that I love her. But conventional wisdom says—"

Alden's amusement died. "You and your by-the-book bullshit."

It was starting to build now. That fucking emergency reckoning. Derek was starting to feel agitated. He *shouldn't* be getting this worked up. Alden's ex-girl had just died. Been murdered, for fuck's sake. This wasn't a good time, and besides, Alden was right, because Derek did love Toni, and it didn't make sense to keep fighting it.

But no one was supposed to be able to fall in love in two weeks. Especially when it was founded on a lie. He should leave now. He should leave, then apologize to Toni and accept she would never want to see him again. That was it.

But something kept nagging at Derek, sitting there in the back of his mind where he couldn't see it well enough to make out what it was. What it meant.

"Don't be a baby. You love her. There's no *maybe* about it. Admit it." Alden was being too aggressive and Derek bristled, but held his reaction in check. Alden was grieving. Alden was the one who'd had a shock.

Right?

Derek shook his head. "She doesn't actually like me. She likes *you*." *You're bad. I'm good. You're bad—*

Not everything is black—

Shut up and leave, damn it!

He didn't understand why he was so angry. He didn't understand what that thing was, that kept telling him he was supposed to understand *something*. Something important.

Alden *pffed* at him. "You were only pretending to be me. Even though she's angry with you, she still likes *you*, pretending to be me, which is really you, anyway, because you're a shit actor. What are you so worried about?"

It was like a poisonous cloud, expanding too fast, pushing at the edges of his skin. It fogged up his vision and he had to close his eyes to keep it from leaking out that way.

"I don't get it," Alden prodded. "Who cares if you fell in love with her using my name? It's just a—"

"Because I don't want her to like *you*!" The words practically exploded out of him.

Holy shit. That was what had been nagging at him. He wanted to say he didn't mean it. But he did. He meant it, and the words only kept coming. The poison kept spilling out now that it had found an outlet.

"I don't want her to like someone who destroyed our family for years. Who made my life a living hell and put me in situations where I had to pretend everything was okay because the only other choice was to fucking crumple in on myself. I don't want you to have spent the past decade being a shitty human being, only to get away with winning over the most beautiful woman I've ever seen. I don't care if it was me all along. *You* got credit for the greatest thing to ever happen to me and *you* didn't do anything right. I did. *You don't get to win*!"

Stop!

The shout in his head was deafening. Derek abruptly stopped talking, and the kitchen fell oddly silent. When had he started raising his voice? *Fuck*, he hoped he hadn't woken Emma.

Across the dinette table, Alden's mouth had dropped open and he was staring at Derek in shock.

Derek *felt* shocked. Had he really said all of that? How could he have been so stupid? Alden was fragile enough. He'd added on caring for Emma almost full-time and he was June's only source of emotional support with Melanie's death, which was still so new and raw. Derek's words might send him back to his life of addiction.

And as much as Derek really did resent how easily Alden seemed to have gotten off, the last thing he wanted was for his big brother to slip back into that horrible life. Those years *had* been long and hard and soul-crushing, despite the happy face Derek had insisted on wearing. Alden didn't deserve that, no matter how angry Derek felt sometimes. He had to apologize *now*.

"God. Holy fuck. Alden. I'm—"

Alden held up a staying hand. "Don't."

Derek's heart sank. His older brother was about to write him off, which was what he deserved, in the end. Even he would admit that.

But Alden surprised him. "Don't apologize. It's okay. *I'm* okay. Hearing it doesn't hurt nearly as much as I thought it would. In fact, it's kind of a relief. At least you finally got it out."

Alden had *known* how he felt? That it was this ugly and petty and twisted?

Even Derek hadn't really understood it until a moment ago.

But Alden continued. "I know I did a lot of shitty things over the years. I'm sure I don't remember even half of them, either, which makes it even worse. And I'm sorry."

Derek opened his mouth to tell Alden it was all right, but Alden went on.

"But I also deserve a chance to be seen as a good guy. I'm not perfect. I'll never be perfect, but I can be good most of the time and right most of the time and as goddamn fucking decent as I can be. I know I won't be able to achieve that every minute of every day for the rest of my life. I know I won't be able to make up for the years I was a sad excuse for a person. But *not everything is black and white*. In fact, *most* things aren't. I'm not the bad twin. You're not the good twin. Seeing the world that way…well, I don't think you've been on the happy side of the emotional divide for most of this time. No matter what kind of front you put up. And you *can* be forgiven for your mistakes."

Derek bowed his head, feeling exhausted all of a sudden. He needed to think. He had to apologize to Toni, but he didn't want to call her up or text her with an apology, or even a demand to see her in person. He owed her much more than that.

But first…he needed to apologize to someone else.

He lifted his head.

"I'm sorry, Alden. Not just for what I said tonight. But for not believing in you more. I'm sorry for trying to turn you into a bad guy. And I'm sorry for not being the brother you deserved."

Alden looked at him for a long time before answering.

"I forgive you. I am grateful you're my brother and I'm honored to be yours." He said it simply and directly, and Derek felt the weight of years come off his shoulders.

"And," Alden added, "I think Toni will forgive you, too, for what it's worth. Be honest with her. Be *yourself*."

The next day, he sent her flowers at the office.

I'm sorry. I miss you. Please forgive me.

They were signed *Derek*.

Toni took the card out and put the arrangement in the company kitchen. She let the card hover over her wastebasket, nearly slipping from her fingers…

But she pulled her hand back before it could fall. She slipped the card into her purse, instead.

She tried for the rest of the day to forget about it, but thoughts of Derek hovered constantly in the back of her mind.

I'm sorry. I miss you. Please forgive me.

It was such a simple apology, but what more could he have said? She wanted to forgive him.

But she was so afraid.

She'd thought about it last night, alone in her bed. She understood why he'd lied at the start. When it came to sacrificing for one's brother, she understood all too well.

But wasn't she worth the truth? Hadn't he thought at some

point that she was worth telling?

Apparently not. And that was what kept her from calling him up and offering him forgiveness. That was what kept her from going to the station, or to his house, and asking him to kiss away her hurt.

Although when she took her keys from her purse at the end of the day, her fingers stroked over the edges of the card.

I'm sorry. I miss you. Please forgive me.

But she shook off the desire to see him and drove straight home, instead.

Chapter Twenty-Six

She hadn't called him after he'd sent the flowers.

So he called her on Friday, but she didn't pick up. He didn't leave a message.

He spent the weekend writing her a long letter, grumbling over his sloppy handwriting, ripping his way through several sheets of paper, trying to put into words how sorry he was and how desperate he was for her to forgive him. He missed her. He wanted her. He *loved* her.

He didn't write that part, though. If he was ever lucky enough to get the chance to tell her in person, he was going to save the words for then. He went to her office on Monday morning to deliver it to her—a place he'd been able to enter multiple times without trouble when he'd been posing as Alden—but ironically, as himself, he couldn't get in. The security guard at the front called up to Toni's desk and shortly afterward informed Derek that she wasn't available for visitors.

He didn't leave the letter then.

He cajoled Alden into letting him accompany his brother to Sentinel that night for the after-hours cleaning shift and left it on Toni's desk, then suffered through the next day, waiting for her to call.

She didn't.

He wasn't sure what else to do. Using his brother to get access to her desk was already bordering on stalker behavior and he didn't want to push it any further. But he wasn't going to give up yet. He needed to give her some time, he knew, and space to decide whether he was worth believing in again.

It was hard, though. It was really fucking hard. He wanted to see her and have her smile at him again. He wanted to kiss her and take her to bed and make her moan and shudder in his arms. She was the greatest thing to ever happen to him, and he wanted to spend the rest of his life showing her how amazing she was.

But he didn't know how to make it happen. He'd blurred all his carefully drawn lines and there was no longer a clear path laid out for what to do next.

He trudged into work for the afternoon shift, and when Chief Travers told him to take the patrol that included passing by Toni's house, he saw it as a sign. Maybe she'd be home already. Maybe she'd be standing outside when he drove by and he could use it as an excuse to at least wave to her and say hello. To introduce himself to her as Derek, her lover. The man who loved her already.

The first time he drove by her place, though, there was no one home. No cars in the driveway, and the house looked silent and empty. It was the first time he'd seen where she lived, though, and he slowed down and studied it for a second. Bars on the ground floor windows. Signs in the window that the house was equipped with an alarm system.

Precautions against Sal.

But Sal hadn't made any more threats since that night he'd called and Toni and her parents had gone to a hotel. Maybe he'd OD'd and now was just waiting to be found. Wouldn't be the first time something like that had happened.

He kept his phone close, in case. But by six o'clock, he had resigned himself to her not calling at all.

When he drove by her house close to seven o'clock, there were two cars in the driveway. He almost didn't slow down, having changed his mind about wanting her to see him. Not when he was feeling so downtrodden.

But a movement along the side of the house caught his eye.

Derek slammed on the brakes. Backed up.

There was nothing there.

227

But he could have sworn he'd seen a man in the shadows.

Should he drive on?

He idled for only another second before pulling his cruiser to the side of the road and getting out, then hurrying up the walk to the front door, instinct propelling him forward.

Maybe Toni wouldn't want to see him, but he had to make sure she was okay.

He rang the bell, and a minute later an older woman with dark hair pulled back answered, looking surprised and confused and a little wary. It had to be Toni's mother. He could see her in this woman's face.

"Good evening, ma'am. I'm Officer Derek Brewer, Greenbriar Police."

From somewhere past the woman at the door, inside the house, he heard a feminine gasp.

The woman standing there turned to look at someone out of sight, then she turned back to face him. "What can I do for you, Officer?" she asked.

"I, uh—" *I'm in love with your daughter and I'm here to protect her and those she loves.*

Probably not a great lead-in.

"I'm doing a routine patrol and I saw something suspicious outside your house, along that wall." He gestured to his right. "Do you mind if I come in for a moment and look around?"

The woman's eyes went wide and she shook her head, stepping back to let him in. "I don't mind. Please come in."

He walked into the foyer. The door shut behind him.

And then he heard her.

"Is this some kind of sick ploy, Derek? If you're pretending again, it's not okay. This is *not* okay."

He turned to see Toni standing in an archway that joined the foyer with a living room. She was visibly shaking. He wanted to close the distance between them and run a hand down her back, to soothe her and tell her everything was going to be all right.

Instead, he took off his cap and shook his head.

"It's not a ploy, Toni. I promise. I saw—" He was very aware of the older woman still standing in the foyer, who had to be Toni's mother. He didn't want to scare her.

Toni's face went white. "Not Sal?"

Her mother pulled in a startled breath and Derek grimaced. "I don't know for sure. I saw something that appeared to be a man, running along the outside of the house. But when I double-checked by looking from the street, I didn't see anything. I thought I'd warn you first and try to secure the inside before doing a sweep outside."

"What's going on here?" A man joined them from another room. A man whose eyes and chin looked like Toni's. Her father, Derek assumed.

"I'm Officer Brewer from the Greenbriar Police Department," he began, but at that moment, all the lights in the house cut out, and he immediately knew things were about to get dangerous.

Toni could feel her heart practically beating out of her chest.

When she'd gone into the office that morning and found his letter on her desk, she'd managed to avoid opening it for the first hour. But it had taunted her the entire time from the top drawer of her filing cabinet, and before long she'd been tearing into the envelope, scanning the paper like her life depended on it.

By the time she'd finished reading all the things he'd written, she was still angry. But instead of being upset with his lies, she wanted to rage at Derek for making her fall in love with him.

Despite what had happened between them, he was *fighting* for her. He hadn't abandoned her like all her loser friends had in the past. That's what she'd realized through her relationship with Derek—that the people who had left when the going got tough were worthy of *her* friendship, and not the other way around. Derek was different. She loved him, and she could no longer deny how much she missed him.

She just hadn't been ready to forgive him yet.

So when he'd appeared on the doorstep a minute ago, at first she'd been angry that he seemed to be trying to force her to forgive him sooner than she was able to. But now…

Derek was here and he'd seen something suspicious. Derek was here, and the lights were out.

Derek was here.

She rushed to him, forgetting her remaining anger, and wrapped her arms around his waist, trying to calm herself with his solid presence. She felt the breath escape him, the relaxing of his muscles, and he brought one hand up to stroke through her hair.

"It's going to be okay," he whispered.

Her eyes had adjusted to the darkness, and his must have, too, because he took her hand and still managed to gather her parents close and hiss a whispered, "Go get behind the couch." He prodded them all toward the living room. "Crouch down and don't make a *sound*."

Above their heads, they heard something creak.

Oh God oh God oh God.

"Now. Go. Get down and stay down," he whispered, and her parents raced to the couch. She started to move there, too, but saw Derek grab his gun from its holster.

"Derek," she whispered, and her anguish must have come out in her voice, because he tipped her head to his and pressed a hard kiss to her mouth before saying, "I'll do everything in my power not to kill him, Toni. I can't make any guarantees, but what's important to you is important to me, and I'll do my absolute best to keep him alive."

What's important to you is important to me.

That was what she'd wanted to hear all along. That someone cared enough about her to suffer through the rest, because what was important to her *mattered*. He'd said as much in his letter, but hearing the words from him directly made it even more meaningful.

"Be careful," she whispered, and went to join her parents behind the couch. Mom and Dad were holding each other tight, and Mom offered an arm to Toni, but she shook her head. Instead, she crouched down but peered around the side of the couch, watching. Waiting.

The shadow of Derek loomed large and imposing in the middle of the living room. She could feel how tense he was. How alert. His gun was cocked and in his hand, posed at the ready.

Creak.

Someone was at the top of the stairs.

Don't hurt him. Don't hurt him.

But she wasn't even sure who she was thinking of anymore.

Both of them, really. Sal and Derek. She loved them both.

She *loved* Derek.

When this was over, she had to tell him that. He had to know. If this kind of shit was what they'd be up against, whether because of her brother or simply because of Derek's job, she'd tell him every day for the rest of their lives that she loved him. So he could be sure of her.

Soft footsteps started to descend the stairs.

A shadowy leg came into view. And then the outline of a torso, and a head…

Sal.

And he, too, held a gun. Where were all these guns coming from? Was this a thing in the world of junkies? How did someone let a guy like Sal have a fucking gun?

It enraged her. He wasn't supposed to be armed. Without a gun, it would have been so much easier. Derek would have had the upper hand and could have taken him down without killing or even hurting Sal, she was sure. But this changed everything. Sal wasn't supposed to be making her *choose*.

Sal had moved so he was hidden behind the short wall that separated the living room from the hall where the stairs were. From where she was, she could see Sal clearly enough to know he had a gun. But could Derek see that?

What if he couldn't? She'd asked him not to kill Sal. She'd asked him to care for what she cared for. And if he went into this blind, Derek would end up getting hurt. Possibly even dying.

She was *not* going to allow that to happen.

She stood as quietly as she could, but Sal must have heard something, because he whipped around, staring into the darkness where she was standing.

"Who's there?" He started to stalk toward where she was, frozen in place. Not just with fear, but with resolve. She was going to distract him from Derek. Maybe she couldn't save her brother, but she sure as hell could do the right thing by the man she loved.

Sal didn't seem to see her, though. His head was swinging around, and the gun in his hand was swinging with him. Erratic and out of control. It worried her. What if his finger slipped and he accidentally shot something? Or one of them?

He was nothing like Derek, whom she could see a few feet behind Sal now, laser-focused and so steady she found herself wondering what kind of training he'd had in deadly combat. She thought about the way he fight-fucked and how she should have known who he was simply by his skill in not letting things go too far. She wondered if Derek preferred to shoot circle targets or ones shaped like men. If he ended up shooting Sal, would *he* have to go to jail? Would Sal really shoot him? What would she do if—

Shut up!

Her thoughts were all over the place. They didn't make any sense, either. She shouldn't be thinking about those kinds of things while their lives were being threatened.

She blinked in the darkness and realized...

Sal had stopped moving and was pointing his gun straight at *her*.

No.

He pulled back the hammer to cock it.

No.

"Drop it." The words rang out in the silence from behind Sal. Derek's words, Derek's voice. He was turning Sal's attention on him.

No.

Sal's gun was already cocked and ready.

No.

Her brother whirled around and she knew what was going to happen. Derek wouldn't aim to kill. Sal would.

"No!" she shouted, the word tearing out of her in a maniacal shriek as she vaulted the couch, adrenaline powering superhuman strength through her as she practically flew in front of Sal, pushing Derek aside as two shots rang out.

And then all she knew was pain.

Chapter Twenty-Seven

Sal was on the ground, screaming, but Derek didn't give a goddamn fuck about the man he'd shot.

What he cared about was the way Toni was half laid across him, whimpering. Like she was hurt.

Like she'd been shot.

If she'd taken that bullet Sal had meant for him...

No. He didn't want to think about that right now.

"Toni?" He gently ran his hands over her, trying to figure out in the darkness whether she was bleeding or even conscious enough to answer him. His fingers hit something wet and sticky high on her right shoulder at the same time her body jerked in pain.

The fucker had shot her, after all.

He needed to get an ambulance there right now. He yanked his radio off its clip and shouted into it, at the same time ripping off his shirt to tie her wound, trying to stop the bleeding as much as he could.

"Are you okay? Toni. Are you okay?" He was desperate, repeating the question like it would be some kind of magic to keep her sane and there with him, but she wasn't responding. Was horribly, wrongly silent, in fact.

"Derek." Her voice was weak, but he could hear the satisfaction in it. "You're okay."

He gave a half laugh, half sob. God, if the guys saw him like this... Countless cases he'd been on and he'd always kept his cool, but this was the woman he *loved.*

"I'm okay," he made himself say, trying to reassure her. "But *you've* been shot, Toni. You gotta hang on for me. Do you hear me?"

But she didn't reply, and he started to panic. "Do you hear me? I love you, baby. Don't—"

"10-69, Brewer. Ambulance en route. Five minutes." The dispatcher's voice crackled through his radio, pulling him back into action.

He struggled to get Toni to sit upright, leaning her back against his chest as he relayed more details as quickly as possible to dispatch. Her head lolled to the side, scaring the shit out of him. At least he could feel her heartbeat, even though it was weak.

Dimly, he registered the black shapes of her parents coming out from behind the couch, her mom crying as they tried to move through the darkness.

"I've got Toni," he told them. "But Sal is down and needs attention."

Sal's screams had turned into pained groans. Mrs. Park started to make her way toward her son and Derek looked back down at Toni, trying to make out the details of her face in the low light.

A moment later, Toni's mother gasped and murmured something, but Derek was too focused on Toni to really register it.

"Mr. Park. Can you get the lights back on?" He barked out the question, then registered that Toni's dad wasn't there anymore. Two seconds later, the lights flipped on. He must have already been on his way to restore power.

Derek blinked, and after a second he could see again.

Mrs. Park was crouched over Sal, pressing down on a cloth—a throw blanket, from the looks of it—pushed against her son's side. Derek could see the fabric was already soaked with blood. Mr. Park came running back into the living room, screeching to a halt when he saw Toni leaned up against Derek. His head swung back and forth from his daughter to his son, and his face went white.

Derek felt for the man. Both of his children, wounded and bleeding on his living room floor.

He locked eyes with Toni's dad. "I'll do everything in my power to save her," he said.

She deserved every last effort he had to give, and so much more. He'd beg, borrow, and steal for her. Fuck good and bad and all the neatly drawn lines. She'd sacrificed herself for him, and there was no way he was going to let her down.

Her shoulder hurt really bad.

Toni kept her eyes closed as she slowly regained consciousness. She was sitting up in bed somehow and there was something stuck into her arm that hurt. But not as bad as her shoulder hurt.

She tried to move her right arm, but even the thought of it made her wince in pain.

"Toni? Are you awake?"

Oh. Alden was here.

No, wait. He was Derek now.

She opened her eyes. Slowly, because her eyelids felt heavy and all her muscles ached—even the ones on her face. The room light was off and the shades were drawn, but there was light coming in from the hallway, and she registered where she was.

She was in a hospital. Because she'd been shot.

Now she remembered.

She turned her head to the side and saw Derek standing beside her bed.

"Oh, shit. Toni. You're awake. Thank God." His voice was hoarse, his hair was sticking up every which way, and he was wearing a rumpled T-shirt.

She'd never seen a man more sexy.

I love you, baby.

Those were the last words he'd said to her, back at the house. She remembered her promise to herself then, too, to tell him every day—

"I love you."

She was surprised to hear the words come out in such a croaking voice. She'd expected them to be clear and loud, the way she felt them in her heart.

"I love you, too," he croaked back.

Oh. He really did feel the same way she did. Well, that was all right then.

"And I'm so sorry, Toni. I'm sorry I lied to you. And I was lying to myself. I kept thinking I was playing a role and that I could step out of it any time with no one getting hurt. I didn't understand how *I* could lie to you and be okay with it, and I convinced myself it was the act taking over, that it wasn't really me, so it was somehow all right. But I *am* that guy. And I like being that guy and I have you to thank for showing me there's so much more to my life than I was allowing myself to have."

She looked at him, at his stricken face, and felt her heart expand. She already knew those things—he'd said them in his letter. But on top of all of that, he'd come for her, he'd *stayed* for her, and she'd fallen in love. "I forgive you," she told him.

"Thank you." He sounded relieved. "Thank you for that. And for—shit—taking a bullet for me. I can't believe you did that. Don't *ever* do something like that again."

She smiled because laughing would hurt too much. "Are you saying you didn't want to be saved?" she teased him.

The somber look he gave her tore at her heartstrings. "Not if it meant living without you."

They stared at each other for a long time, and then she gestured him forward to kiss her. The kiss was soft and sweet and entirely too little for her, but she could tell he was holding back out of concern for her wound.

She should never have doubted this man was perfect for

her. After all the years of loneliness and not being able to find someone—even a friend—who thought she was enough to be worth sticking around for, it was almost fitting that the perfect man for her would start out as an impostor. But he was perfect for her. He'd renewed something in her she'd thought was long gone. She was worth someone loving completely and truthfully, for herself. Derek had given that part of herself back, and she would be forever grateful.

That was why, when he pulled back, she whispered against his lips, "Thank you for saving *me*." And then she grinned and added, "But if you ever lie to me again, I'm kicking you to the curb and finding someone who thinks that the sun rises and sets with me."

He barked out a laugh at the warning, then tipped his head to hers. Her eyes were sparkling with amusement, but he had no doubt that she meant what she'd said. "I always thought the sun rose and set with you. I'll never lie to you again, because I only ever did it to begin with because I thought it was the only way to spend more time with you. I love you and I don't want to be without you from now on."

He kissed her again with such a tender, gentle heat that she found herself increasingly frustrated at being confined to the hospital bed. She couldn't wait until she was recovered enough to shudder beneath him, to cry out his name—his *real* name—when she came.

"How long do you think it'll take until they let me out of here?" She made her tone as suggestive as possible, despite the fatigue she could feel creeping in from expending even a small amount of effort.

He ran his hand down her left arm and took her hand with a smile. "A few more days, probably. Sal will be in here longer, though. They've got him sedated because he was thrashing around so much from withdrawal pains. Kept ripping out the IV."

Oh, God. Sal. She couldn't believe she hadn't thought to ask about him yet. "Is he in bad shape otherwise?"

In a way, she was glad Sal had been shot. Not because she would have ever actively wished that on him, but because he was getting help for his addiction in a way that would hopefully cause him as little harm as possible.

Derek shook his head. "The shot went straight through on his left side. It missed anything major. The surgeon only cleaned and stitched it and shipped him off to recovery upstairs. Your parents are with him right now."

Good. Sal needed them. And a part of her believed that they still needed him, too.

"How are they holding up?"

"Surprisingly well," he said softly. "They were here with you until about an hour ago. We've all been talking. They remember Alden and wanted to hear about him, and about me, and…us." He squeezed her hand.

"What did you tell them?" She could hear the sleepiness in her voice and knew it wouldn't be long before she succumbed again to whatever pain medication was probably being piped in through her IV, but it wasn't only her body that felt much more relaxed now than when she'd first awoken. Her mind and heart were also at peace, and she was sure that had everything to do with the man at her side.

"I told them everything," he murmured.

She gave a weak gasp. "*Everything?*"

His soft laugh soothed her. "I told them that I love you. That *you* are everything. They seemed to think that was all they needed to know."

She felt her mouth curve upward and wanted to tell him again that she loved him, too, but it seemed she could no longer summon the energy to say the words. She registered in some far corner of her mind that her eyes had closed, too, when she felt rather than saw his hand reach up and stroke her hair. She could feel the warmth of his skin against hers, and she let out a contented sigh.

"I think it's time for you to get some more sleep, baby," he whispered. "But I'll be here when you wake up. I'm not going anywhere. I hope you know I mean that in every way."

I do know. I trust you. I love you.

Those were her last thoughts before she fell back asleep with a small smile on her lips.

Epilogue

Six months later

"Can we talk?"

Derek froze at the sound of Toni's voice, solemn and serious. He turned from where he was washing dishes in the sink and watched her walk into the kitchen. She'd moved in with him last month, which had finally spurred him to get the last of his boxes unpacked.

He eyed her warily. "What is it?"

"Sal wants to see me."

"What? In jail?"

Over my fucking dead body.

After Sal had been deemed well enough to stand trial, the judge had sentenced him to ten years in prison with a possibility for parole after five. Sal had cursed Toni and their parents then, heaping so much vitriol on them that the bailiff had finally had to wrestle Sal out of the courtroom. The physician assigned to Sal's case had explained that he was still in the early stages of withdrawal and unable to manage his emotions very well, that paranoia might be playing a role in his outbursts and that the needed to give it time, but Derek had seen how hurt Toni had been at Sal's words.

What if she went to see him and he did the same thing during the visit?

Toni nodded. "Yeah, in jail. He wrote me a letter. He apologized for what he'd done and he's really clean now. They've been giving him treatment and he's been feeling better. Stronger."

"I don't know…" Derek frowned. Maybe he was being

overprotective, but this was the woman he *loved*. He would do anything to keep her from getting hurt again.

"What's the worst that can happen, Derek? I go and he says something upsetting and I leave? I'm prepared for that possibility and it's a risk I'm willing to take. I owe it to him."

He shook his head. "Oh, baby, no. If you think that him getting in jail is your fault—"

But she interrupted him. "I don't think that. I don't mean that I owe him because I did something wrong." She reached out and took his hand, pulling it to her lips for a kiss. "Just like you didn't do anything wrong with Alden," she said gently.

"Then why?"

"Because he's my brother. Because I still have hope in him. Just like you held out hope for Alden all those years. And look at your brother now. Who would have thought he'd grow his business to such success?"

It was amazing. In these few short months, what had started out as the only way to find work for a high school dropout had become a solid, thriving business. Brewer Janitorial Services now had several regular clients and Alden had hired a few employees.

Derek shrugged. "I guess I'll concede that it's possible."

Toni pressed on. "Even if Sal never does anything like Alden did—apart from the fact that he's got at least a few more years to serve, anyway—he's already done more than I had thought he could, back in those dark days. Mom and Dad have never looked so good, either. We're all in a good place, Derek. It's time to start repairing my relationship with my brother."

Derek stood for a moment, mulling it over, before finally dropping his head in acquiescence. "Okay. You may go see him. But I don't like it."

"I wasn't asking for your permission." She didn't say it with any rancor, but rather the quiet determination of a woman who knew what she was worth. What she deserved.

Derek opened his mouth to argue, but stopped. She was

right. She didn't need his permission to do something that he knew was physically safe. And her emotions belonged to her. So instead, he grinned at her confidence as she smiled at him and stepped forward and added, "But I'm glad I have it. And I was hoping that you would come with me. Even if all you do is stand behind me and look intimidating."

She tugged on his hands, pulling him to her, then leaned up and wrapped her arms around his neck. Derek hugged her back, feeling the press of her breasts against his chest and letting the now familiar heat between them flare.

"I'll come with you," he murmured against her lips.

She squeezed him hard for a brief moment. "Thank you for being there for me." She was looking at him with so much love that his heart nearly burst out of his chest.

"Always," he whispered.

And that promise was the last word that either of them spoke for a long time afterward.　　　　•

About *Giving It Up,* Pushing the Boundaries book 1

She dominates his body and his mind…but can he give up control without handing over his heart?

If Beatrice Lawrence didn't know better, she'd swear the universe is out to make sure she is totally, completely screwed. It's not enough her family's restrictive rules drove her away from home at a young age. She had to go and fall for a guy whose mere presence heats her body like Death Valley.

Except he seems to harbor a special brand of dislike, just for her. He even seems intent on ruining one of her biggest wedding photography gigs by dodging every key shot to make a phone call.

It's not that SWAT officer Warren Davis isn't attracted to Beatrice. He is. *God,* he is. But between supporting his parents and helping raise his single-mom sister's kid, there's no time to build a relationship.

Besides, Beatrice is too innocent for some of his darker…appetites. Until she catches him on the phone with a professional Domme. He must be crazy to let her talk him into hiring her instead. Even crazier to risk letting their professional relationship get personal…

Warning: Contains an out-of-her-element, wannabe Domme who has no idea the power she wields, and a SWAT officer who can't wait to show her just how deeply he needs her command. Buckle up and keep your safeword handy.

Other books by Audra North
Lucky in Love Series
Hard Driving Series
Stanton Family Series

Acknowledgments

Every time I finish a book, I find myself marveling at how many people are involved in making in its creation. My infinitely patient and understanding family has provided me with time and space to write, my befri stend Jenny Holiday critiqued the life out of this story, my editor Christa Soule took a half-baked idea and worked her magic to turn it into something of substance. To all of these people I am deeply grateful. I could never have completed this book without them.

Thank you, too, to my readers, who inspire me every day with their enthusiasm for stories about hope, love, and all the good things that make the world a wonderful place in which to live.

www.ingramcontent.com/pod-product-compliance
Lightning Source LLC
Chambersburg PA
CBHW020602180626
46810CB00007B/2614